Young Blood and Old Paint

Young Blood and Old Paint

William Frank

Terra Nova Books

SANTA FE, NEW MEXICO

Library of Congress Control Number 2021937761

Distributed by SCB Distributors, (800) 729-6423

Terra Nova Books

Published by Terra Nova Books, Santa Fe, New Mexico.
www.TerraNovaBooks.com

ISBN 978-1-948749-81-7

To Carl Barks, who wrote the best stories ever, and to the three grand ladies of Albuquerque who taught me how to read them: Rebecca Menaul Frank, Mary Menaul Rowe, and Edith Menaul.

A **wail like a keening banshee pulled Tom McNaul back to conscious-**
ness. As the howl of the Boston police cruiser faded into the urban
din, he reached across the bed. The tangled sheets were damp, but
Colleen was gone.

Failing November light struggled through the lone hotel window. Tom
gathered scattered clothes and set them on the desk next to his gun as
Colleen emerged from the bathroom and turned on the lights. His wife
stared at him like a vampire contemplating dessert, her shimmering black
dress clinging like a sailor's dream. Flowing ebony hair framed a pale
Irish face with faded eyes and black lips. She gave Tom a pensive frown
while tilting her head back and to one side, as if estimating the return
on her twenty-five-year investment. Her mouth curled into what was
technically a smile. Tom read it as a decision to sell short, but he never
could tell. She moved in for a cautious snuggle and a nip at his neck.

Tom pressed his cheek against the crown of her head, enjoying the
familiar scent of her perfume and the tickle of hair brushing his bare
chest. There was a certain thrill in enjoying a tryst with your own wife,
but it was poor compensation for living two hundred miles apart.
Colleen would fly home to New York after her opening, while he would
return to Washington when the operation was over. Not the best of
arrangements, but only for one more year.

Colleen pulled back to elbow range and dug her fingernails into
Tom's arms, fixing him with a fierce stare, her eyes flashing like fire
opals. "I hate this. I thought you transferred to Art Crime to cut back
on the undercover work."

He shrugged. "I'll be fine."

She landed a no-smear kiss and grabbed her black cape and red
beret. "Is it still going down at six?"

"Allegedly. I'll call when it's over. When do you get home?"

She instinctively glanced toward her watch without really looking
at the dial. "The flight gets in just after eleven. I took the late one in
case the show runs on."

"Break a leg."

She laughed and tossed her hair over her shoulders. Her opening at the J&M Gallery was a major event for Colleen, her first shot at the lucrative Boston art market. Her New York debut five years ago was a smashing success, in large part through the influence of Justin and Mona Mellon, owners of the J&M. They were long-time players in the New York art world, and more recent ones in London and Boston.

Tom glanced at the disheveled bed. "We're too good at this to live in separate cities. You've got your gallery contacts now, so why don't you and Cassidy move down to Washington?"

Colleen's trace of smile vanished before he finished. "We've talked enough about that. It's my turn now." She spun toward the door and left without a word.

Tom stowed his clothes in a duffel bag, showered, and dressed in a conservative European-cut suit that seemed appropriate for his new role as master art appraiser. He stood at the window and scanned the sidewalk in front of the Marriot. An early Alberta clipper was driving snow squalls across the harbor and unlucky pedestrians down State Street. A cab swerved across two lanes scattering people and cars, its tires spraying a sheet of slush onto a woman maneuvering a stroller with more wheels than a semi. Rival drivers honked their appreciation as the cab lurched to a stop and discharged a short woman wearing a dark topcoat and a hat with an expansive brim. Clutching her hat against the storm, she snatched a receipt from the driver, flipped him the finger, and entered the hotel.

Tom opened the door and stepped aside as his partner for the operation, FBI Special Agent Katherine J. Bacon, marched into the room and shook snow from her hat. She started to sail it onto the bed but spotted the ravished sheets and aimed for the desk instead. Sliding out of her stylish coat, she turned to face Tom and struck a pose with arms akimbo. "Well?"

Tom barely recognized her. Kate Bacon could be an attractive woman, but at work her appearance was pure utility. She maintained an air of energetic grimness often found in drill sergeants. Short and muscular, she relentlessly fought off every trace of fat. Tom wondered if the obsession resulted from teasing about her name, but he knew not to ask. The Kate that Tom knew stood no more than five-four in flats and kept her blonde hair in a tight ponytail. The current version was taller, sleek, and elegant. Her hair was stylishly coifed, and she wore a continental suit worth a month's pay. The rented diamonds would cost that just to insure. She looked at Tom from her unaccustomed height, surprisingly steady perched on the spike heels. Subtle makeup added at least five to her thirty-five years while pretending to do the opposite. Kate looked every bit the wealthy society woman her Boston Brahmin parents once expected. Just the sort of woman who might have a few million bucks to spare for an art toy.

"I guess you'll do."

Kate faked a pout as she kicked off the heels and glanced at the sheets. "I take it things are going better with Colleen."

It wasn't really a question, so Tom let it go. Colleen had always been a jealous lass, but she and Kate were friendly once. That ended abruptly when Colleen moved to New York, leaving Tom alone in Washington. Now the pair scrapped like the famous two cats from Kilkenny, though only Colleen's family actually hailed from the banks of the River Nore.

Kate and Tom pulled chairs to the tall window and sat watching the storm disappear into darkness. The heat was off in the room, and water had condensed on the inside of the glass. Kate tilted her chair precariously onto its back legs, her arm brushing Tom's. She began to draw a heart on the window with her big toe but smeared it with the side of her foot when she heard the door lock click. Joe Samuels and Tony Cabrera, young agents from the Boston office, let themselves in. They would be the primary backups tonight. Each wore a blue suit and an earnest smile, but there the resemblance ceased. Joe was lanky as a cowboy with squinty blue eyes and a blond buzz cut. He towered over his darker, stocky comrade. Tony would stand eyeball to eyeball with Kate, if he could get that close.

Tom stared out at the storm as Kate rehashed the plan. It was a straightforward sting. Kate was playing the rich buyer. When the phone in her room rang, the caller would direct her to a remote site. Tom, cast as the appraiser, would drive her there, with Joe and Tony shadowing. When they reached the eventual rendezvous, the caller would show Kate proof that he had the painting. With luck, the proof would be the painting itself. For a work this pricy, pictures and documents weren't going to cut it. If all went well, Tom and Kate would take the bastards down.

He suppressed a sigh. Not bloody likely. When word had reached the FBI Art Theft Team that yet another anonymous party was shopping a piece from the Gardner theft, there were groans all around. Police, private investigators, the FBI, and Interpol had worked the famous case for more than twenty years, but all thirteen pieces stolen from the Isabel Stewart Gardner Museum were still in the wind. This seller claimed to have Vermeer's "The Concert," the most valuable piece taken. It was easily worth a hundred million. The customary underworld price would be 5 to 10 percent.

Tom's review of the case had revealed hundreds of fruitless tips and several near-miss sting operations on both sides of the Atlantic. No one was betting this time would be different. Still, the seller described details of marks on the back of "The Concert" that jibed with museum records. His account seemed accurate, so they had to try.

Tom glanced at Kate as she wrapped up her monologue. "OK. The call's due at six in my room. Stand easy." Kate was registered across the hall as Mrs. Dorothea Braun, the young wife of a German hedge fund manager. After an early three-year post in Berlin, she was adept at feigning a German accent. Her room faced the Columbus Waterfront Park north of the hotel, and there was a chance her window was under surveillance, so the four kept vigil in Tom's room.

At 5:45, Kate checked the hall and crossed to her room. She looked back as Tom entered on all fours to avoid being visible through the window. "Heel, Fido."

Tom snapped his teeth at her and sat on the floor beside the window, his back to the wall. Kate turned on the lights and sat at the desk, plainly visible to anyone in or beyond the park. She leaned her phone against the brass desk lamp and made a show of opening a book: a Norwegian mystery, Tom noticed. Kate's taste in fiction kept to the dark side.

At 6:05 Willie Nelson began singing "Whiskey River" on Kate's cell. Samuels was asking for a status check. Kate barked him off. Tom figured Joe must be the one keeping an eye on Kate's rented jewelry.

Two minutes later the hotel phone rang. "Yes, I am Mrs. Braun." Kate listened and then wrote down an address. "How far is that from here? All right, but that will take some time, you know. We will be there at seven o'clock." She paused again. "I have no intention of driving there by myself. My appraiser will drive me." After hanging up, she pretended to make a brief call, then put on her coat and turned out the lights.

Kate's eyes scanned the small team. "It's a motel near Lexington. The Minuteman Inn. Just north of the I-95 exit at the Concord Turnpike." The four agents exchanged glances and silently checked the loads of their Glock 23s. The men returned their pistols to shoulder holsters while Kate stowed hers in a rented Gucci bag.

"Showtime," she said.

Tom maneuvered the black E-Class Mercedes through Friday traffic and blasts of snow. They reached the outskirts of Lexington just before seven. Joe and Tony cruised well behind them watching for any cars that might be tailing the Mercedes, while two other surveillance teams maneuvered on their flanks. Kate worked the secure radio from the passenger seat, coordinating their small wolf pack as they converged on the target. Tom glanced at her. Although he was ten years older than Kate and had more FBI service time, she was the logical team leader for the operation. Her eight years on the Art Crime Team trumped his two, and she was the lead agent on the Gardner case. Tom was impressed by her relentless dedication to the operation, and he found her more attractive by the day. He was careful to suppress the feelings, though maybe not careful enough. Colleen obviously sensed something.

Kate silenced the radio and pulled out her muted cell phone. "Yes?" She nodded toward Tom. "Say that again, please." She scribbled briefly on a small notepad and read the directions back to the caller. "You know, this really isn't ..." She smacked the phone down on the seat. "The bastard hung up." Kate activated the radio and directed the team to a new destination in a rural area northwest of Lexington. Tom slowed to let the other cars adjust their relative positions.

Ten minutes later he turned onto a two-lane road and wound through a forest of new-growth pines. They passed the entrance to a gated community and several driveways leading to upscale houses on pastoral lots. After rounding a sharp curve, Tom slowed and turned right onto a narrow drive next to a real estate sign. The tires crunched gravel as he wound through a dense stand of older trees that gave way to a broad lawn. He eased to a stop. The headlights illuminated an aging blue farmhouse with a long covered porch extending along most of the front. The porch was empty except for a hulking shape resembling a man standing by the front door. It reminded Tom of a leftover Halloween decoration. The hulk and door disappeared as Tom killed the motor and lights. Faint light eluded the curtains of one window on the ground floor.

Tom felt Kate's hand slide the radio onto his lap. Leather squeaked in the darkness as she leaned back. He pocketed the radio, unbuttoned his suit jacket, and got out. For a moment the dome light illuminated them both. He helped Kate out and took her arm, less for appearances than to help her navigate the snowy sidewalk in her unaccustomed heels. A light flared briefly on the porch, and he watched the hulk light a cigarette and flip the match into the snow. A small orange glow remained and hovered near the door at least six feet above the porch. Big fellow.

Kate clutched Tom's left arm as he steered her to the front door. The hulk with the cigarette emerged from the shadows. "Just the lady from here on." His looks had not improved with proximity, and Tom noticed that the man's coat was unbuttoned despite the cold.

"What are you saying?" snapped Kate. "I'm not agreeing to anything without my appraiser examining it."

"He can come in later." The hulk turned toward Tom and gave him the once over. He didn't seem impressed. "You stay out here with me."

Kate's face tensed to a glare that would have routed a gargoyle, but the hulk didn't flinch. She hesitated, but the game was on. With a final twitch of one cheek, she gave a brief nod of assent, and the hulk opened the door. She stepped into a dark hallway leading to a dimly lit room as the door closed behind her.

The hulk stepped back into the shadows next to the door. Tom was worried and unsure of his next move. The request wasn't unreasonable. Whoever was inside wanted to size up the buyer before trotting out the goods, but sending Kate in alone wasn't the plan. He couldn't use the radio. Hopefully, the surveillance teams were close enough to hear Kate's wire. He edged down the dark porch until only the glow of the hulk's cigarette remained visible.

Kate clicked open the clasp on her bag and headed toward the light. She entered a large living room furnished with expensive, worn leather and unevenly lit by an assortment of brass lamps. There were no personal items visible. A short, round-faced man in a pinstriped suit stood in front of the unlit fireplace. He beamed a patrician smile and waved her toward the two winged chairs flanking the hearth.

"Mrs. Braun, I presume? Please join me." His voice was high-pitched and raspy, but he had the practiced diction of private schooling.

Exeter, perhaps. Kate nodded to the smile. As she started toward the left chair, the man's cell phone rang.

"I'm sorry. Excuse me just a moment." He turned toward the curtained window and walked slowly away from Kate. "Yes?" He stopped near the window and listened for several seconds. "I see." He replaced the phone inside his jacket, and as he turned to Kate, his hand was holding a pistol. The smile was gone.

Tom heard a cell phone ring once inside the house. A few seconds later Kate's voice was audible, but her words were garbled in the howl of the storm. He heard two closely spaced shots and froze for a tic, then instinctively stepped to his right and reached for his gun. The tic was almost fatal. He saw two orange muzzle flashes as sharp reports shattered the night. Tom felt a blow to his left side and a burning sensation. He sank to one knee as the hulk fired a third shot which struck wood. Tom exhaled as he squeezed off three quick rounds aiming a foot below the orange glow. He heard a grunt followed by a soft thud. Smoking's bad for your health.

Tom struggled to his feet and clutched his left side as he staggered forward. He tripped over the torso of the motionless shooter but regained his balance and yanked open the door. Pain stabbed his side. He raised the Glock in his right hand and shuffled down the dark hallway.

As Tom emerged into the light, time slowed. Kate lay on her back to the left of an empty fireplace, and blood was pooling on the pine floor. A small man in a pinstripe suit was kneeling beside her, looking intently at her face. His left hand was on her chest near the throat, and his right was hidden behind his thigh. He looked up at Tom, his eyes widening, and he spun away. Tom put two bullets in the man's back. He heard an object slide into the stone fireplace as the man did a face plant on the bare floor and began twitching.

Tom sank to his knees beside Kate. She was trembling and sucking air through a hole in her chest. He grabbed Kate's open bag. Her pistol fell to the floor as he pressed the soft leather into the wound. Shaking his head failed to clear the dizziness. He fumbled for the radio and heard footsteps running down the hall. Strong hands grasped his shoulders from behind and pulled him back from Kate. He saw Tony move in to take over the first aid. Tom collapsed into a sitting position and inched backward along the floor until he felt the sofa behind him.

Joe leaned in close, staring at Tom's eyes until they focused. "Stay with me, Tommy. Help's coming."

"I'm OK. How's Kate?"

"Don't know yet, but there's nothing you can do."

Car doors slammed outside as Joe peeled Tom down to his skin and examined the wound. "Doesn't look bad. It passed through—looks like a deep slice. Probably didn't hit much you can't spare." He wadded Tom's shirt and pressed it to the wound. "Hold this tight."

The backup team members ran into the room and swarmed over Kate. One of them tossed a bandage kit to Joe, who applied a quick field dressing to Tom's side and then joined the others. Tom closed his eyes and tried to focus as his energy drained away. All my fault. She shouldn't have been alone in there. Urgent voices roused him, and he sat emotionless for a long time watching the others fighting to keep Kate breathing. After twenty minutes or so, a distant siren grew louder. More car doors slammed, and he heard rapid steps as an EMT team raced into the room with a stretcher. He stared as they loaded Kate onto it and carried her to the waiting ambulance. No one looked his way. He shivered in the cold room as he scanned it looking for the painting, a photograph, any sign that the dead men had the Vermeer, but he saw nothing. Sirens wailed again as Kate's ambulance sped into the night.

Tom climbed onto a wooden chair and draped his bloody suit jacket over his shoulders against the chill while Joe and Tony left to search the house and grounds. Ten or fifteen minutes later, Tom heard more cars arriving and shouts outside. Local police were setting up a perimeter. The turmoil settled into the grim, familiar pattern of a crime scene. A second ambulance arrived with a slender young paramedic who checked Tom's side. She smiled through a field of acne but seemed disappointed to have missed the main action. The medic was upgrading his repair job when Joe and Tony returned.

Tony knelt to take a look at Tom's wound. "They had a motorcycle parked around the back. Must have been their exit plan. There's a rough track heading into the trees behind the house. The locals are looking for a car or truck parked along a road beyond the woods."

Tom nodded. "Find anything in the house?"

"Just an envelope. It's a standard business envelope, about nine by twelve. Feels like there might be a photo in it, but it's sealed, so we'll let the CSI folks open it."

"No painting?"

"Nope. I suppose there could be something in their car, if there is one. Doubt it, though. They weren't going to haul it over here on a bike."

No, they wouldn't. Tom looked across the room. Joe was biting his lower lip and fidgeting.

"Tommy, do you know that guy?" Joe nodded toward the only corpse in the room.

"No clue. I take it you do?"

"He's Sean O'Neill."

Tom shrugged. "So?"

Joe exercised his lips more vigorously. "He's the nephew of Paddy O'Neill. That would be Congressman Paddy O'Neill."

The name meant nothing to Tom, and he was growing too numb to care. He looked at the pool of Kate's blood on the floor and closed his eyes. This isn't going to end well.

~ 3 ~

Joe was alone when he pulled the blue sedan up to the door of the emergency department. Tony was driving the rented Mercedes back to the dealer. A muscular orderly, seemingly impervious to the swirling snow, rolled Tom out to the curb, loaded him into the passenger seat, and disappeared back into the hospital. Tom leaned against the headrest and stared out the side window into the night as they headed eastward toward Boston. His wound wasn't serious, but he was floating on painkillers. He could have used some pain to push back the emptiness.

The storm seemed to be easing, and they cruised for a while in silence. Joe glanced sideways at his listless passenger. "They found a van parked behind the woods. No art in it—just a ramp to load the motorcycle."

Tom rolled his head toward Joe. "What about Kate?"

"Nothing new. She came through the first surgery pretty well, and the bullet didn't hit any arteries. Missed her spinal cord. The docs were talking about moving her to Mass General, maybe tomorrow, but they weren't willing to say much about the long term."

"Just one bullet? I heard two shots."

"They found one in the wall."

Tom stared through the windshield at snowflakes streaking out of the darkness and around the car. The headlights lit a moving sphere of white. He felt like a Santa in a snow globe. Dry snow was deepening on the road, and he could hear it crunching beneath the tires. "So who was that guy in the pinstripes? You said O'Leary or something?"

"O'Neill. Sean O'Neill. His Uncle Paddy's been a congressman for twenty years or more. Respectable old-Boston family and all that. But Paddy's kid brother, Jack, is a lawyer who does some business with the shadier sons of Erin."

"Irish mob?"

"Yeah. We've been watching Jack for a couple of years now, but we've never nailed him for anything. He seems to handle their more-legiti-

11

mate business. His kid's a bit of a punk, though. At least he was until tonight. He seemed to be trying to make his mark with the boys."

Tom was having trouble focusing. "It doesn't make sense. It was like an ambush. Why? They didn't even have the goddamn painting. Why were those hoods even there? Who sets up an ambush for the FBI?"

Joe shrugged. He knew Tom was in trouble. "Look, why don't you come home with me tonight? Elka and I don't have anything on this weekend, and you don't want to sit in that hotel room till Monday. The doc ordered two days of rest and a checkup before you leave town."

It took a moment for Tom to realize what Joe had said. "Uh, thanks. Just tonight, though. Where do you live?"

"We've got a place in Brookline. Spare bedroom. No kids, no cats."

"That must mean a Saint Bernard." Tom was attempting to reenter the world of the living. He felt like a drunk trying to fool a clergyman.

"It's a double bed. You'll both fit."

"If it's a female, Colleen won't like it." Colleen. Tom needed to call her. "What time is it?"

"About ten-thirty."

He searched pockets for his phone but couldn't find it. Probably in the effects bag the orderly had given Joe. He gave up. Colleen wasn't home yet, and he pictured her tired, still excited from her opening, and picking up the phone: Hi toots. Hope your show was better than ours. No sign of a painting, and Kate and I got shot. He rolled his head to look at Joe. "Any update on Kate?"

"You already asked that. Get some sleep. We'll be there in ten."

Joe made a quick call to his wife. He didn't say anything about the botched mission or the condition of their unexpected guest.

Tom was ushered into a ground-floor apartment in a converted row house. It was traditional Boston brick on the outside and all things Scandinavian within. Every surface was white—even the Cy Twombly print on the living room wall was mostly white. The seating was chrome and white leather. The only signs of color were a cluster of irises in a glass vase on the kitchen counter and a red Swedish Dala horse on top of a bookcase. The source of the decor was instantly apparent when Elka entered the room. Flowing blonde hair split over her broad shoulders, and her bearing suggested a pure bloodline back to the Vikings. Though she was barefoot, she was no more than an inch shorter than Tom's six-two. She greeted him formally with a strong handshake and a deep Wagnerian "Welcome." As Joe related the tale of their evening, Elka's mood crashed like a bear market. Tom was whisked off to bed in a blur of proper kindness punctured by Elka's frequent glares at her husband. The guest room proved to be free of Saint Bernards, and Tom felt secure under the white down comforter. He heard voices from the kitchen, restrained but tense. Joe's in for a long night.

*　　*　　*

It was quarter past ten by the time Tom worked his way to the kitchen. He limped favoring his left side. It ached, but he didn't dare take any more painkillers. His mind was still reeling from the drugs he'd had, and he needed to clear it for what had to be coming.

Elka was seated at the kitchen table reading the Saturday Globe and drinking a dark, viscous brew with an aroma resembling coffee. She didn't look up but nodded toward the stove. "Still hot."

Tom searched in vain for an acceptably large mug and settled for a small white porcelain cup well camouflaged in the sea of white. He eased into the chair opposite Elka and waited for some sign of civility. He knew his appearance was appalling. Joe's clothes were several sizes too small, so Tom wore the remains of his own bloodstained shirt. He sat with his right side toward Elka hoping she might not notice the condition of his left. At least the blood had dried. He needn't have bothered as Elka continued to stare at the front page.

"Sorry," she said. "Look, I know it's part of the job, but Joe's never had to use his gun before."

"He still hasn't. It was all over before he and Tony got there."

"Yes, well." She put down the paper and looked Tom over. Her eyebrows arched and then dove toward her nose as she took in the remains of his shirt. "How do you feel?"

"OK. Doesn't seem to hurt except when I move." Tom looked around for signs of Joe.

"He's not here. He went downtown to turn in his report. He said he would drop by your hotel this afternoon if he can get away. If you're up to it, I can drop you there on my way to work." Elka looked at his torn, bloody shirt, and her face softened. "You're welcome to stay here, you know."

"That's good of you, but I need some time alone." He peered closely at her but saw no sign that Joe had filled her in on the worst of the details. "Good coffee," he lied.

"Let me get you something to eat." Elka fetched two white plates and a package of plywood crackers. She reached into the surprisingly bare refrigerator and emerged with a glass jar filled with chunks of a white substance. The jar landed before Tom with a proud thump.

Herring! There was no legally obtainable foodstuff Tom hated more, and his stomach was still queasy from the drugs. He forced what might pass for a smile and accepted a portion that was small enough to starve a Dane but depressingly large to him. He carefully prepared for each bite to avoid shivering. Flaccid chunks slithered down his throat. The smell of fish oil cleared his sinuses as he excused himself and shuffled toward the bathroom.

An hour later Tom waved to Elka and entered the Marriott, covering the bullet holes in his topcoat with the sports pages. The cover worked well enough to get him past the front desk with only the mandatory welcomes from the staff. He nodded back, but his head spun from the slight movement, and he nearly fell.

Back in his room, Tom staggered into the bathroom and threw up the remnants of the herring. He felt marginally better, at least in principle, and eased himself onto the freshly made bed. Through the window he could see sunlit cumulus clouds speeding across the harbor. The core of the storm was now offshore, harassing sailors and trailing frigid winds it its wake. Jesus! Last night the four of us were standing here fondling our guns like the Earp Brothers. What a total fuckup! He closed his eyes and started replaying the shootout at the farmhouse. The show rolled by at least half a dozen times before the room phone rang. It was Joe.

"Tom? I'm not going to be able to stop by the hotel."

"That's OK. You've got stuff to do."

"No, that's not it. I was told not to talk to you today."

A chill settled over Tom, clearing his mind. "Go on."

"A supervisor from Washington flew in this morning. Not anyone I know. He left here a few minutes ago heading for the hotel, and he didn't want you talking to anyone before he gets there."

"You said he?" That meant it wasn't Susan Parker, the head of the Art Crime Team. They were sending someone higher up the food chain.

"Yeah. Look, he didn't tell me what they're thinking at headquarters, but they seem to be in a hell of a hurry—not even waiting for you to fly back Monday. Hang in there, Tommy. The guy may be a little rough on you, but it was a shootout. He'll huff and strut, but you'll survive."

But there's history. "Thanks for the heads-up. You'd better stay clear. I think I can weather this, but no sense you getting bloody too. And Joe, don't tell them you called."

Tom lay on the bed and tried to figure out what was stirring up the brass. Sure, there's always an investigation after a shooting, but this seemed like a pretty clear-cut firefight. And why did they want to question him away from headquarters? Probably on my way to Guantanamo. He pulled out his phone and checked for messages. There was one this morning from Colleen. He started to call her back but stopped when he realized it was after twelve. She always left the loft for lunch and usually met someone. Better to wait until after the big cheese rolled through.

He didn't have to wait long. There was a knock, and a few seconds later the door clicked open. Must have Joe's key. A trim, clean-shaven man stepped into the room. His creaseless trench coat and carefully tilted fedora suggested he and Bogie had stopped after the first whiskey. "Agent Thomas McNaul, I assume?" Seeing a slight nod, the man quickly removed his coat and hat and placed them in a neat stack on the luggage stand. When he turned back, Bogie's pal was gone, and Tom was facing a standard Bureau blue-suit with two-inch hair. "Agent McNaul, I'm Peter Myers."

Tom nodded again. The name was familiar, someone a few levels up the flow chart from the Art Crime Team, but Tom didn't recognize him. He slid his legs off the side of the bed and winced as he moved to a chair next to a small table. Myers sat down facing him and proceeded without small talk.

"I've already received a briefing on the mission from the other members of the operation, but I want you to tell me exactly what happened after you arrived at the scene. This is not a formal hearing, though it's only fair to warn you that you've got a lot at stake." Myers spoke in a monotone that suited his stone poker face. Tom had trouble breaking eye contact with him. He felt like he was frozen in the stare of a predator, and he had to measure his breathing to keep focused.

"Do I need a lawyer?"

"No. I'm not here to investigate you. I'm here to make a deal. If you want to go through formal procedures, that's your option, and I was only here to ask about your health. I'd advise against that."

"A deal? What the hell is this? Look, I'll make a detailed statement later, but I'm not guilty of anything except letting Kate go in alone. She went inside the house. A phone rang. It must have been the shooter's phone since Kate doesn't use stock ringtones. It sounded like Kate was arguing, and then I heard two shots. The guy in the shadows opened up on me and I put him down. When I got to the living room, Kate was on the floor, and the guy who shot her had one hand at her throat and a gun in the other. He spun away and I shot him. That's it. What was I supposed to do? Read him his rights while he finished off Kate?"

Myers bent forward, unleashing a burst of cologne. He leaned on the table with both arms, his baleful stare intact. "I'll give you the guy on the porch, McNaul. But the guy inside didn't have a gun in his hand. It was in his shoulder holster. I'm sure ballistics will confirm that he shot Kate, but he must have put the gun away before you got there. You managed to shoot an empty-handed man in the back. Twice. And I think by now you know that it wasn't just anybody."

Tom started to protest but froze before uttering a sound. He looked down to his right as he replayed the action in the living room. Did I really see a gun? He had to have had it. He focused on the shooter's position. Where was his right hand? I can't remember. Shit. A cold wave rose in his chest. He looked back at Myers. "Have you talked to Kate?" Tom realized as he spoke that Kate was probably unconscious by the time he'd reached the room.

Myers relaxed his expression and pulled back from the table. "She's out of intensive care, but we're not going to talk to her before Monday. She won't be able to speak to your actions anyway." He waited in vain for Tom to respond but soon gave up. "Let's cut to the chase. A lot of things can happen in a gunfight, but you've got two priors. Same pattern each time. You hesitate and let the situation get out of hand. Then you shoot too fast. You survived both previous investigations, barely. No one's going to cut you any slack this time."

Tom tilted his head to one side, unleashing another wave of dizziness. He braced his hand on the table until the spinning stopped. "So why are you here? Why not just wait till I get back to Washington and fry me by the book?"

"Too high profile. This one's already filling headlines, and the editorials will hit the Sunday papers in the morning. Investigations take time, and we want this to go away ASAP." Myers paused as if deciding whether to say more.

Tom stiffened. He was cooked, and was impatient now to get it over with. "You mentioned a deal." He thought Myers looked relieved, but it was only the faintest of tells.

"You've got twenty-four years of service, just ten months left before you're eligible to retire. We can pull a couple of strings, put you on temporary disability leave that would last until you retire. You leave now, quietly, and never come back. Go somewhere far way from the liberal Eastern press while we go through the formalities of an internal investigation. Without you around, the story will die soon enough. It's a pretty damned good deal if you ask me."

"And if I fight it?"

"Formal investigation with full press honors. You get locked in a file room somewhere until they terminate you with no pension. The Bureau gets a blacker eye, not welcome in this age of budget hawks."

Tom stood up and took small steps to the window, trying not to show the pain. He stood with his back to Myers and watched low clouds scurry south. The taste of herring still fouled his palate. There wasn't much to say, but he felt he deserved to take some time saying it. "What's this about getting away from the Eastern press? My wife and daughter live in New York."

"Too close, Tom. You need to be far away where the reporters won't knock on your door." For the first time, Myers began to look uncomfortable. He flexed his fingers and avoided Tom's eyes. "And there's another issue. Sean O'Neill was a punk. His congressman uncle couldn't stand him. Considered him from the wrong side of the family tracks or something. But the kid had friends in low places, and so does his old man."

"You saying they'll come after me? Seems like I might be better off keeping the badge."

"I made a phone call to the kid's dad, Jack O'Neill, this morning. I knew him in law school. He's damned upset, but he understands it was the kid's fault. He said he'd try to keep a lid on it so long as you get the hell out of Dodge and stay out. He might be lying, but I don't think so." Myers crossed his legs and assumed the smug look of a man laying down a full house.

There didn't seem to be an option. Tom turned to face Myers. "OK, but I've got a condition."

Myers stiffened. "You're not in a position to bargain, Agent McNaul."

"Maybe not, but I've got one, and it's not negotiable. If I go back out west, I'll need to work. No law enforcement agency is going to touch me. I've got a half-brother who's a private investigator, and he'll let me join his firm if I have a P.I. license in hand. You've got enough heft to get me that. The full thing, including the concealed carry permit."

"For a guy canned because he shot too many people? Dream on, McNaul. What state would do that?"

Tom smiled for the first time that day. "New Mexico. Such things go down easily there."

~ 4 ~

Tom awoke with a jolt. He had no sense of time, but the room was dark and he was lying on a bed. As he began to reorient, the horns of taxis working the harbor area told him Saturday night in Boston was still young. He rolled over and felt a stab in his side as he sat up. It was 7:40 according to his watch, 2:17 a.m. on the flashing bedside alarm clock. The watch seemed like the better bet. He pictured the smug Myers walking out the door with his deal and the end of Tom's career in hand. That was seven hours ago. It was time to get moving. The hotel might not be safe. He flipped on lights and located his phone. Three more calls from Colleen, all in the last two hours. He took a cleansing breath and called her.

"About time, Tommy. I was beginning to wonder. Did you bag any big ones?" Tom hadn't told Colleen they were after a piece from the Gardner heist, but she'd guessed right away that Art Crime wasn't sending an FBI team to Boston for anything small-time. Her voice was airy, and she seemed anxious to tell him about her show.

"The news isn't so good, toots. The sting went bad in a hurry, and Kate got shot. I think she'll live, but I haven't heard anything for a while." He couldn't think of anything else to say. Colleen soon picked up the slack.

"Kate? What happened? And what about you?"

"We're still trying to sort out what went wrong. I'm OK. I got a nick but it's nothing, like the kind the marshal gets in a TV Western."

"Jesus, Tom! And you didn't even call?"

Tom's status was switching rapidly from victim to perp. He had to get off last night's fiasco and talk to her about his deal with Myers. "Look, I'm sorry, and I'll fill you in later, but I need to tell you something else. I'm leaving town and the FBI. I'll be moving to Santa Fe in a few days." He could hear Colleen breathing hard and knew she was already seething.

"What the hell are you talking about?"

"I haven't got time to explain. Trust me, hey? It'll work out." He struggled to think of soothing words but knew it was hopeless. "It won't be so bad. Santa Fe's a big-time art market. The schools are, well, they have some. It'll be OK for us."

Her words came slowly and were colder than Friday's storm. "I don't know what you've gotten yourself into, but there's no way in hell Cassidy and I are leaving New York for some mud-house backwater. Not now. Not later. I hope you're really OK, Tommy, and I'll say a prayer for Kate, but as for the rest, you're on your own."

She waited until he uttered a pathetic "Colleen?" before she hung up. It was about what he'd expected. She wouldn't be praying for Kate anytime soon—the last time he saw her pray was at their wedding, and she was probably faking it then.

Right. Got to move. The bandage on Tom's left side showed no signs of bleeding. He stuffed his few clothes and the shoulder holster into the wheeled duffel bag and his pistol into the right pocket of his topcoat. The odds some punk would be coming after him while he was still in Boston seemed slim, but he wasn't taking chances. Myers said he'd discussed the deal with Jack O'Neill, and that meant the word was out—he would be losing his FBI status. Tom hoped the mob boys wouldn't know the timing.

Tom left the lights on in the room and exited the hotel by a side door without checking out. The Bureau would be picking up the tab for another two nights. The sidewalks and street were clear of snow, but the winds pierced his coat and numbed the exposed hand dragging the duffel. He tried to walk normally as he worked his way to the Harborside Inn by an indirect route. After surveying the sidewalks from the lobby for twenty minutes, he grabbed a cab and checked into a Holiday Inn a few hundred yards from Mass General. The woman who answered the phone at the hospital was sympathetic but refused to confirm that Kate was there—not surprising considering the media interest. He called Joe.

"Yeah, they moved her to Mass General late this afternoon. She's doing pretty well, considering. She's not in intensive care anymore, but the nurses keep the press at bay. Can you tell me what happened with the big shot from Washington?"

"Better not. Let's just say the next time you see me, I'll probably be talking like Philip Marlowe. See you around, and thanks."

*　　*　　*

Mass General had no formal visiting hours, so Tom grabbed an early breakfast and arrived on Kate's floor before seven, hoping to see her before anyone from the Bureau showed up. The duty nurse's broad body tapered with height to a square head with closely cropped hair. She reminded Tom of a chess rook and moved like one, but she seemed friendly enough. A smile and his FBI badge were enough to get him a brief summary of Kate's condition and five minutes alone in her single room. Kate heard the door close and opened her eyes.

"Tommy?" Her whisper was barely audible. He stepped to the bed and judged her right hand to be the only part of her body safe to touch. Tubes and wires emerged from beneath bandages and sheets. They connected her to monitors, an IV, and who knows what else. There were beeps accompanying dancing electronic lines and flickering digits, and he could hear the sound of some sort of pump. A small bouquet of gift-shop flowers was too small to compete with the smells of alcohol and antiseptics. Kate's breathing was fast and shallow. He lifted her hand an inch off the bed and held it there, squeezing gently. She took a slightly deeper breath and winced. "What happened?"

"I was hoping you could tell me." He felt a surge of guilt as he thought of sending her alone into the farmhouse. "The nurse said you're doing really well. Tell you the truth, though, you've looked better."

"So lie," she whispered.

Tom hadn't spent much time next to hospital beds, but he took her attempt at humor as a sign she was at least coherent. "I heard a phone ring in the house," he said. "Just once. I heard your voice but couldn't understand the words. Then there were two quick shots inside. The ape on the porch and I had our own shootout, and I came out a little better. By the time I got to the living room, you were down. Do you remember anything?"

"The guy answered his phone. Didn't say anything to me. Just pulled his gun." She paused long enough to take three labored breaths. "I said something. Went for my gun. Too slow."

"Any idea who called?"

"No." She rolled her eyes toward Tom. "Catch the guy?"

"Dead on the field."

Kate went back to staring at the ceiling. "Why, Tommy?"

"It's beyond my ken. Just doesn't make any sense." Tom glanced at his watch and knew his time was up. "They really did say you'll make a full recovery. You cut it a little close, but you'll be back kicking butts in no time." No one had said anything of the kind, but at least they didn't say otherwise. Kate closed her eyes and drifted off.

Tom lowered her hand to the bed. He took a chance and maneuvered through the tubes and wiring to place a soft kiss on her forehead before leaving. The nurse nodded from her station as Tom bypassed the elevators in favor of the stairs at the end of the corridor. He had to ease his way down using the railing, but he didn't want to meet any agents coming up to see Kate.

The emergency room was quiet, a lull after the usual Saturday night action. The wounded, overdosed, and otherwise impaired were beyond triage. A weary resident in need of stronger coffee and a closer shave reluctantly examined Tom's stitches and pronounced him likely to live another day. It was too early to call anyone, so Tom retrieved his bag from the hotel and headed for Logan Airport.

*   *   *

By 2 p.m. he was surveying the contents of his tiny furnished studio. The owner was serving a tour somewhere in the Middle East. The size wasn't an issue since Colleen and Cassidy never came down to Washington. He had depressingly few possessions in the place. Most of the accumulations of their years together were in the New York loft. He repacked the duffel with a change of winter clothes and loaded a large, lockable metal case with an assortment of electronic devices and weaponry. There was a little space left in the case, so he added a few photos and books. He tossed in a baseball autographed by the Cleveland Indians during a spring training visit with his dad. Everything else went into cardboard boxes from U-Haul, and he arranged to have the lot shipped west in a small pod.

Tom knocked on the third door down the hall to ask Sandy Delane if she'd oversee the movers. Sandy was a computer tech in the State Department who dressed like a country-western star to remind folks she was Texan. Two years ago, on the day he moved in, she engineered a key swap with Tom so they could look after each other's plants and cats. It proved to be a one-sided deal—Tom possessed neither while Judy's apartment resembled a tiny rain forest teeming with bonsai tigers. Still, he liked having someone to talk to now and then.

Sandy swung the door open with a smile that faded when she learned he was leaving town. "Sure, I'll keep an eye on your stuff, but it'll cost you a fancy dinner."

"All redheads seem to run a tab." He agreed to the terms, as usual, but insisted on limiting the damage by taking her to an inexpensive bistro just around the corner. It was a ritual—they always ended up at Mario's, and they always split the tab. For an hour they pushed away their troubles with rich pasta and cheap Chianti. Sandy never asked why he sat down so gingerly. They promised to stay in touch.

After dinner Tom sat alone at his kitchen table fingering his phone and trying not to finish an IPA. He gave up and emptied the bottle with a long tug. No more stalling. It was time to call Willie, and there was no telling how that would go.

Tom knew it was a shade presumptuous to tell Agent Myers of his impending job with Willie. The brothers had last spoken a year and a half ago at Aunt Jane's funeral. They got along well enough, but Willie was twelve years older, and they had different mothers. Mark and Frances McNaul were professors of anthropology and English, respectively, at the University of New Mexico. After eleven years of marriage and one child, they divorced for reasons that became apparent when, six months after the decree, Mark married one of his graduate students, the former Elizabeth Wilson. Willie was nine and stayed with his mother. He grew up convinced that Liz was a home-wrecking little whore and spent his life shunning father and step-mother alike. When Tom arrived, three years after the remarriage, the women called a truce of sorts on behalf of the two boys. Willie surprised them by befriending "the twerp," and the two maintained a distant brotherly affection.

Willie answered on the eighth ring, his norm. It was 8:45 on a Sun-day evening in Santa Fe, and while the sidewalks were not fully rolled up, they were curling around the edges. "Yeah? That you, Twerp?" Willie never trusted his caller ID. Tom could hear electrified Dylan blasting at high volume in the background, a sign that Rosanne wasn't home. "Yo, Bro. You got a minute?"

"Sure. Hold it a sec." The sec turned into a couple of minutes, Willie not being inclined to talk until the song had ended. The harmonica howled like a coyote pack fighting over the bones as Dylan finished off the tenth verse of "Desolation Row" and rolled on to the finale. "OK, what's up?"

"I'm in a bit of a jam, and I need a favor. The FBI's giving me the bum's rush, and I need a job, at least for a while. You willing to take on a partner?"

"What the hell happened? You've been an agent forever. Forget to wear a blue suit one day?"

"Something like that. Look, I'll have a New Mexico P.I. license, and I've got some savings. I could buy in, or just share some office space if you'd rather stay solo. But I need to know now. What do you say?"

"You're on, Twerp. When ya coming?"

Tom could picture Willie's face from the tone of his voice. The grin would be so wide he'd have to be careful not to swallow his phone. "I'm not sure—a few days, I think. I'll get back to you. Thanks, Willie."

"Seriously, are you OK, Tom? This isn't like my junior G-man."

"I'm well enough for now. I'll call in a day or two."

Tom hung up and sagged into his chair. He never even hesitated. Tom was ashamed he had doubted Willie, but you never knew. Relief brought on exhaustion, and he decided he could risk this one night in the apartment. He climbed into bed with his Glock on the night table and set the alarm for six.

*   *   *

Monday morning arrived with a woman on NPR earnestly talking about global warming and polar bears clinging to shrinking ice floes. Tom crammed his duffel bag and metal case into the small Prius hybrid forced upon him by his wife and daughter before they abandoned cars altogether in favor of the New York City Transit Authority. He couldn't spot anyone tailing him as he joined the tide of lemmings already flowing along the beltway toward their chosen cliffs.

Tom rolled into a Super 8 just south of downtown Baltimore, his safe haven for the coming night. The only room available was friendly to dogs and—worse—smokers. The carpet felt damp and smelled from alternating doses of competing liquids. He left the bags in his room and lingered over a breakfast better suited for bolting down as he waited for the Toyota dealer across the street to open its sales office. Fortunately, the car title was in his name, and he was able to exchange the Prius and a few bucks for a new Tacoma pickup. It was painted a color resembling New Mexico dirt but called something else. He was feeling better but not well enough to drive the truck across most of the country by himself, so he dropped it at a corrugated steel shack next to the Baltimore railyards. The shack housed an auto shipping office staffed by one bored woman in a Baltimore Hon hairdo. She stopped reading

People long enough for Tom to buy the truck a ticket to Albuquerque. He rode a cab to the rental car facility at BWI Airport, selected the most generic white car in the lot, and headed back to his equally generic motel for the night.

*   *   *

With the aid of an elderly porter, Tom maneuvered his bags into a Superliner Roomette on the Capital Limited at Union Station. It was just after three-thirty on an unusually sunny afternoon for November in Washington. He spent the half hour before train time settling into his compartment and checking out the route to the dining car. Tom was partial to trains. When he was a kid, the Santa Fe Railway tracks ran just two blocks east of the McNaul house in Albuquerque's north valley. On the days that Willie came over, he told Tom wild tales of hobos and train wrecks, and showed him how to mash pennies on the rails as the freights rumbled and screeched through the neighborhood. This trip wasn't for railroad nostalgia, though. The metal case contained things that wouldn't fly with the airlines. Technically, they weren't legal on Amtrak either, but nobody ever checked.

Tom stuck to his room as the Limited rolled northwest, swaying and lurching as it negotiated the aging track bed. The train reached West Virginia and darkness at almost the same time. He wedged himself into the tiny lower bed using pillows and blankets from the upper bunk to keep his body from rolling along with the car. He was tired enough to sleep through most of the whistle-stops, but there was no ignoring the longer stays in Pittsburgh and Cleveland. Toledo pushed him over the edge. He gave up and folded the beds for the final three hours into Chicago. Thanks to the stubborn survival of luggage lockers in train stations, he was free to walk about without bags, but there was nowhere to go. He avoided the food court and settled in the waiting room. There were six hours to kill, and he preferred diesel fumes and ozone from the locomotives to the smell of frying burgers.

*   *   *

The roomette on the Southwest Chief was no larger than the one on the Limited, but this time he was tired enough to sleep through anything. Just twenty-four hours to Lamy, the nearest station to Santa

Fe. Tom had been surprised to discover that the famed Atchison, Topeka & Santa Fe Railway never actually had passenger service to Santa Fe—its trains passed twenty miles south of the city on their way to Los Angeles. So did Amtrak's.

As the train rolled south through bare Illinois cornfields, Tom stumbled to the lounge car and ordered Irish whiskey on the rocks. He settled for bourbon. A train buff in a striped engineer's hat was brandishing a 1939 timetable and announcing to all comers that the Santa Fe Super Chief used to do the Chicago-L.A. run two to three hours faster than Amtrak. Ah, progress. But not really fair. The Super Chief was an express. Tom managed to avoid the amateur dispatcher and took the snort back to his room, barricaded the door with the metal case, and called it a night. He was sleeping comfortably in predawn darkness as the conductor watched a man in a black leather coat step from the shadows of the Dodge City platform and climb aboard the Chief.

Tom's eyes sprang open. The tiny room was still dark and rocking, but something was wrong. He listened but there were no unusual sounds he could separate from the background whine and classic two-step beat of steel wheels on jointed rails. Gun in hand he carefully sat up and peered around the edge of the curtain covering the glass door. His metal case was wedged so the door couldn't slide more than half an inch if someone managed to unlock it. The door was still latched, but the paper sticker he had placed across the door and frame was loose on the frame side. There was enough play in the hardware for the door to slide a quarter of an inch while latched. The door fit snugly, so it wasn't likely the rocking of the car that had moved it. But passengers caroming through the cars were constantly lurching and bracing their hands against the walls. Could have been a midnight toilet run. Maybe.

By 7 a.m. the train was awake, and Tom checked out the dining and observation cars. The former was choked with disheveled passengers who looked as if they were in shock from what they'd paid for a two-foot-wide bed. The lounge car was already packed with sightseers hoarding their seats for the day, noses and cameras pressed to the windows. One man in the rear of the car was reading a book with no dust jacket. A folded leather jacket lay on his lap, and there was a small briefcase near his feet. Tom kept a close watch on the man while he strolled the aisle, bending low to peer at the bleak landscape. They were rolling across the dustbowl corner of Colorado. After five minutes the reader had not turned a page. Tom went back to his roomette and closed the door and curtain.

By quarter to three the Chief was running twenty minutes late as it slowed for its one-minute stop in Lamy. There was nobody on the platform as the conductor helped Tom maneuver his duffel bag and case down the steps. No one else got off. The conductor saluted, and the train disappeared toward the southwest. Tom stood with his back to the tracks and surveyed the quiet scene. For a brief time in the 1940s, the little platform swarmed with scientists and military personnel en route to and from the secret city of Los Alamos. That era had passed quickly, and in recent years, only a single passenger arriving was not unusual. The old mission-style station remained, but the nearby Harvey hotel was long gone. Along the tracks to Tom's left stood a boarded up adobe church. Maybe they backed the wrong deity. A variety of homes and a couple of hopeful enterprises were trying to make a go of it among the rolling, dusty hills. Tom stared down the tracks past the old church and across the high plains. There was more dirt than plant life, and the tough little junipers and piñons didn't block much of the view. A first-time visitor from the green hills of New England might have felt he'd stepped into the set of a Sergio Leone western, but to Tom it was home. And he could see forever.

Where's Willie? Tom's eyes again swept the empty platform and the sparsely graveled parking lot. An ancient red pickup with the rounded fenders favored by Santa Fe landscape painters was the only vehicle at the station. He took a few steps to his left to see through the intense sun glint on the windshield, but the truck was empty. The still life with truck was interrupted when a tall blonde woman in jeans, flannel shirt, and ponytail strode out of a restaurant beyond the lot and waved at him. His heart lifted. Laurie! Tom and Laurie had been high school sweethearts. They drifted apart when Tom went east to M.I.T. while she stayed in Albuquerque to study journalism at the University of New Mexico. He hadn't seen her in almost twenty years. From her faithful holiday letters, he knew Laurie's marriage hadn't lasted long enough for kids. She'd eventually moved to Santa Fe and became a reporter for the New Mexican. Tom stood on the platform as she approached with a glistening white smile and traces of life under the New Mexico sun crinkling around her eyes. Prettier than ever.

"Hey, big guy. Willie sent me."

"It's great to see you, cowgirl. Been way too long." He felt a pang of remorse—he was the one who'd called off the relationship after he met Colleen. "I didn't know you still hang with Willie." During their high school days, Willie had returned from a stint in the marines and taken up the job of mentoring the young couple during their coming of age rites. They'd survived with relatively minor scars.

"It's a small town." Laurie walked straight into him without slowing and gave him a fierce bear hug. She grabbed the duffel bag and began wheeling it toward an aging white Subaru covered with faded stickers.

Laurie stayed off the Interstate and ten minutes later pulled into Jack's Tavern, a popular eatery on Old Las Vegas Highway. The place was nearly empty in the late afternoon. Over a pitcher of pale ale, they alternated abridged tales of their past two decades. Tom paused his story at the time he'd joined the Art Crime Team and Colleen had split for the Big Apple. Laurie dove into her final segment describing her ongoing investigation of corruption in the oil business. While corruption and oil were seldom separate, she was working on a bribery case that would be eye-popping even by New Mexican standards. Laurie named no names, but it was clear that it involved major players in the state government. She leaned back from the table and drained her glass, flipping a line of foam off her lip with a finger. "OK, get to the point. What the hell are you doing here? Willie said you'd be coming in on the choo-choo and asked me to pick you up." She moved her chin forward an inch and arched her eyebrows.

Tom resumed with an account of the failed sting, his sudden career change, and Colleen's decision to remain in New York. When he was finished, he stared at Laurie, waiting for a reaction, but she merely blinked five or six times. "Well. That's it. I'm moving here, effective now. I figure I'll stay with Willie and Rosanne for a couple of days while I get set up. We haven't really worked out the job details yet."

"They're out of town—down near Ruidoso. Willie's working some case connected with the racetrack, and Rosanne went along to see a cousin. I'm supposed to make sure you don't get lost before they get back on Thursday." She cocked her head to the right and assumed a wary expression. "You can stay at my place for a day or two if you don't think it'll cause a scandal back at the ranch. I've got a second bedroom. No big ideas, OK? And Willie left me a key to his office. I can drop you there in the morning. Myrna, his assistant, won't be there—she's off a couple of days while the boss is gone."

"Sounds good." Tom knew Colleen wouldn't like it, but under the circumstances, he really didn't give a damn.

Thirty minutes later Laurie pulled into the driveway of a small adobe house in the South Capitol area. The exterior's sizeable dose of Santa Fe charm included a sagging portal and a finicky lock on the front door that did its best to prevent entry. A punched-tin sconce shielded the door from most of the light produced by a single forty-watt bulb. They managed to drop the luggage inside and proceeded to Juanita's for Tom's official homecoming ceremony—blue corn enchiladas, served flat in the northern New Mexico style and smothered by a volcanic flow of red chile. They tempered the chile with the strongest margaritas sold without a prescription on the high plains. These were a popular hazard for visitors from lower altitudes who weren't accustomed to the combined effects of tequila and the 20 percent reduction in oxygen at seven thousand feet. Tom was a lowlander now, and he crashed instantly after Laurie steered him to her guest room bed.

*　*　*

After a brief bagel and coffee breakfast, Laurie handed Tom a key and dropped him on Staab Street. The building before him was of unclear ancestry and could be classified as either pueblo revival, territorial style, or none of the above. It was an old house subdivided into tiny offices with external doors opening in random directions. The sidewalk once had known better days but now was just irregular bits of broken concrete separating the entrances to competing ant colonies. Tom approached the door facing Staab Street and found a hand-lettered sign written on a piece of paper ripped from a spiral notebook. The sign was stuck to the door with blue duct tape and read: "McNaul Brothers, Private Investigators. Inquire within." The key worked, and he stepped into Willie's world.

The entry was barely large enough to host a four-peg coat rack and a framed poster advertising a Santa Fe Opera production of La Bohème. Willie would only attend an opera at gunpoint or as a security guard, but Tom rather liked the art deco rendition. The adjoining room sported a surprisingly fresh coat of paint in a dark shade of red resembling Beaujolais. On second thought, it was closer to blood. A large oak desk supported a computer station and two pictures of kids who probably belonged to Myrna. One wall was lined with four-drawer metal file cabinets, no two matching. Tom opened the top drawer of each and found only two containing paperwork, plus one housing coffee paraphernalia. Two sagging leather chairs with chrome supports flanked a square table in one corner. Tom tried the left chair and found himself staring between his knees toward the desk. The walls were spattered with an assortment of framed documents that resembled diplomas but were cleverly hung too high to be read by persons of modest stature. The only frame at eye level contained a copy of Willie's investigator license.

A solid white door in the rear wall was unusually outfitted with a brass Marine Corps knocker complete with eagle. Tom rubbed the eagle's beak as he entered Willie's emerald green office. He walked past a long, well-stocked bookcase and settled into the rickety knockoff of a designer office chair behind Willie's desk. From this vantage point in the green room, he could see past the open white door to the red wall opposite Myrna's desk. The resemblance to the Mexican flag had to be intentional. He wasn't about to prowl through Willie's desk—many things were best left unknown, particularly by brothers. The surface was bare except for a cup of unmatched pens, a phone, and a brass lamp. A worktable was pushed up against the room's lone window. There seemed to be space for another desk, but the table would do for now. He checked out two doors in the rear wall and found a largely bare supply closet and a full bath, complete with a claw-foot tub which appeared to have contained neither bathers nor gin for at least half a century.

The room also contained a conference table with three wooden chairs and a battered faux-leather sofa from Goodwill or a nearby sidewalk. He'd slept on worse. There wasn't anything to do for the next couple of hours, so after checking under the sofa cushions for stale food and mouse droppings, he settled in for a short nap.

*   *   *

Downtown Santa Fe is compact, and Tom knew it is best navigated on foot. By noon he had consumed three cups of coffee, posted a $10,000 surety bond, arranged for the required million bucks of liability insurance, and picked up his P.I. license with related documents. The old boy network was alive and well. He expected to be subjected to at least a ceremonial butt chewing and lecture, but apparently no administrator considered him worth the time. The envelope with his license contained a note saying Lieutenant Eddie Romero of the Santa Fe Police Department would like to have a welcoming chat with him. That didn't sound pleasant, so Tom decided to ignore it. Tom and Eddie went back to high school and had been good friends until they got into a fight over Laurie. Eddie could bloody well track him down if he still had issues. Tom celebrated the new job with a dripping, foil-wrapped burrito from a cart on the plaza.

The office phone was comatose when Tom settled into Willie's chair, and it stayed that way for most of the afternoon. No sultry blondes with broad-brimmed hats and pouty red lips came up the sidewalk. He made a note to check into the firm's advertising budget. He spent an hour on his cell phone calling rental agencies and made an appointment to view a promising condo the next morning. The day's work done, he located a dog-eared Agatha Christie on the bookshelf and settled onto the sofa. The office phone finally rang just after four. It was Laurie. Her oil story sources were hiding successfully, and she was ready to pick him up. They stopped at a small pizza place on Guadalupe Street before heading home. The pizza was prompt and the beer was beer, with the odd twist that the price per ounce increased as the mugs got bigger. They each ordered two smalls.

Laurie finished her first glass and pushed it aside. "Well, let's see it."

He took out the license. "Not very impressive, is it? Any luck with your story?"

She twitched one side of her mouth. "I'm getting closer. A woman in Las Cruces said she'd email me copies of some land records tomorrow. I don't know if they'll show anything, but something must be working. And I got my second death threat yesterday."

Tom's hand flinched, almost knocking over his second glass of Italian beer. "What?"

"Not to worry—just the usual anonymous note in the mail. They aren't rare in the newspaper business, you know."

"But you said two?"

"Yeah, about a week apart. Maybe a crank, or maybe someone trying to back me off." She snorted into her beer. "They can't be too serious. I don't know enough to be dangerous."

"Yet."

"Yeah, yet."

It was dark by the time Laurie turned the Subaru into her driveway. The porch light must have burned out. She handed Tom a tiny flashlight from her purse, and he leaned his head close to hers as she worked at the lock with her key. A car was approaching from the east. The sound of the engine faded, and Tom realized it was stopping. He was turning toward the street when he heard the crack of a shot and splintering wood as a bullet hit the door. He pushed Laurie hard, sending her sprawling across the porch as he dropped the penlight and dove the same way. The car sped off with lights extinguished. Grabbing the light, he saw the key still in the lock. He gave it a few hard twists and shakes, shoved the door open, and went back for Laurie. He managed to lift and carry her into the house, kicking the door shut behind him. Pain bit his side as he twisted and lowered her onto her couch. She was fighting back sobs but losing badly. He closed the living room curtains and turned on a light. Laurie was bent forward with a hand cupped over her right eye.

"Let me see it." The shot had hit the door inches from their heads, and Tom suspected she might have a splinter in her eye. He spread her eyelid with his fingers and tried to examine the eye with the penlight, but he couldn't hold her still. He gave up and called 911.

The first police car pulled up ten minutes later and was soon followed by two more. Tom answered questions while trying to keep Laurie from rubbing her eye. When the ambulance arrived, he stopped talking until she was on her way to St. Vincent Hospital. He turned back to the two patrolmen on the front porch and repeated the story for the third time. "I didn't get a good look at the car or driver. I think there was only one guy. He turned his lights off when he slowed under that tree, and the streetlight wasn't on him. Laurie never turned his way—that's why she got the face full of splinters."

The uniform on the left rechecked his notes. "Not a lot of drive-bys in this neighborhood. You sure you don't have any guess who it was?"

"No. Sorry." He decided not to tell them about Laurie's death threats. He hadn't actually seen the notes, and Laurie could fill the cops in when she got back from the hospital if she wanted to. The police let him go inside while they finished photographing the door and looking in vain for a shell casing. After they left, Tom found her spare set of keys on a peg in the kitchen and drove to the hospital

Laurie turned out to be in pretty good shape but hardly looked it. There were no splinters lodged in her eye—just a slight scratch. The result was a black eye patch that stood out against her ashen complexion. A couple of minor splinters had lodged themselves in her nose, resulting in a humorously placed Band-Aid. Tom considered snapping a photo with his phone but refrained. She flinched when they reached the damaged front door of her house but seemed stable enough until she collapsed onto the couch. Tom found a bottle of Jack Daniel's, poured two tall ones, and joined her.

"I'm sorry, Tommy. You could have been killed." She stared at him with the available eye. "I've had a lot of notes like those before, and nothing ever happened."

Tom didn't reply right away. He didn't want to upset her any more, so he silently tilted his glass her way and made a good start at emptying it. I'm not so sure he was shooting at you, babe.

They sat for more than an hour talking about anything but what had happened. The second round was as tall as the first. Laurie regained a bit of color, and the shakes were coming less frequently. They decided to turn in, with Laurie taking first shot at the bathroom.

Tom switched off his light and began replaying the shooting to no avail. He had turned too slowly to see anything but a dark figure in the car. He wasn't even sure the shooter was alone. He pushed away the images and fell asleep in seconds.

A few minutes later he was startled awake. The covers pulled away slightly, and the side of the bed sagged as Laurie slid in beside him. He felt her shudder as she snuggled her back against him, and he could tell from the sniffles that she'd been crying. He curled his left arm around her and held her quietly in the darkness as her breathing slowed into a gentle rhythm. His arm was beginning to fall asleep when she rolled over to face him. She tilted her head upward, and he took the cue and met her with a long, soft kiss. They made love gently—at first. It had been more than twenty-five years, but as they lay together, spent and fading, it felt comfortably familiar to Tom. Neither of them said a word. Sometime during the night, Laurie disappeared from his bed.

~ 6 ~

Tom hid out in Laurie's guest room listening to the sounds of a standup breakfast being prepared and slurped. The smell of coffee finally flushed him. They chatted in cheerful tones for several minutes while avoiding eye contact, and then Laurie rushed out the door for a morning staff meeting. It was obvious that however the day went, Tom would be spending the night elsewhere. He packed his bags while consuming bagel and coffee and was ready when the doorbell rang promptly at nine.

Mary Ortega seemed somewhat taken aback when Tom stuffed his bulging duffel bag and locked metal case into the back of her SUV. Unless the condo she was showing him was uninhabitable, he'd take it. Ten minutes later she turned into a small parking lot adjoining a cluster of condos on Paseo de la Cuma, a largely unpaved road that ran along a ridge a few blocks north of the plaza. Neither or them had a clue what "Cuma" meant, but the location was great.

Unit 17 was available and unfurnished. According to Ortega, the owner had sold his soul for a job in Houston but refused to sell his split-level foothold in Shangri-La. Who could blame him? A cursory inspection showed the usual Santa Fe style—tile floors, beam and latilla ceilings, a kiva fireplace in one corner, and punched-tin cabinet doors in the kitchen. It was small but had two bedrooms. The upstairs master had a porch large enough for two people if neither wanted to sit down, and a thirty-degree wedge of view through trees toward the west. The setting sun might be visible during some months. Technically, he had a mountain view—a small volcanic cone that Ortega identified as Tetilla Peak. It resembled the Grand Tetons in name only.

Mary Ortega was happy to take his check and multiple signatures in exchange for a set of keys and a copy of the lease. They shook hands, and Tom waited until her Lexus disappeared back onto the paved streets before locking the door and walking down the hill to town. The condo was only five minutes from either the Staab Street office or the plaza at the brisk pace he preferred.

The pod with his furniture wasn't due for another four or five days, so he turned up his coat collar and walked fifteen minutes past his office to the REI at the railyard. He outfitted himself with a backpacking pad, a down sleeping bag, and an LED camping lantern, and lugged them back to the condo. A second trip down the hill ended at DeVargas Mall, where he located decent coffee, assorted victuals and libations sure to evoke Colleen's scorn (particularly the single-malt Bushmills), and the cheapest toaster he could find. A stainless-steel industrial-strength toaster was coming in the pod, but he couldn't wait. That left him a coffee pot short of breakfast, but he could make do with the spare in Willie's file cabinet. His addictions to toast and coffee were a source of constant friction with Colleen, who was a prophetess of the low-carb faith. Tom had managed to preserve the marriage until this week by always being the first one out of bed in the morning.

It took him three minutes to set up his new digs with the foam pad aligned to maximize his view through the sliding porch door. A brief stroll through the condo confirmed that he wouldn't be hosting any parties until the movers arrived. It was time to get to work.

The winter sun was passing high noon when Tom arrived at the sidewalk leading to the McNaul Brothers office. Meandering chalk marks wound through the fractured concrete, forming some type of grotesque grid. He finally recognized it as a particularly daring hop-scotch court where a misplaced foot might stir up a battalion of angry red ants. There were no kids in sight, though he could hear shouts from an elementary school playground one street away. After two quick hops on his right leg, he swayed off balance and felt a jab in his wounded side as he planted his left foot hard on a particularly active anthill. He hobbled up the steps bent over and brushing tiny infantry off his left shoe. The duct-taped sign was gone, and the door opened as he was reaching to try the handle.

He stood up to face a pale smirk with green eyes and blazing lipstick that was the only thing in sight redder than the explosion of curls. "I thought he was just being mean when he called you the twerp. You OK?"

"Yeah." He abandoned any attempt at salvaging dignity and extended his hand. "Myrna, I presume?"

"Indeed." She stood looking slightly up at him from her position atop knee-length boots with uncomfortably steep heels. Myrna smiled and led him through the tiny entry toward her desk. Tom performed a thorough appraisal as he followed. Forty pounds ago she would have been a knockout, and dressed to prove it with too-tight sequined-butt jeans, a plunging white linen shirt, and long earrings dangling amid the red curls. Now she looked like a Texas trophy wife gone to seed with only her walk unchanged.

Myrna shimmied around the desk, leaned back in a swivel chair, and crossed her boots on an inverted mesh wastebasket. She saw him staring at the pictures of two tweeners, a boy and a girl, in drugstore frames. "Yeah, mine. Only a single mom would be desperate enough to work for Willie. Take a load off, Tommy. It's good to meet you."

"Likewise." Tom glanced at the sagging chairs in the corner and opted to stand. A sudden sting caused him to swat at his left thigh and pinch a tiny lump under his jeans. He felt a slight crunch as the ant's body yielded to the pressure. "Partisan activity. Think I got him, though." Myrna seemed puzzled but said nothing.

Willie's voice boomed from the back room: "Come on in, Twerp." Tom complied, resisting the urge to try out the brass knocker. The brothers stopped four feet apart for the mandatory once-overs. Willie was the same height as Tom but twenty pounds heavier and a good deal hairier, with shoulder-length gray hair and a full, closely trimmed beard. They shook hands silently—the McNauls were not a hugging family. Tom sat on one end of the sofa and scanned the room while Willie poured two mugs of steaming black coffee. A small oak desk and chair now faced the window, with the worktable forming a right angle. The desktop was bare except for two items. The first was the essential basis of the modern workplace, a surge protector with eight outlets. The second was a black six-inch statue of a scowling bird standing on a block. Tom recognized it at once: The Maltese Falcon. He choked. It was one of Willie's favorite possessions, a souvenir acquired during a stopover in Malta on his only trip to Europe.

Willie pulled one of the wooden chairs over and sat on it backward. "OK, Tommy. Let's hear the whole truth." He stared at the floor, his folded arms resting on the back of the chair, while Tom reported the events of the last six days. Willie only interrupted twice to clarify small details. When the tale ended, he nodded and looked up at Tom.

"Let's work backwards from last night. Who do you think the guy in the car was shooting at?"

"Don't know. Laurie is sure she was the target. It makes sense, given the death threats, but I don't know much about her investigation. Do they really play that rough out here?"

"Oh yes. Laurie's onto something big enough to be dangerous, but she's holding her cards close." Willie stared off to his left. "It's not quite the way I'd expect the oil crowd to intimidate a lone woman. More likely they'd send a couple of tough guys to corner her in the dark somewhere and scare the hell out of her. She mention anything like that?"

"No, but these days it's hard to find good help."

"Wiseass. Well, she might be right. I'll talk to her and see if I can get some names to start with, but she may not talk. Sources and such." Willie looked back at Tom. "What if he was after you?"

"The FBI had a deal with the Boston boys. They'd let bygones be if I headed west. I don't figure the bosses have anything to gain by taking me out—it would just bring on the heat. But the dead punk may have had a buddy."

"Working overtime?"

Tom nodded.

"What about the guy on the train?"

"The guy reading below grade level?"

"Yeah."

"Couldn't say. He just looked suspicious. I've got nothing on him, and anyway, he didn't get off in Lamy."

Willie didn't look satisfied. "I'll make some calls. Meanwhile, let's get some lunch and figure out how we'll work this soon-to-thrive enterprise."

They squeezed into a cozy booth in a downtown enchilada emporium and avoided talking money until they reached the sopapillas. Willie grinned as his little brother extended his open hand over the table, palm down, with the squeezable honey bear clinging like a stalactite. "No thanks." He leaned across the aisle to grab a cleaner one from an empty table and loaded up the hollow fried puff.

Tom peeled the plastic bear off his hand and stuck it to the table. He didn't know much about the structure of small businesses, but he needed to take the lead on this to make sure Willie didn't suffer from taking on a partner. Willie was proud and likely to offer more than he could afford. To the dismay of Tom's mother, Tom had inherited half of his father's rather substantial estate in 2006. Willie got nothing from the old man, and he had no source of income other than the business. Frances did not remarry and was still in good health at eighty-eight, holding tightly to her portfolio.

After dipping a paper napkin in his water glass and removing some of the honey, Tom wiped his hands on his jeans and looked Willie in the eye. "I feel like I'm horning in on you. Is there really enough work for two P.I.s? I can go it alone, maybe even move once the dust settles."

"The dust never really settles here." Willie squirmed, trying to get comfortable in the wooden booth. "The answer is, I don't know. Just enough people come through the door to keep Myrna and me paying taxes, and we don't turn many away. I work with lawyers, both lawsuits and criminal cases. The odd missing person. Can't afford to be picky, and yes, I even do divorce work."

Tom nodded. He knew he would have to carve out a completely different niche, and he'd come prepared. "Do you work with stolen property?"

"Nah. There isn't any money in it. The burglars are mostly junkies who fence TVs for twenty bucks if they're lucky. The cars get chopped for parts or otherwise trashed. Now and then, someone steals some jewelry, but there's no way to trace it unless they're dumb enough to pawn it in town."

"What about art?"

"Everyone asks that after looking at the prices on Canyon Road. But here's the thing. Knocking over a Santa Fe gallery is easier than stealing a kiss from a blind woman, but then what? There's no way to sell the stuff. You can't deal an abstract landscape from the back of a pickup. It takes ambiance and salespeople who can spin the art dream. Hell, the contemporary place where Judy works—she's Laurie's niece—is full of smart young women in slinky black outfits. Kind of like the time I was in L.A. and walked into a Swedish Dux bed store."

"Sounds more like your last trip to Bangkok. I take your point, but you're talking about the local art world. Internationally, art crime is a big-time game, and I know how it's played. Here's my idea. We'll share the office and expenses, and Myrna if you can spare a piece of her, but not any of your cases. I'll work solely on stolen property—art and antiquities—and related crimes. What do you think?"

Willie closed his left eye while arching his right eyebrow. "Sounds nuts. How many stolen Rembrandts do you figure to dig up in Española?"

"Two, maybe three, but the world's wired now. I can work cases anywhere in the world from an office here. There are massive online databases, and I've got twenty-five years of contacts in the FBI and Interpol. Some of them will still talk to me."

"Still sounds nuts, but deal." Willie reached a paw across the table for a ceremonial shake without showing any regard for the honey.

"Tell me, though, do you really figure it's good business, or is this some kind of cause for you? You've always been something of a Don Quixote type."

"Little of each, I guess. Art's important to me. It's part of our culture, and it pisses me off when people steal it—particularly from the public. The money bothers me, though. So much money for old paint on canvas, all because rich folks want it. It's not always easy to give a damn when someone pilfers their prize specimen."

"Well." Willie reached for his coat and began sliding out of the booth. "I do admire your sense of justice, little brother. But as Woody Guthrie used to say, some guys will rob you with a fountain pen. You'd do best to remember that."

* * *

Tom borrowed Willie's truck and Myrna. They spent the afternoon buying and installing devices that plugged into the surge protector and every other available outlet. By the end of the day, the office computers were networked and Willie had gone home in symbolic protest. Myrna stopped by Tom's desk to say goodnight and caught him playing with the falcon.

"You take good care of that black bird, big boy. It's ugly as sin, but Willie loves it. Don't ask me why." She started to leave but changed her mind and settled on the sofa, angling her head until she peered at him over the fur ruff of her coat and through a red curl. "Willie said you were going to work on catching painting poachers, or something like that. True?"

He failed to suppress a grin. Myrna was keen as a samurai blade and well educated to boot, but she insisted on playing Mae West. "Something like that. I'm not a cop, though, so my job will be to bring the paintings back alive, not lasso the poachers."

"You'll be carryin' a gun, though?"

"Yeah. The poachers don't always let go easily."

"Heard you're pretty good with one."

"Not good enough sometimes."

She nodded and switched her expression from femme fatale to concerned comrade. "Willie told me about your partner. Kate was her name?"

"Is her name. She's going to make it."

"Glad to hear it." Myrna weighed her options for a moment and decided to leave. "Good night." She strode out of the office with plenty of motion.

"See you, Myrna."

There wasn't much to go home to, so Tom logged on. He spent three hours poring over online databases for art stolen in the western U.S. during the past two years. There was no overriding reason to confine the search to the U.S., but a guy had to start somewhere. Hunger increased to a roar, and the Plaza Cafe was still open. By the time he'd downed a green chile cheeseburger and two cups of coffee, a cold front was roaring through with forty-mile-an-hour gusts. His hat and gloves were still in the office, and he hurried there with hands in his coat pockets and ears stinging. After a five-minute thaw, he charged up the hill to his lair and made for the upstairs bedroom.

Tom turned out the lights and sat on his sleeping mat with his back against the wall. He stared at the night sky through the glass door and listened to the wind howling around skylights and through the rails of the tiny balcony. A hell of a week, but the worst seemed to be over. He'd call Colleen in the morning. They would work it out somehow. Then he remembered Laurie.

Tom vowed to put off thinking about women until morning and settled in to get some sleep. He stretched out and was arranging the pillow when his cell phone rang. It was 10:45, and he didn't recognize the local number.

"Yeah?"

"Is that you, McNaul?" The male voice was vaguely familiar.

"Who's asking?"

"It's Eddie. Romero. That would be Lieutenant Romero to you."

"Oh, hi Eddie. Sorry I didn't call you yet. How've you been?"

"Never mind that just now, let me in. I'm outside your front door. Myrna gave me your address."

Tom pulled on a shirt and jeans and padded barefoot across cold tiles to the door. Eddie hadn't lost much but hair color since they'd last met. He was shorter than Tom, about five-foot-nine, and built like a middleweight. He walked past Tom without speaking and came to a sudden halt staring around the empty rooms. "Jesus, Tommy, how broke are you?"

"Nice to see you too, Eddie. What're you doing here?"

"About an hour ago, a guy was dropped off on the sidewalk outside the St. Vincent emergency room. He had two broken legs, various contusions, and a right hand that looked like someone ran a truck over it. You know anything about this?"

"No." Tom was being truthful, but his mind raced ahead. Willie. Oh shit. "Why are you asking me?"

"Don't bullshit me, Tommy. You've got a reputation, and don't think anyone here likes the feds passing you off on us. You were only in town a few hours when the drive-by guy shot up Laurie's front door last night. Now this. You telling me there's no connection?"

"Not one that I know about. And I figure the drive-by was shooting at Laurie. Who is the guy, anyway?"

"Some Irish punk with two sets of IDs, one of which turned out to be real. Some arrests in Boston but no convictions. He lawyered up and just wants to go home. We'll have to let him go when he's able. Sure you haven't seen this guy?" Eddie held up his cell phone with a photo of a man who hadn't had a good day. The undamaged parts of him looked like the slow reader.

"I saw a guy who looked like that on the train, but I don't know him. Honest, Eddie." The lieutenant grimaced. During their high school days, an Albuquerque car dealer called Honest Eddie advertised relentlessly on TV. Eddie Romero had inherited the nickname, and it lived on after he joined the police force. There wasn't anything more to say, so they repeated themselves two or three times and Eddie left. Tom added the battered reader to his list of things not to think about before morning and poured a glass of whiskey to help him get there.

~ 7 ~

There was no hiding from the New Mexico sun in a house with no curtains. Tom slithered out of his makeshift bed feeling somewhat seedy but absent the misery of a true hangover. It was only six-thirty. Jesus.

Within half an hour he was bundled to face the ten-degree wind chill and out the door carrying his third cup of coffee in a travel mug. Santa Fe at seven. About as lively as Chaco Canyon. Five minutes later he settled at his desk and placed a call to Colleen. After eight rings her voice told him he was being exiled to voicemail, as usual. Colleen hadn't picked up one of his calls for two or three years—the etiquette of the times—though she always seemed to answer when her gallery called.

Tom pretended he wasn't killing time by adjusting the tension knobs on his desk chair. When he ran out of knobs, he pondered the falcon on his desk. It wasn't as large as the one in the famous Bogart film, but it was a reasonable likeness and a whole lot cheaper. One of the four statues made for the movie had brought a cool million at a recent auction. Fools and their money form an unstable state. Of course, an original Maltese falcon—the annual rent the Knights of Malta allegedly paid for their island—would be worth far more. He made a note to check the stolen art lists for filched falcons.

When Tom's phone rang, it showed Colleen's number. He set the falcon back on his desk and waited four rings before answering. "Hi, toots."

"Hi, Tommy. Sorry I didn't call earlier."

"It's OK."

"No, it's not. But I needed some time to settle down before we talked." She waited for Tom to say something, but he waited her out. "How are you? And for that matter, where are you?"

"I'm fine. It wasn't much of a wound, and it only seems to hurt when I play hopscotch. I'm in Santa Fe." He passed on an abridged version of the week's events, leaving out the drive-by shooting, the sex with Laurie, and the case of the slow-reading man.

"What the hell? How long are you planning to stay out there?"

"I signed a year's lease yesterday. Rented a nice little condo up in that group on the ridgeline north of the plaza. We looked at a place there a couple of years ago when we were thinking of getting a vacation home, remember?"

"A year?"

"That's just the lease. I'm here for the long haul. I've had it with the East, and not just because of the Boston Irish."

Colleen's pause seemed a little too short, and her words sounded well rehearsed. "Tommy, I can't just drop my life and run out to New Mexico. I've waited more than twenty years to break into the real art market. I followed you around to one FBI hellhole after another trying to sell my paintings from tents to yokels who wanted something yellow to match the sofa. No way I can leave New York now. And Cassidy's got one more year of high school. She couldn't leave her friends."

"Yeah, I know. But it's not so different, really. I was going to be in Washington another year anyway. I'm just a plane ride instead of a drive away. Look, I think we could make a good life out here. Can you and Cassidy come out for a visit? How about Thanksgiving?"

"I need more time to think, Tommy. Justin says he needs at least six new paintings for a show in December, and I've only got two. Maybe Cassidy could fly out for a couple of days. I'll talk to her."

Justin. As usual, her gallery owner was calling the shots. "Well. OK, ask her, then. She hasn't been out here for five or six years."

"I will. Oh, how's Kate doing?"

It was a pro forma question, but Tom felt guilt pangs because he didn't really know. He should have checked up on her. "I'm not sure. I haven't talked to her since Sunday, but I'll let you know when I hear something."

Colleen made her excuses and hung up. It didn't sound promising, but at least she sounded concerned about Kate. Her tone seemed pretty lame after twenty-five years of marriage. He was reaching to set his phone on the desk when it rang again.

"Yeah?"

A weak but cheerful female voice responded: "That you, Tom?"

"Kate! Nice surprise. How the hell are you?"

"Been better, but I've moved over to rehab. I'm learning to breathe deeply again and that sort of stuff. They didn't have to remove any of my lung, so they say I should make a full recovery. I'll probably toss my two-piece bathing suit, though. My skin looks like an abandoned railroad track."

Not the worst result—Kate didn't have a two-piece figure anyway. "You can swim faster in a one-piece. Hey, anything going with our case?"

"Not much. We figure the two guys you took out were moonlighting—some kind of scam. Their photo of the back of the Vermeer seems genuine, so at some point in the past twenty years, it was probably in the hands of someone in the Boston underworld. Can't prove it, though. It's possible they never had more than a photo someone sent them trying to sell it."

"What's your take?"

She was silent for several seconds. "They had it, or at least saw it. The print was from a Canon inkjet printer, and the lab says the inks used weren't around more than five years ago. The photo could be older than that, but I doubt it."

"Sounds right. Any idea who called the guy in the house?"

"No. The call came from a disposable. By the way, don't talk to anyone about that call. It's one of the holdbacks. That's why it's not in the papers."

"Too bad. Well, I wish you luck with the chase. We took a good shot at it, so to speak, but I'm moving on to lesser things out here."

"Sorry how it turned out for you, Tommy. You got a bum deal."

"Thanks. Salvaged some pension at least. Come west for a visit sometime, and don't push yourself too hard with the rehab." Useless advice to be sure. Kate would work out at the Olympic Training Center if they'd let her.

*   *   *

At nine-thirty Willie and Myrna arrived together in Willie's Ford F-250. Roseanne McNaul shared the common female weakness for horses. She and Willie lived fifteen miles from town on twenty acres zoned for any type of known animal. When Myrna's husband split for the coast, she and her two kids moved into an apartment in Willie's former tractor barn. She helped pay the rent by apprenticing the kids to Roseanne as stable hands.

When the coats were hung, Tom followed Willie into their office while fending off an already-customary wink from Myrna. He shut the door and wheeled his swivel chair over to Willie's desk. Willie opened the bottom drawer for a footrest and leaned back. "What's up?"

"What the fuck, Willie? What did you do? My first night in the condo and I've got Honest Eddie at my door."

Willie shrugged. "Not much. I made a few phone calls. Spent the evening working on bikes with Rosanne." They were restoring a pair of vintage Indian Scout 45 motorcycles, and had one in approximate running order.

"Keep talking."

"OK. I didn't get anywhere sniffing around Laurie's story. Didn't expect to, really. The oil people cover their tracks too well to be flushed out by phone calls. But I did find someone who saw a man get off your train in Albuquerque. Black leather jacket and a briefcase. Had to be the slow reader. Turns out he rented a car an hour later, and the agent recommended the Quality Inn in Santa Fe. A few bucks got me the info."

"And you beat the guy half to death?"

Willie assumed a concerned look that just might have included a trace of sincerity. "Is that what happened to him?" He took his feet off the drawer and leaned forward over his desk. "No, as a matter of fact I didn't. I have a couple of acquaintances who owed me a favor—never did get paid for saving their uncle's farm. I told them some bastard took a shot at my friend, Laurie, or maybe at my little brother on his first night in town. Asked them to talk to this fellow to see what he knows. Sounds like maybe they did."

"You know damned well they did, and they almost killed him in the process."

"Probably because you're my brother. Family ups the ante around here."

Tom found himself shaking his head. "Well, did they find out anything?"

"Not much. Tough little bugger. He's not from these parts. Lives in Boston, or somewhere near there. He had a gun on him, though. Even had a silencer in the briefcase. I told my guys they could keep the stuff."

Willie considered this a done deal, so Tom rolled his chair back to the desk by the window. The Boston connection meant the gunman was stalking him. The guy probably had hoped to hit Tom while he was asleep on the train and get off in Raton or somewhere. But was he working alone, or did someone send him? If Boston ordered the hit, they might have sent someone to pick the guy up when he got off the train. He was alone in Albuquerque, but maybe he hadn't planned to get off there. Probably stayed on the train after he couldn't get through Tom's door in the night. Thinking about it wasn't going to help. Tom knew he would have to make some calls, but they could wait a couple of days. The slow reader wouldn't be a problem anytime soon.

A few minutes later a steam whistle blew two lonesome howls from somewhere inside the office. It sounded like the whistle on an old Lionel locomotive. Tom scanned the room but couldn't find the source. Willie looked up from his newspaper and took a walkie-talkie from his center desk drawer. He turned it on and pressed the send button. "What's up?"

Myrna's voice squawked back amid static worthy of a five-dollar radio in a thunderstorm. "Tracy Lee's Bimmer just rammed the curb out front."

"Shit. Tell her I'm not here." Willie exploded from his seat, pushed Tom hard enough to send his chair rolling across the room, and climbed onto the desk in front of the lone double-hung window. Tom dragged his heels and stopped the chair short of the bookcase. His brother was on hands and knees struggling to break the grip of the last coat of paint on the window. Each upward heave was accompanied by a mighty grunt. Willie retrieved a Swiss army knife from his pocket and hacked at the paint. Tom rescued the teetering falcon just as Willie rammed the lower window upward against the frame with a thwack loud enough to silence the voices in the front room.

A second later the office door burst open and rebounded against the wall, rattling the brass knocker. A high-striding red cowboy boot entered the room followed by the attached cowgirl. Tracy Lee was tall, dark, and angry. Forty-plus years of Texas sun were etched on her face. Her long hair was stretched back and clamped by an inlaid silver comb big enough to let everyone know it wasn't a rubber band. Her western outfit was pure opulent horsewoman, and her demeanor suggested she left the wounded behind. She came to a stop staring at Willie's behind as he crouched on all fours on Tom's desk. "Going somewhere?"

"Just cooling the place off a bit, Tracy." A blast of frigid air and dust cleared the papers off both desks.

Tracy Lee looked like the kind of woman whose laugh should blow out bonfires, but it came out as alternating giggles and snorts. "My ass. Damn, Willie. I'm not even here to talk about my ratfink husband."

Willie closed the window and slowly backed off the desk, keeping his butt squarely pointed at Tracy as he dismounted. He turned to face her and swung his arm toward Tom. "Tracy Lee, allow me to introduce my new partner, and long-time little brother, Tommy McNaul.

Tom took a short step forward to shake hands before realizing he was still holding the falcon. He stopped just out of range. Nice to meet you, Ms. Lee."

Tracy looked him over as if she were considering him as an understudy for her tennis pro. "Likewise, I'm sure. But my last name isn't Lee." She didn't elaborate.

"Make that Tracy Lee Jackson," said Willie. "What can I do for you, Tracy?"

"Some asshole stole my soup can."

Willie and Tom looked at each other in obvious bewilderment. It seemed somewhat surprising that Tracy Lee would eat canned soup, and far more so that she'd give a damn if someone lifted a can. Willie broke the silence: "Someone must have been pretty hungry. Doesn't sound like much of a loss, though. What kind of soup was it?"

"Campbell's Tomato, of course. I always go for the best."

Dawn broke on Tom's face. "You're not talking about somebody's lunch, are you?"

"Of course not. Nice to see the McNauls didn't reach a dead end at Willie. It's a print. A genuine Andy Warhol silkscreen. Bryce—that would be my husband—gave it to me for my birthday. I've been in Dallas a couple of weeks, and when I walked into my kitchen this morning, no soup can."

"The kitchen?" Tom's mind raced. Ah, the Warhol soup can prints— late 1960s. Two sets—each with ten varieties of soup, but tomato was the prize—Andy's trademark. But what fool would hang one in a kitchen?

"Yeah, the kitchen. I mean, where else would it belong? I needed some red in there."

Tom decided to hold his fire. The soup cans were printed on relatively lightweight paper compared with Warhol's later prints. The paper was extremely sensitive to changes in temperature and humidity which caused it to expand and contract, eventually damaging the image. Then there was the greasy smoke.

Willie got back in the game. "That's a police matter, Tracy. Didn't you call the cops?"

She snorted. "Bryce did. They gave him the usual runaround, but they'll never find it. They haven't got the time, not to mention the inclination."

Willie glanced at Tom and then back to Tracy Lee. "Maybe it's your lucky day. I don't do stolen property, but young Tom here happens to be an expert. Direct from the FBI Art Crime Team to you. I'll just leave you two to discuss it." He made his escape through the more-conventional door.

Tracy Lee eyed Tom with suspicion. "Is that Willie's usual load of bull, or do you really know something about art?"

Tom was done with shy. "Willie's right this time. I'm as good as you'll find, Ms. Jackson. Maybe better than you deserve. You're right about the police. The only city force with a full-time art detective is L.A., and they don't care squat about New Mexico. Art theft is an international business, and the FBI team is the only real group working it this side of the pond. I was with them up until a week ago."

"So what are you doing here?"

"They thought I was too much of a straight shooter."

"I haven't a clue what that means, but what the hell? You want the job?"

"OK."

"Such enthusiasm. What do you charge? Same as Willie?"

Tom realized he had no idea what Willie charged. "I don't know yet. Give me the rundown, and we'll talk about it."

Tracy sized up the available options and settled on one of the wooden chairs as Tom returned to his desk. "Last May Bryce bought a set of the soup cans, the first set. He knows I like Warhol, so later on he pulled the best one from the portfolio and gave it to me for my birthday."

"Tomato Soup?"

"Yep. It sells for three times what the others go for. Well, except for Chicken Noodle; that's somewhere in the middle. As I said, I got back from Dallas and it was gone. Bryce said the cops were out yesterday and found a jimmied window. The alarm had gone off, but they got in and grabbed my print before the cops got there."

"Kind of an unusual grab and run. A framed Warhol print is pretty big."

"Uh huh. The cops figured they had a car and shadowed someone through the gate, but nobody saw anything."

"Was it insured?"

She nodded. "Bryce figured there wasn't much chance of getting it back, so he filed a claim. He says I should just forget about it."

"You obviously think otherwise."

"Damned straight. I don't care that much about the money, but it really pisses me off. You don't mess with Tracy Lee Jackson." She stuck out her jaw, daring him to disagree. He didn't.

"Let me do a little homework. I'll check to see if anyone's selling soup on the black market, get an updated appraisal, and so on. I'd like to come out and have a look at your kitchen tomorrow morning, and I'll figure out what I'm charging by then. That OK?"

"Sure, but make it after ten."

Tracy Lee gave Tom directions and the code for the neighborhood gate before squealing off in her red BMW convertible. A few minutes later Willie reappeared from somewhere. "Well, well," Tom asked. "Any chance you'll tell me why you were heading out the window?"

Willie looked chagrined. "Tracy hired me to find out if her husband's been playing around. He is—the guy's a well-known tomcat—but I didn't want to tell her yet."

"Because?"

"Well, it's partly that she pays well and I need the cash. But mainly, it's because his current mistress is a friend of mine. Lola Cisneros. She manages a gallery a few doors down Canyon Road from the one Tracy and Bryce own. There'll be hell to pay if Tracy Lee gets wind of her, and I'm hoping Bryce will just rove on to some other babe before she does."

Tom fired up his laptop and checked the international stolen art database for a recent surge in stolen Warhols. They were popular targets, but he saw no obvious trend. He checked the most recent auction results. Tomato Soup was indeed selling for three or four times the price of the others. The most recent sales averaged thirty grand, a nice profit for somebody since they sold for a couple of hundred back in 1968. It was an edition of two hundred fifty. They were signed in ballpoint on the back and numbered with a rubber stamp, also on the back.

Tom called Tracy Lee on her cell. "Ms. Jackson? Do you know the number of your print? I'm asking because you said the print was framed, and the number's on the back."

"I know all that, but the framer left a cutout in the mat so you could see the signature. Not that you can read it—Andy really scrawled on this one. The number's visible too. Nine. It was Tomato Soup number nine."

~ 8 ~

Tracy Lee's directions turned out to have a left that meant right and two numbers inverted in the code for the security gate. Otherwise, it was a fine November morning. The only break in the blue was a small cap cloud parked over Santa Fe Baldy. Tom was stuck idling at the gate in his rented Chevy and dialed Tracy for a more-useful number. Her phone was still ringing as a silver Mercedes pulled up behind him. Its driver immediately laid on his horn and kept up a steady rhythm of blaring bleats. You'd think for that much money the horn would at least honk a chord. Tom got the code from Tracy and tested it. The gate swung open. He unfolded the morning New Mexican and began to read as the gate closed. When the honking stopped, he looked in the mirror and saw a short, bald man in an Irish sweater slamming the door of the Mercedes. Tom tossed the paper on the passenger seat and punched in the code again. The gate opened just as the increasingly ruddy-faced man reached the window of Tom's Chevy. With as big a shit-eating grin as he could muster, Tom hit the gas and squealed off to Jackson Manor.

The sprawling single-level house backed onto a golf course with lush fairways and traps so bright they might have been ripped off from White Sands National Monument. A few golfers were braving the chill in colorful attire apparently styled to keep them from taking the game too seriously. Tom lost sight of them as he wound up a paved driveway and parked before an imposing entryway leading to massive double doors. They were flanked by tall, turquoise flowerpots filled with casualties of a hard frost. He was searching for a bell when the right door swung inward and was replaced by Tracy Lee. She was a study in scarlet, snugly covered by blazing red warmups with matching runners and holding a tall Bloody Mary, complete with celery stalk.

"Come in, Mr. McNaul." She turned before he could reply and led him down a tiled hallway that skirted a huge room with dark leather seating and a fireplace large enough to roast oxen two at a time. They entered the doorway to her kitchen and a short time later reached the other side. The room had a twelve-foot ceiling, steel appliances designed to evoke a restaurant kitchen, and a marble-topped island that reminded Tom of a carrier flight deck. He saw two wine cabinets, and an open door led to pantry large enough to store his Washington condo. The southern wall of the kitchen contained several floor-to-ceiling windows overlooking the backyard and the seventeenth fairway.

"It was up there." Tom turned to see Tracy Lee pointing at the wall opposite the windows. The green diamond plaster above the smaller of two sinks was indeed bare. Two lonely screws stuck out of the wall about eight feet above floor level. Tom could see a faint outline where the print had hung—the grease border. He looked back at the tall windows and judged that the lower portions of the print would receive direct sunlight during the winter, a slow but sure death for the volatile inks used in silkscreens. This is crazy.

"How many people knew you had it?"

"Oh, lots. Bryce hung it on my birthday, and we had a bash that night, maybe seventy-five people. Not counting the caterers and such. A few other people have been over since."

"You said you found it missing yesterday morning, but your husband had already reported it?"

"Yes, the house alarm went off late Thursday morning, the day before yesterday. The security company called Bryce. He drove home and called the cops from here."

"Which door was jimmied?"

"The sliding one from the dining room to the patio." Tom looked it over, but there wasn't anything remarkable. There were scratches and pry marks on the frame near the lock. Only seconds were required to open a patio door, not that it mattered. He turned as if to leave.

"That's it? Aren't you going to do any tests or something?"

"There wouldn't be any point. The police report will cover that."

"So what are you going to do? And how much will it cost me?"

"Fifty an hour plus expenses, and I get twenty percent of the print's value if I bring it back alive. I'll have Myrna get in touch with you about a small retainer."

"Fair enough. You want one of these?" She waggled her Bloody Mary.

It was barely eleven. The obvious move was to smile and split, but Tom had a few questions. Tracy Lee seemed pleased and mixed him a tall one with at least as many fingers of vodka as she had on one hand. Tom wisely set the glass on the coffee table before almost disappearing into a plush white leather sofa. Tracy balanced her freshened glass as she expertly sank into the other end.

"Tell me, Ms. Jackson. . . ."

"Tracy Lee."

Tom tilted his head a few degrees to the right. "Tracy Lee. I understand you and your husband own a gallery on Canyon Road."

"I own it. Bought it eight years ago with my own money. You see, I come from a wealthier family than Bryce, and we keep our family monies separate. I inherited quite a bit when my father died, and I used some of it to buy the business. Bryce has a small interest, but it's basically mine, even though we call it the T&B Jackson Gallery."

"Who runs the place?"

"Bryce. He's the manager, and he draws a salary plus a small share of the profits. I keep an eye on the books, and I have final say on any big purchases or sales, but I don't like day-to-day business. Bryce is good at that."

Tom maneuvered through the undulating folds of leather until his drink was within reach. He took a healthy slug. "Do you sell a lot of Warhols?"

"No. Andy's paintings are beyond the price range of what sells in the Santa Fe market. Now and then we get in some of his prints, though. Bryce likes to buy a set of prints and then sell them individually. I think he usually gets them from some gallery in Philadelphia."

"Do they sell well?"

Tracy flexed one shoulder. "Pretty well. Quite a few go locally, but we also ship some, even to Europe."

"If you don't mind me asking, is the gallery doing well overall?"

"I don't mind. Sales have been pretty weak for the last couple of years, but they're starting to heat up again. We sell high-end art, Mr. McNaul."

"Tom."

She smiled. "All right. As I was saying, our buyers tend to be rather well off. They seem to be bouncing back from this recession more quickly than the economy as a whole." Tracy Lee stared at Tom to judge his reaction. He didn't notice any "aha" expressions, so perhaps his poker face was intact.

"One last question: Who insures your gallery?"

"Art Insurance International—AII. We use them for our personal collection as well."

Tracy Lee drained her second glass and was frowning toward the liquor cart. Tom decided to move the investigation to drier ground and left.

* * *

Tom found the office empty with no notes in sight. Willie had said he usually came into town for a while on Saturdays, but he didn't seem to have many cases just now. Tom looked over Myrna's desk and noticed a doorbell button attached to its left side with thin wires disappearing through a small hole in the floor. He pressed the button and heard the train whistle wail in the inner office. After a few minutes of searching the back room, he found wires coming up through the floor near the end of the bookcase. Behind a few paperbacks was an old twelve-volt doorbell transformer with wires leading to a single piece of three-rail track. A black, well-used Lionel tender sat alone on the track. It was probably the only surviving piece of Willie's toy train. As a kid he'd been prone to staging train wrecks, blowing up tracks and bridges with illegal M-80 firecrackers.

With one mystery solved, Tom moved on to the can caper. He knew he should try to get a look at the police reports, but the chances of a runaround were high, so he put that off for a while. He called Laurie instead.

"I was beginning to think you're the kind of guy who never calls after. What's up?"

Tom filled her in on the theft of Tracy Lee's print. "Heard anything about it at the paper?"

"No, but I've been working my own story pretty hard. We're way understaffed these days, and I doubt if anyone cared enough about a straight-up burglary to dog it. It'd need at least one person getting shot to rise above a line in the daily police log."

"Figured as much. Feel like lunch?"

Laurie was always up for lunch and, to the irritation of her friends, had a metabolism rate that left no traces on her long, shapely frame. She ordered the Saturday special—a two-handed green chile cheeseburger—and ate all the fries. Tom noticed her eyeing his sopapilla and handed it over.

"It's nice to know a man with manners."

"More like a man who knows what's good for him. Mind if we talk about art awhile? That way we can write this off on our taxes."

"Would anyway, but shoot."

"Santa Fe's supposed to be the second or third largest art market in the U.S., but I rarely saw reports of major art crime here. Most of what I did see involved dealing illegal antiquities. Don't people steal things out here?"

Laurie laughed. "We hold our own in the crime rate department. Mostly small-time stuff, though. If you own a flat-screen TV, you'd best chain it to something heavy, but that's mostly junkie and gang stuff. Someone lifts a small piece from a gallery now and then. Not many big pieces, though. What would you do with them?"

"That's pretty much what Willie said."

"I did a story a few years ago about some Hopi pots missing from the collection at what used to be the School for American Research. Didn't go anywhere, though. Nothing was recovered. There were some O'Keeffes stolen from that museum back in 2004, but that was before I moved up from Albuquerque."

"Before I joined the Art Crime Team too, but I did hear about the case. Inside job, from what I read in the papers. What I don't get is why someone would go to the trouble of stealing a Warhol print, and only the print, from a house with an alarm system and located in a gated community."

Laurie shrugged. "Maybe Tracy Lee pissed somebody off. She's pretty good at that."

Tom took a long route back to the office. He walked up the stretch of Canyon Road where the galleries held sway and strolled through several of them just to regain the feel of the place. His last trip to Santa Fe had been five years ago, but the changes seemed modest. He walked along Palace Avenue until he was back at the plaza and stopped at a couple of galleries near there. It was almost three when he entered the New Mexico Museum of Art. The young woman at the entry desk smiled him into an annual membership, and he took a quick tour of the galleries. He loved the classic architecture of the place. A few blocks later he arrived at the Staab Street office. The back room now contained Willie, so Tom filled him in on the meager developments of the morning and leaned back in his chair. Willie stared at the ceiling for several minutes, then swiveled to face Tom.

"Doesn't sound like you learned much from Tracy. And she's right; the cops won't waste time trying to find her soup can. What's your plan?"

"The place to start is the insurance company. Sooner the better. I've got to talk to their claims agent before they actually pay off the Jacksons."

Willie scrunched his brow. "Why's that?"

"I have to find the print while Tracy Lee still owns it or I won't get paid." Willie's expression didn't change.

Tom rocked forward. "The world of art theft involves a little known, and occasionally shady, relationship between the insurer, the thieves, and law enforcement. Once the insurance company pays off on a stolen piece, it becomes their property. My commission from Tracy would disappear faster than Dad's Pontiac that time he missed a payment. I might be able to work with the claims agent to find the print before they pay out, but once it belongs to AII, I'm out of the game."

"Strange world you work in, bro, but what's shady about it?"

"Once the claim is paid, the insurers may try to ransom the piece back from the crooks at a bargain rate. Hell, if the art happens to be underinsured, they could even make a tidy profit by selling it at auction. But crooks are skittish, and they won't deal with the insurance company if they smell the law. The ransom usually has to be paid under the table, and that's illegal—dealing in stolen goods."

Willie's eyes began to wander, and he made a show of tugging his whiskers. Tom took the hint and turned to look out the window. He knew it was not uncommon for the police to look the other way during an art ransom, particularly if the piece was important enough to qualify as some sort of national treasure. Better to recover a masterpiece than put a thief away for a year or two, the sentences for stealing art being rather light in most countries. Tom's problem was that Tracy Lee's print didn't rise to that level of distinction.

Willie relaxed. "Too convoluted for me, but good luck. I think I'll head back to the ranch. Why don't you come out for dinner tomorrow? Six?"

"That'd be great. Thanks."

Willie left and Tom looked up the number for Art Insurance International. Twenty minutes and four transfers later, he was talking to Margery Montgomery, the claims adjuster assigned to the Jackson case. He'd expected some kind of brush-off and wasn't disappointed.

"I haven't got much to say to you, Mr. McNaul. I talked to your local police, and there isn't a chance in hell they'll find the print. They won't even look—no point. It might surface someday, but we can't sit around hoping someone lists it on eBay. I've been waiting for the OK to pay off the claim."

"I don't suppose you can tell me the amount."

"No, but they only insured that set a few months ago."

Tom figured that was a polite way of letting him know they were insured for something close to current value.

"Thanks. One more question—are you guys going on the prowl for this one, or is it a write-off?"

"I really don't know and wouldn't tell you if I did. However, I've never known them to mount a search for anything in this price range."

Tom wasn't impressed by his remaining options. He figured he could honestly log a few more hours making inquiries before giving up, but if next month's rent wasn't to be paid by another savings debit, he needed a new case. He leaned closer to the window but didn't see anyone coming up the office sidewalk, so he spent the next half hour searching internet art-sale sites. As expected, nobody was hawking this particular soup can. He saved his favorite site for last since he knew the owner, Debbie Ryan. She was a pioneer in the online art business and was still running Internet Art World. Unlike Colleen, Debbie always took his calls.

"Hey, Tommy. Good to hear from you. I heard you moved west."

Debbie knew everything that went on in the art world, but Tom was still impressed that this bit of news had reached her. He didn't ask how. "Yeah, I'm in Santa Fe now, working for clients instead of the feds. Make that one client—I'm just gearing up. How's business?"

"Starting to fly, my friend. Someone must be building empty walls again. What can I do for my favorite agent?"

"Someone stole a rich girl's Warhol soup can print—Tomato number nine from the 1968 set. Any chance someone's tried to list that with you?" Tom was expecting a quick denial but instead got a long pause.

"Let me look a sec." Debbie was gone for two or three minutes, fortunately without muzak. "Mary took a call about a Tomato Soup print a couple of weeks ago, but it was from a guy in Germany who was looking to buy one, not sell. He placed a print-wanted ad with us. Nobody's tried to sell one recently, at least not through us. So are you chasing a hot one? I could use a little excitement."

"Yeah, but your German buyer doesn't seem to fit. Mine was only stolen two days ago, and I'm hoping someone will be looking to sell it soon."

"That's too bad. It might have been fun."

"Let me know if you hear anything more, will you? Even if it's not number nine."

"Sure will, Tommy. We get a lot of calls, but some of the sellers are pretty fuzzy with the details. It's mostly because they're worried about paying taxes—checking to see if we report sales to the IRS."

"Do you?"

"Wouldn't do much for sales if we did." Debbie rang off to take more-lucrative calls.

Tom understood the tax issue. Profits from dealing in art didn't qualify for the reduced capital gains rate applied to stock sales. As a result, a lot of art collectors became libertarians of convenience when they found out they'd be hit for their full marginal rate, along with the hefty commission, when they sold a painting. But burglars weren't all that likely to be dodging taxes, so the chances of Tracy Lee's soup can turning up on Debbie's website seemed slim.

Saturday night in Santa Fe coming up. Should have asked Willie where to find the nightlife. Assuming there is any. Tom set off searching for dinner and tried his luck at a small Thai place. The service was slow, but the pad Thai was good. He managed to drag dinner out until six-thirty but was still five hours short of his usual bedtime when he reached the condo. Now what? Calling Laurie didn't seem right. He tried anyway but hung up after four rings.

Across town Laurie was curled up in her leather cocoon chair watching Annie Hall on Turner Classic Movies. The phone on her coffee table rang, and she recognized Tom's number. She was still staring at the phone's screen when the light went out.

~ 9 ~

Tom signaled his approach by kicking up a jaunty rooster tail of dust as he sped down Willie's long driveway. He braked hard and spun the wheel, putting the little Chevy into a controlled drift and coming to a halt a few feet from the gate. He waited until the westerly breeze blew the dust off in the general direction of Santa Fe before climbing out. Rosanne was standing on the front portal watching the dirt swirl through the rippling sheets on her clothesline.

"Sorry, Rosy. I didn't see the linen."

"Mmmmm."

As Tom skipped up the steps and gave Rosanne a hug, Laurie's white Subaru turned off the paved road and began its own dust storm. Tom felt a brief surge of adrenaline suppress his sense of marital duty. Rosanne had filled out a dinner foursome. She always had a plan.

Willie emerged from the barn pushing his classic Scout 45, and the four assembled near the gate to admire the handsome motorbike. Laurie ran her hand down its length as if it were a pet retriever. "This beast running yet?"

"Mine's ready to go. Rosanne's is a little behind."

Rosanne countered with a low growl. "He means he strips mine for parts, and he's too cheap to go buy replacements."

Willie stomped the bike to life, and they all nodded approvingly as he revved the engine four or five times. He switched it off and leaned the bike against the fence. The rising roar of an engine short a muffler caused the group to look toward the paved road as a veteran red pickup with two men inside approached from the east. It was bearing down on a brown mongrel dog with matted hair that was investigating a road-kill carcass in the near lane. The little dog looked up at the truck and ran onto the shoulder, but the driver swerved after him. They heard a loud thump as the dog spun off the roadway and lay twitching. The truck weaved back onto the pavement and sped away.

Willie grabbed his Indian and began rolling it toward the road with Rosanne in close pursuit. He leaped high and kick-started the bike while twisting the throttle. The motor caught, and he raced the engine. Rosanne screamed for him to stop and launched herself into a desperate tackle. She grabbed Willie with both hands and hung on as the bike wobbled and dragged her off the driveway. Willie lashed his left forearm at her face, but she kept her grip until the bike skidded onto its side and came to a rest with the front wheel spinning. She let go and lay sobbing face down in the dirt. Willie struggled but failed to stand up, and sat down hiding his face with both hands. Tom thought he heard a sob from his brother, but he knelt to help Rosanne first.

Laurie eased Rosanne into a sitting position and held her as she buried her face against Laurie's neck. Tom turned to help his brother, but Willie gained his feet and staggered toward the barn. Nobody said anything until Willie was out of sight. The front wheel of the Indian was still turning.

"He could have killed them." Rosanne's voice was barely above a whisper. "Killed them both." Tom and Laurie helped Rosanne into the house. She had scrapes on her legs and a few other spots, and Laurie took her to the sink to clean up. Tom headed to the barn. He found Willie sitting on a hay bale with his head hanging and his hands clasped between his knees. The barn smelled of aging hay and manure with an overlay of spilled motor oil. Tom dragged another bale out so he could sit facing Willie who continued to stare at the ground. They sat in silence. Tom stole occasional glances at his watch. After ten minutes Willie gave a shallow sigh, raised his head, and looked Tom in the eye. "Let's eat."

*　*　*

The roast chicken dinner was consumed without further incident. No one spoke of the death of the dog until the dishes were cleared. Tom stood up first. "I'll bury the little guy. It won't take long." He headed for the tool shed.

Willie grabbed a small flashlight and left to retrieve his bike. From the kitchen window, Rosanne and Laurie could see the light bobbing. Willie was holding the flashlight in his mouth as he rolled the Indian toward the barn. Laurie scraped chicken scraps into a pungent garbage can outside the back door while Rosanne filled the sink with suds. When Laurie returned, Rosanne dried her hands and looked out the window again. The lights in the barn were on. "He'll be out there a long time, I expect."

Laurie slid dishes into the warm water. "I know he loves dogs, but I've never seen him like that."

Rosanne bit her lower lip. "He's been that way longer than I've known him—since he was a kid."

"Did something happen?"

"He'll be mad as hell if he finds out I told you. He wouldn't tell me for years, but we killed a fifth of Jack Daniel's one night in bed and he opened up. I'm not even sure he remembers that night."

"You don't have to tell me."

"No, it's good for you to know. Maybe you could tell Tom sometime. I can't seem to do that." Rosanne checked the lights in the barn. "When Willie was little, maybe five or six, the McNauls lived next to a family of true, badass rednecks. The mother was OK while she lasted, but she died when her twin boys were eight or so. There was a third boy, two or three years younger, I think."

Rosanne twisted the wet dishtowel until it squeaked. "The boys picked on Willie. He tried to stay away from them, but one day they took his dog. It was a little pup from the pound that his folks gave him for his birthday. The boys turpentined him."

"I don't understand."

"They doused the little dog with turpentine and lit it. The dog didn't know what to do, so it ran around screeching, fanning the flames. The boys just laughed and held Willie—made him watch until it collapsed. Then they left. Willie had to kill the dog after."

Laurie collapsed in a chair and covered her mouth with her right hand. "How can anyone do something like that?"

"I don't know. Frankly, I think some kids are just born bad, but I guess you have to blame the old man to some degree."

"What happened to them?"

"Not long after the wife died, the old man moved them to someplace out in the sticks. I'm not sure exactly where, but it's somewhere east of the Sandias. I think Willie still runs into the boys now and then. It doesn't sound like they've improved much."

Rosanne saw the lights go out in the barn. "Not a word to Willie, now."

Laurie nodded and headed to the sink. Willie came into the room and pulled a fresh bottle of Bushmills and four glasses out of a cabinet. The first round was over by the time Tom returned from burying the dog.

* * *

Tom squinted in the dim lantern light and realized the bottle was down to an amber puddle. The four were huddled around a small table on the portal. The temperature was near freezing, but the wind was down and warm whiskey is a siren on cold, still nights. A round or two back, Tom realized he wouldn't be driving to town before morning. Neither would Laurie. Willie and Rosanne called it quits and steadied each other as they staggered to their bedroom. Tom stared at the rising last-quarter moon and realized it was near midnight. "Come on, cowgirl. Let's walk some of this off."

"OK. Some water first, though." After two tall glasses each, they trudged off on a slow lap along the perimeter fence line.

They'd gone about halfway when the stillness was torn by a sudden cacophony of yips and barks as coyotes said a blessing over their kill. Death in the moonlight. Tom looked to see if Laurie's hand was within reach, but she still had them both jammed into her coat pockets and was looking straight ahead. The coyotes shut up as they got down to the serious business of eating. Tom tried to think of something witty to say but gave up. "You OK?"

"Yeah. Let's sit a bit, though." They cut back toward the barn. Tom found the light switch and collapsed onto the same hay bale he'd occupied before dinner. He closed his eyes for a moment, but his head began to spin, so he tried to focus them on Laurie instead. She was sitting on Willie's former bale, leaning back slightly and bracing herself with both arms. She was staring at a haystack to her left. Tom thought he detected a slight smile when she turned back and saw him staring at her, but it could have been wishful thinking. She suddenly broke eye contact and rolled to the right, throwing herself face down across the bale with her head hanging off the far side. Tom fought to keep his own stomach steady as he listened to the sounds of Laurie purging her system of whiskey and chicken. She scraped a handful of hay over the mess, but it didn't stifle the odor. After resting a moment, she rolled back to an upright position. "Sorry. I should learn." She wiped her lips with a finger, but there was nothing there.

"Yeah. Me too. It's not like you to OD on the hard stuff, though. Something wrong?"

Laurie clenched her teeth, took a breath, and told Rosanne's story of Willie and his dog.

"Shit. Poor Willie. Didn't our dad do anything about it?"

"Doesn't sound like it. Not much anyway. The boys were still minors, and the cops wouldn't have done anything but growl at them."

Tom recalled a distant story Willie's mother had once told Tom of a fight when Willie was in high school. It occurred after baseball practice when one of the infielders kicked a stray dog hanging around the backstop. Willie beat the kid senseless. The coach kicked Willie off the team even though he was their best hitter. There were other signs, now that Tom thought about it. His big brother was strong and deliberate but not often violent. Except when a dog was involved.

Laurie cleared her throat. "You know, Willie told me once the only charities he supports are the animal shelters in Santa Fe and Española."

"I can't say I fault him for that." Tom looked at the moon through the open barn door.

"No." Laurie waited until Tom looked back toward her. "Tell me about Colleen."

"There isn't much new to tell. She's staying in New York. Indefinitely, I think. I tried to get her to come out for Thanksgiving or thereabouts, but she's too busy with fall shows."

"You know what I mean."

He did. "Things aren't going that well. Colleen may never come out here. I don't know—maybe it's for the best, but I don't want to face up to that right now, not on top of everything else. And there's Cassidy."

"Who's almost grown."

"Yeah."

"You need some time, Tommy."

"Yeah."

They stood up with some difficulty and decided not to resume the lap of the property. Laurie led the way out of the barn, and Tom cast a wistful glance at the haystack as he switched off the lights. Snores and the ticking of the McNaul family mantel clock were the only sounds in the house. Laurie headed down the hall to the guest room while Tom arranged pillows on the couch.

*   *   *

Tom was the first one up in the morning despite the remorse chaperoning his hangover. He managed to make a pot of coffee and start the toast by the time Laurie appeared, looking somewhat less haggard than Tom felt. Several nods and grunts later, she scrawled a note to Rosanne on a Post-it, and they climbed into their respective cars.

After a brief repair-and-refit session at the condo, Tom walked down the hill to the office. The only coat on the rack was obviously Myrna's—he recognized the pink-feathered boa around the collar— and a whiff of breakfast burrito riled his stomach. Myrna was not alone. A thin, swarthy man with a nose like a flying buttress was being swallowed by one of the low-slung chairs. His expensive yellow dress shirt was tucked into tight jeans and partly covered by a silk tie with a pattern resembling a tray of vegetables. A leather bomber jacket was folded on the other chair. The man stood up with surprising grace considering his initial position. He extended a hand to Tom before Myrna could swallow her mouthful of burrito. "Mr. McNaul?"

"Yes, I'm Tom McNaul." The man had a delicate hand but a firm grip. "What can I do for you?"

The man held Tom's hand for longer than seemed necessary, but he eventually let go. "My name is George Hayek." His accent was subtle and vaguely foreign though Tom couldn't place it. "I am the owner of Southwest Cultures. It's on Delgado Street, just off of Canyon Road. We deal in indigenous Southwestern art and artifacts."

Tom didn't know the place but feigned recognition. "I see. Nice to meet you."

Myrna regained speech capability and broke in: "Mr. Hayek has been robbed." Both men turned toward her. "He came to talk to Willie, but I explained to him that for stolen goods, you were the man." She emphasized "man."

Tom ushered George Hayek into the inner office and closed the door against Myrna and the burrito. They sat at the small table. "When did this robbery occur, Mr. Hayek?"

"Early Saturday morning."

"This past Saturday? That's just two days ago. Isn't it a little early to be hiring a detective?"

Hayek presented a rationale nearly identical to Tracy Lee's. Maybe the cops were saving time these days by telling people upfront they wouldn't find their goods.

"How did it happen?"

"The gallery's alarm went off around two in the morning. I live a few blocks away and got there before the police. They showed up about twenty minutes after I got the alarm call. Someone rammed the side door with a pickup truck. The door and part of the wall were bashed in. The thieves backed the truck out, ran in through the hole, and grabbed the goods. They left the truck behind."

"Was the truck stolen?"

Hayek nodded. "How did you know?"

"It's a fairly common technique. What did they take?"

"They mostly went for our Navajo rugs and the larger pots. They had a pretty good eye for the best quality."

"Jewelry?"

"Only some of the cheaper items. The expensive pieces are kept in the safe at night."

"I see. About how many items were taken?"

"Twenty-two rugs and twelve large pots. They also took some smaller, less valuable items, but we're still checking the inventory on those."

"Uh huh. That's quite a load to carry out in just a few minutes. Do the police have any idea how they did it?"

"Yes. They wrapped the pots in the rugs and put them in some kind of cardboard barrels. Apparently they had a second truck to haul the barrels in and out."

"How did the cops figure all this out so quick?"

"They left one of the barrels behind. It was half full of some lesser pots and a few kachina dolls."

"Nice of them. One more question. Have you noticed anyone suspicious wandering through your gallery recently? Someone who didn't look like a typical tourist or art hound?"

"No. My brother and I keep a close watch on the customers, and one of us is always there. We have good noses for shady types. Aaron and I have been dealing for many years now, Mr. McNaul."

Tom thought for a while as Hayek began to fidget. "This sounds like a contract job, Mr. Hayek."

"What do you mean?" Hayek ratcheted up the fidgeting.

"These guys didn't go in and browse. They knew exactly what they wanted and came prepared to get it all and pack it away in fifteen minutes. There were probably three or four guys in the two trucks. My guess is some local cased your place and hired a team to come in from out of town to make the grab."

"You don't think the head man was with them?"

"No. Leaving the barrel behind was too sloppy. That had to be the work of paid snatchers. Someone surprised them, or maybe they just went over their time limit. Either way, that's a pretty nice setup for the cops to start with."

"Do you think the police will find our wares?"

"No, and neither do you or you wouldn't be here. They don't have the resources. Are you well insured?"

"We're insured, Mr. McNaul, but we didn't anticipate a crime of this magnitude. I'm afraid our theft coverage tops out well short of full value."

Tom did some mental calculations while Hayek looked around the office—his eyes pausing for a moment when they got to the falcon on Tom's desk. "OK, Mr. Hayek. I think I might be able to help you. I'll see what I can find out from the police, and I'll start checking my sources. No guarantees, of course, but I'm not that expensive. Talk to Myrna about setting up an account. And this is important: Stall your insurance company as long as you can. You don't want them paying off on the claim while we're still looking for your goods. You're underinsured, and the company might try to take advantage of that."

Hayek assumed a wry smile. "I know how the game is played, Mr. McNaul." He shook Tom's hand, more briefly this time, and went to the front room to haggle with Myrna. Tom closed the door and called the Santa Fe Police Department for an appointment.

* * *

By noon he had read the report on the burglary, talked to the lead investigating officer, and outlived his hangover. There seemed to be no discrepancies in Hayek's story. He hadn't expected any. The only additional information of note was that the marooned packing barrel was a standard commercial type made of a fiber material resembling cardboard. A stamped label near the bottom said it would hold thirty gallons. It was made in Paducah, Kentucky, but there was no label identifying the retailer—just a rough, slightly sticky area on the side where one might have been. No moving companies or suppliers of shipping materials in the Albuquerque and Santa Fe areas admitted selling a truckload of fiber barrels. Some of them were checking their more-distant branches, but it sounded like the barrel lead was heading into a box canyon.

When Tom arrived at Southwest Cultures, the hole in the side of the building had been patched with plywood. Two workmen in hard hats and orange vests were installing steel-reinforced concrete posts to protect the side of the building against future kamikaze attacks. The posts were about as decorative as tank traps but would probably stop the average pickup. The gallery was close to the street, and the truck had had plenty of room to build up speed before the driver steered it off the road. There would be no problem gathering enough momentum to jump the low curb and bash through the old wooden door. Many Santa Fe galleries would not be so vulnerable to a ramming attack, as they tended to front onto narrow, congested streets.

Southwest Cultures was open for business, and George Hayek was attending to an elderly couple who were the only customers. Tom admired the flair with which he flipped open a large Ganado red and floated the rug to rest in front of the admiring pair. Tom waved and took a quick look around on his own. There was no doubt the Hayek boys sold high-end goods, at least in terms of price.

There were two phone messages waiting when Tom returned to the office. His new Tacoma was waiting at the Albuquerque depot, and the pod with his Washington belongings would be delivered Wednesday morning. Myrna offered to drive him down to Albuquerque in the morning, but Laurie had a meeting in Old Town, and he booked a ride with her. Myrna pouted for the rest of the afternoon. When she left at five, she leaned into Tom's office, arched one eyebrow, and followed with a sly wink.

Has Laurie become a morning person? Tom stared into the pre-dawn blackness as her aging Subaru hurtled down the interstate toward Albuquerque. She picked up steam on the downhill at La Bajada and was pushing ninety. For peace of mind, he avoided looking at the speedometer but did venture a glance at his watch. Five-thirty. He'd assumed Laurie's meeting would be at some civilized hour, perhaps after they'd shared a leisurely breakfast, but she called him at quarter to five saying she needed to be back in Santa Fe for a 9 a.m. meeting. The knock on his door came fifteen minutes later.

Tom's stomach growled with enough gusto to rival the road noise. His toast was home cooling its crust next to the dormant coffee pot. Laurie grinned without looking his way. Her mission was to pick up an envelope of photocopies from a skittish source who distrusted the communists staffing the U. S. Postal Service. Grab and go in five minutes. She'd probably be sitting around a table at the New Mexican before the railroad freight depot opened its office.

Laurie dropped him on the curb in front of a small coffee shop staffed by two sluggish workers still turning on the lights. The Central Avenue sidewalks were as empty as a shark's eyes and about as comforting. Lonely red and green lights swung in the wind and tinted patches of dew on the pavement as they directed nonexistent traffic. It reminded Tom of the aftermath of a Christmas party. He waved through the cafe window and smiled the young waitress into letting him inside. The short-order cook was just firing up the grill, and the coffee pot was still yawning. Tom retrieved part of yesterday's Albuquerque Journal from the top of the cleaning cart and settled into a booth with a view of the kitchen.

At seven he pushed back the sparse remains of a breakfast skillet the menu had labeled "The Dog's Dinner." The only other customers were a young couple consuming bagels and coffee at the counter, looking like escapees from Hopper's Nighthawks. Ten minutes of brisk walking got him to the firmly locked depot. He found a diner down the block.

After a fresh paper and enough coffee refills to make the owner scowl, Tom noticed that the depot was open. A listless man with greasy hair and two buttons on his work shirt grunted when Tom showed him the invoice. "Truck's parked in the holding lot. About a mile from here." He pointed down the tracks.

The wind kicked dust in Tom's face as he turned down a long dirt driveway. It ended at an ancient trailer attached to a green cinderblock building with a cardboard OPEN sign in one window. Tom knocked on the wooden screen door, trying not to push it off its remaining hinge. Generous swaths of duct tape were stuck on the screen at odd angles, patching spots where flies had breached the defenses.

A short, skinny man with a black patch over his right eye swung the solid door inward and edged the badly wounded screen out a few inches. His army fatigue jacket was loose enough to suggest that the airborne patch on the sleeve once belonged to a larger soldier. Tom managed to exchange a receipt for his keys. His pickup was the only vehicle in a small rectangular lot surrounded by a chain-link fence. The barbed wire strands at the top only extended around three sides. A crust of khaki dust lay between Tom and the shiny truck paint, but the interior retained a hint of pleasant, though probably toxic, new-car smell.

Tom parked in the lot of a convenience store, bought a large coffee, and called Myrna. "Hello, handsome. Find your truck?"

"Sitting in it now, my little chickadee. I'm going to stay down here and make a few house calls on barrel salesmen. Probably won't be back in the office before tomorrow."

"Ooh, I'll miss you, but didn't the cops already do that?"

"They didn't find any records of sales to individuals around here, so they moved on. But I'm not so sure these barrels were sold in the conventional sense. The police gave me a list of the places they checked, and six of them are in Albuquerque. I'm going to sniff around a bit."

"I'll tell Willie."

*   *   *

By two-thirty Tom was having second thoughts about second-guessing the cops. The first four barrel sellers confirmed that they hadn't sold any fiber barrels to individuals within the last six months, only to businesses that were regular customers, and no barrels were missing from inventory. A two-note bell announced his entrance into number five, a corrugated metal building on South Broadway with the unlikely name of Universal Shipping. A forty-something woman with long, dark hair and more tattoos than Popeye was sitting on a folding chair outside the counter reading People magazine. She stood up, revealing a form trending more toward squat than petite, and placed the open magazine face down next to the register. "Can I help you?"

Tom leaned down, squinting at the nametag above the woman's left breast pocket and managed to read "Pilar." She responded by thrusting her ample breasts toward his face. Tom recoiled to avoid possible eye contact. "Uh, yes." He fished the new business card from his wallet and handed it to her. "I'm trying to find out if anyone in Albuquerque sold some fiber barrels recently. It concerns a burglary in Santa Fe two nights ago."

Pilar stared at the black silhouette of a man wearing a fedora and trench coat—Willie's choice for their corporate logo. "Are you with the police? I already talked to someone on the phone."

"No, I'm a private investigator. I'm not trying to catch anyone. My clients just want their property back."

"I'm sorry, Mr. McNaul, but no. We do sell that kind of barrel now and then, but all our customers are industrial users. They mostly use our containers to ship bulk dry products—soap powder and things like that."

"I see. Do you have many of them in stock?"

"Quite a few, but I couldn't tell you just how many. They're stored in the old garage around back, and we haven't run an inventory for a while. Want to see them?"

"No, that's OK. And thanks." Tom told Pilar to keep his card and exited to the same bell-tone accompaniment. He stopped next to his truck and edged to his left until he could see her reflection in a side window. She was watching him from behind the counter. He moved around to the driver's side and climbed in. After fumbling with his keys for a few seconds, he glanced at Pilar without turning his head. She was standing at the register talking on her cell phone and waving her right hand in small circles.

Tom climbed out of his truck and reentered the building, patting his pockets as if he'd forgotten something. As he approached the counter, Pilar hung up her phone and set it down next to the overturned magazine. She looked at him with a wary expression. "What's up?"

Tom locked eyes with her and flashed a Bible salesman's smile. His right hand shot out and snatched her phone.

"Hey, give me that." Pilar lunged toward her phone, but Tom spun away, keeping his back to her as he worked the menus with his right hand. She dashed around the counter and clawed at his free arm as it held her at bay. When the last number called appeared on the screen, he memorized it and flipped the phone backward over his right shoulder as he made his escape. Pilar made the save before her phone hit the floor and unleashed a torrent of swearing at his back.

* * *

Tom was finishing an eight-napkin green chile cheeseburger when the Clancy Brothers began singing Whiskey, You're the Devil, an appropriate ringtone he'd downloaded during Monday morning's hangover. It was Myrna. Her sultry voice, detached from the expansive image of its owner, could seduce a cardinal into turning Wiccan. A Santa Fe bureaucrat had no hope. Myrna had converted the number on Pilar's phone into a full biography of its owner in the time it took Tom to down the burger and half an order of fries.

"You ready for this, Tommy?"

"Whatcha got?"

"It belongs to Ike Langston, you know, of the asshole Langstons. The rednecks who used to live next to Willie and your dad one wife back."

"I'll be damned."

"That seems likely enough. Did you know him?"

"No. Bit before my time. They moved away somewhere before my mom and I arrived on the scene."

"Well, I've also got the somewhere, big guy." Myrna reeled off an address south of Edgewood along with the description of Ike on his driver's license. "Anything else?"

"Does he have a tattoo on his butt?"

"Minnie Mouse. It's on the left cheek. Be sure to check it out sometime."

"I'll take your word for it, toots. And thanks. See you in the morning—I'm going barrel hunting for a while."

* * *

The Langston place turned out to be one of the many rural New Mexico properties located nowhere in particular. The navigator on

Tom's phone steered him to a dirt road leading into heavily eroded valleys and ridges running down from the eastern foothills of the Sandia Mountains. The road crossed an arroyo and then disappeared around a bend. He stopped at an open gate to a road leading into a narrow valley. A No Trespassing sign painted on a retired truck tire and a mailbox so riddled by shotgun pellets it appeared to be made of wire mesh guarded the gate. The map said he was somewhere southwest of Moriarty. Seems appropriate. Should have brought Watson. Tom wasn't about to turn into the valley. A bit of reconnaissance turned up an even rougher ranch track leading into the next valley to the north. It was unmarked and free of tire tracks, so he followed it for half a mile and parked at a spot well hidden from the highway. It was almost dark, and the temperature was bedding down for the night. He zipped his leather bomber jacket tight around his neck, donned a black watch cap, and ascended the steep valley wall.

A ten-minute climb brought Tom to a rounded hilltop. He stayed just below the summit as he moved along the ridge. The junipers and piñons offered cover if he needed it, but there were no signs his route was popular. He began to hear the clamorous griping of numerous dogs. As the barking grew louder, he eased his way to the ridgetop and crouched in a clear spot behind a juniper.

Tom looked down at ranch buildings two hundred yards away. They were clustered just past the point where the valley widened into a broad bowl. He saw a sprawling adobe house consisting of a series of brown rectangles attached at random right angles. The flat roof was covered with white gravel to reflect the summer sun, and each roof segment was spotted with dark patches that appeared to be ventilators and swamp coolers. It looked like an abandoned dominos game. Tom could see a ragged garden behind the house and a round patch of grass about the diameter of a sprinkler's range. A short wire fence, no more than a speed bump for the local jackrabbits, circled the garden. Three or four pastures were scattered about the valley—hard to tell given the condition of the fences. There were no people or animals in sight, but the din from the dogs continued unabated. It had to be coming from the large metal barn. The road emerging from the narrow valley entrance curled between the barn and a small corral and then past a doorless garage on its way to the house. A dilapidated outhouse between the barn and garage stood almost vertically and was the only other recognizable structure. Prosperity must have caught a train to the coast.

Tom had no plan and no flashlight, so it was time to withdraw. As he turned to leave, a headlight beam reflected off an outcropping of white rocks at the point below where the road made its final turn into the secluded valley. He dropped to one knee and peered between clusters of juniper berries as a black pickup rounded the bend and pulled up to the house. Two men in cowboy hats emerged from the truck, but Tom couldn't see their faces in the dying light. The house door opened, and he saw the backlit outline of a tall, slender man. The shape fit Myrna's description of Ike Langston—roughly six-two and one-eighty. The tall man came out of the house and closed the door. As the three men approached the barn, the barking increased, and the host disappeared inside through a small door. A few minutes later he reappeared with two large dogs on leashes. Tom couldn't make out the breeds, if any, but he guessed they were pit bulls or close relatives.

As the tall man tried to pass one of the leashes to the passenger from the pickup, the dog suddenly broke away and began running hard directly toward the ridge and Tom, the leash flying loose behind. The wind was blowing Tom's scent toward the barn. He froze. He had no chance to make the truck, so he stepped backward off the ridgetop and away from the juniper to give himself shooting room. His right foot rolled off a loose rock, wrenching his ankle with a popping noise. He stumbled, flailing his arms as he tried to regain balance, and grasped at a dark branch. His left hand closed on a cholla cactus, shooting fire up his arm. Tom fell backward and then rolled to his knees. He reached his right hand around to his back and drew the Glock. There were yells from the valley. After several long seconds, holding his left hand away from his side, he edged back to the juniper and saw the dog loping back to the men.

Tom holstered his pistol and broke a branch off a dead piñon to use as a walking stick. The last of the twilight gave out as he reached the truck. He switched on the overhead light and counted at least fifteen spines protruding from his palm and fingers. The Toyota's tool kit lacked pliers, and Tom wasn't about to risk pulling spines with his teeth. He opened the window, letting his left arm dangle outside in the cold as he steered the darkened truck slowly back to the highway with his right hand. Fifty yards short of the pavement, he stopped and waited until no traffic was visible before flipping on the headlights and turning toward the slow route home up the Turquoise Trail. When the cold wind chilled him to constant shivers, he retrieved his hand and raised the window. It was after eight-thirty when he pulled up at St. Vincent and hobbled into the emergency room. The nurse on duty upped the count to seventeen cholla spines and cooed bemused sympathy while trying not to reveal her mirth as she worked the tweezers.

*   *   *

"So let me get this straight. My little brother, the FBI man, goes snooping around in the hills after dark, gets chased into a cactus patch by a dog, and is hoping to get the Purple Heart?" Willie slammed his palm down on the desktop, threw back his head, and tried to emit a loud guffaw. Laughing out loud did not come naturally to him, and the resulting sound was a strained howl. Myrna rolled her eyes at one or both of them.

"OK, OK." Tom waited for the howling to pass. "But what do we do now?"

Willie leaned forward, folding his arms on the desk. "We?" He tilted his head so far that it looked like he was listening to his right shoulder. "This is your case. Are you asking me to help out?"

"Well, yeah. You know these guys. Have you been out to their so-called ranch?"

"OK, I'm in. And no, I haven't been there. I knew they were out in the scrub somewhere, but I never had any desire to go calling. Run this through again, a bit more slowly." Willie tilted his chair back and locked his fingers behind his head. His boots thumped on the desk, kicking another coffee cup to a crashing demise. It would not be missed—the closet held an endless supply of chipped, unmatched mugs.

Tom repeated his story with full details and honors. Willie kept making involuntary chewing motions with his jaw as he stared at the ceiling, and Tom got tired of waiting. "So this leaves me with lots of questions and not much else. For starters, I figure Pilar has some connection to the Langston hacienda, but that doesn't tell us much."

"Nope."

"I mean, it was suspicious the way she called Ike as soon as I was out the door, but maybe she was just mad at him for not dancing with her last Saturday night. It doesn't prove she gave him the barrels."

"Nope."

"But he might still have the barrels. Do you think we should try to get a look in that barn?"

"Nope."

"Any chance you can speak in sentences of more than one syllable?"

"Yep." Willie swung his boots back to the floor but continued his unfocused stare at the far wall. "Look, Tommy, you don't have much. Sure, the woman might have handed them out to one of the Langstons as free samples. But even if the company does an inventory and comes up short, it won't prove she took them or where they went."

"Nope."

Willie smiled sideways at Tom. "And even if the Langstons did get the barrels from Universal, the goods probably wouldn't be in that barn. If the crooks were on contract, like you think, they should have delivered the goods quicker than an owl's wink."

"Maybe. But if the Langston boys are as dumb as you seem to think, couldn't they still have the barrels?"

"Well, I guess there could be a barrel or two in there, but I don't see another recon trip as worth the risk. They might have seen you last night."

"No, they wouldn't have called back the dog."

Willie nodded.

"What about the dogs, Willie? I didn't see any sign of animals to herd, and nobody needs that many dogs as pets."

"We'll talk about that later." Willie's face turned dark and hard. He stood up and strode out of the office, grabbing his shearling coat as he headed for the front door. "I need to get some air and think. Alone. Be back after lunch though." He slammed the door as he left.

Tom and Myrna sat staring at each other. "Shit," she said.

"What's going on? Did I say something?"

"No. He's not mad at you, Tommy."

He gave Myrna an inquiring shrug but she looked away.

"Come on, babe. What's going on here?"

She tightened her jaw and looked at the floor. When she looked up, her eyes bore into Tom's. "Do you know about Willie and dogs?"

Tom nodded, his heart sinking as he sensed where this was going.

"Well, I don't know for sure, but some of the country people around here are into dog fighting. Rumor has it the Langstons are some of those people. Assholes." She went back to her desk.

Assholes indeed. Always in abundance, even in Shangri-La. Tom stared out the window and took stock of his situation. Two cases. No good leads. No known cash flow incoming. The scabs of Willie's childhood wounds picked open. Nice start.

~ 11 ~

Tom left his truck in the office driveway, grabbed lunch from the carnitas cart on the plaza, and wolfed it down as he ascended the ridge north of town. The shipping pod with his Washington possessions was due to be dropped in his driveway sometime between one and five. He hadn't taken enough napkins to handle the runoff from the carnitas, so as he reached the entrance to his driveway, he wiped his greasy hands on the top of a squat fire hydrant, hopefully a bit above dog level. No sign of the pod. As he unlocked the front door, a young woman in hiking clothes emerged from the adjoining unit with her Great Dane, waved, and headed for the hydrant.

After drying his hands, Tom sat on the half flight of stairs leading up to his bedroom and called Kate's office. Julie, her administrative assistant, intercepted the call. "Hey, Tommy. How are you?"

"Pretty good, considering. Has Kate made it back to the office yet?"

"Sure has, but she's in a meeting now. She should be back in an hour or so. Want her to call you?"

"No, I'm hoping to be busy. Tell her I'll try next week."

"OK, but if you do, be sure to let it ring at least a dozen times."

"Dare I ask why?"

"Well, you know Kate. She moved her phone to the corner farthest from her computer, and she won't use her wheelchair. She forces herself to shuffle over to the phone, and it sometimes takes a while. Says it's part of her rehab, but I don't think the doctors told her to do that. And she turns off her voicemail when she's in the office. Misses some calls but she won't quit."

"That's my Katie."

*   *   *

After three hours, two dozen peeks out the living room window, and eight trips to the top of his driveway, Tom called Myrna.

"Hi toots. Any chance the movers called you?"

"Nah, but don't worry. Not much happens on time in Santa Fe. Pretty quiet here too. Want some help unloading?"

"I'll be OK, thanks. I wouldn't want to bust any backs."

Despite his refusal, people began arriving at the condo. Myrna showed up at four-thirty with both kids and three family-size pizzas. Twenty minutes later Willie and Roseanne arrived with two growlers of IPA from a brewpub on Cerrillos. They were followed closely by a flatbed truck carrying the pod. The driver deftly swung it into Tom's lone parking place using a small crane mounted on the truck. Laurie's approaching Subaru pulled off the road to let the truck escape, and she parked with the others in the tiny, now-full visitors' lot. She walked down to Tom's place with a slender young woman in a black leather jacket and tight jeans. A leash attached the woman in black to a stocky dog about twelve inches high, not counting the oversized, pointy ears. The lack of a tail confirmed the dog was more corgi than not, and it seemed to be in late puppy stage. Laurie introduced the pooch as Stella and the young woman as her niece, Judy. The former was a recent adoption from the shelter, while the niece looked like she'd been around for close to twenty-five years. Both Stella and Judy had short, reddish-brown hair and freckles clustered above warm smiles.

After the first round of pizza and beer, the crew bored into the pod. There wasn't much to unpack but it took a good while. Willie and Tom hauled in the few pieces of furniture while the women dug into each box and bag with unseemly curiosity. When not assaying his goods, they took turns going up to his bedroom in pairs to laugh at the camp-site. Stella curled up for a nap downstairs. After every item had been sufficiently fondled, the crew collapsed into a circle around the coffee table and consumed another round.

Judy Kepler was the daughter of Laurie's older brother, Jake, a for-mer rancher-turned-realtor now living in Las Cruces. She was a painter of what she called expressionist landscapes, trying to make her mark in the art world along with at least a thousand other Santa Feans. Her work wasn't moving well, so she'd taken a job selling other people's art at the T&B Gallery. She seemed focused on finishing the second pizza but looked up when Tom described the case of Tracy Lee's missing soup can. "I remember that print. Bryce pulled it out of the set and gave it to her."

Tom arched his eyebrows a millimeter. Ah, the first witness. "Did you see the print on her wall?"

"Yes. I've only been out there once—about a month ago for a gallery party. Bryce doesn't like to have them at restaurants—costs too much. But he wasn't happy about the way Tracy hung it. She stuck it in the kitchen. That's awful."

"Agreed." Time to look for a second witness.

"Do you like pop art, Tommy?" Judy was clearly not one who believed elders deserved formalities. O tempora! o mores!

"Yes, actually, and that steams the hell out of Colleen—my wife. She considers it a passé movement, but I think Warhol got it just right. Campbell's Soup cans, Brillo boxes, and cold portraits of hot celebrities. He painted the true art of America."

"Whatever. Anyway, we're having an opening Friday night at the gallery—prints by Warhol and Lichtenstein. They've been moving a little slow, and Bryce wants to try a show. Would you all like to come? I don't think it'll be crowded on the day after Thanksgiving. Plenty of cheap wine and cheese."

Conversation halted. Each of them seemed to be stealing glances at everyone else. Willie sized up the problem. "OK, out with it. Who here didn't get invited anywhere for Thanksgiving dinner?"

The sideways glances continued, and hands began edging up one at a time. Willie's hand was the last to ascend, making it unanimous.

"Right. The forgotten ones. The unloved and unforgiven. The outcasts of Poker Flat. OK, Rosanne and I didn't figure we'd do a dinner this year. We thought we'd find a diner somewhere and have hot turkey sandwiches. But what's wrong with the rest of you? I can understand nobody inviting Tom—he's ornery and somebody would likely get shot. A couple of you are nice people, though."

There was a massive outbreak of eye avoidance. Judy broke the silence. "Well, I usually go home to Las Cruces, but my folks are going to be in Cabo this year. And nobody up here asked me." She pointedly avoided looking at Laurie.

"I once had Thanksgiving dinner in a Wegmans grocery store in upstate New York," said Tom. "I was homeward bound from Ottawa, and it was the only place open for a hundred miles. Interesting crowd."

Laurie looked at him with apparent sympathy. "I thought Cassidy was flying out to see you."

"Fell through. No surprise, I guess. Actually, I never heard a word from her."

Everyone turned to Myrna, whose kids were clambering about

downstairs tormenting Stella. "Well, true confessions, I guess. I thought Woody, the guy I've been seeing for the last couple of months, was going to invite me and the kids to his family dinner for the big introduction. But the bastard invited some little tart of a schoolteacher. Maybe he figured we'd eat too much."

Rosanne stood up to rally the troops. "All right, everybody. It's after nine. No stores are open, so this dinner will have to come from what we've got in our larders. Noon tomorrow at our place. Now what do y'all have? Tom, we'll skip you. I've already checked out your kitchen, and even the cockroaches have bailed. Willie and I have one more chicken. Or if I'm wrong, Willie can steal one. So let's make a list."

*   *   *

Even the sun was slow getting up on Thanksgiving morning. A prefrontal cloud band kept the dawn at bay, and Tom managed to sleep until seven-thirty—a record. The morning was cold, and the inside of Willie's house was going to be tight for eight people. Chances were good that a lot of the day would be spent on the portal. He opted for flannel-lined jeans and colorful layers filled with plunder from goose nests.

Tom didn't bother to check his cupboards. He'd have to go out for toast and find some contribution to the dinner that wouldn't be a howler. After an hour cruising past closed supermarkets and open convenience stores with depressing inventories, he spotted a bakery with its lights on. Nirvana. He finished off the last of a breakfast basket and three cups of local dark roast, and left with two loaves of fresh sourdough and a coffee cake worthy of being a prisoner's last meal.

It wouldn't do to arrive early—Rosanne would be handing out the local labor assignments—so Tom went home and killed a couple of hours trying to find where the ladies had hidden his underwear and wiping fingerprints off everything with a smooth surface. He was still fifteen minutes ahead of schedule as he approached the turnoff to Willie's neighborhood, so he pulled off Old Las Vegas Highway to kill the time. The wide, gravel parking area was usually rife with vendors in trucks selling rocks, sad-looking desert plants, and spray-painted ravens made from twisted barbed wire. The holiday apparently had trumped business, as only one battered pickup sat waiting. The driver got out and limped over to Tom with a hopeful look, and he appeared to catch a whiff of the baked goods. By the time fifteen minutes were up, Tom owned a decorative raven and was short thirty dollars and the coffee cake.

The stalling was in vain—Tom was still the first to arrive. Rosanne's bird was dressed and ready for the oven. From its wiry shape, it must have been a free-range chicken, or perhaps a large roadrunner. Willie led the way to the porch and handed Tom one of the half-gallon growlers from the previous night's party.

"I thought we finished all the beer."

"We did."

Tom opened the bottle, releasing the soothing aroma of Irish whiskey. Rosanne appeared with three small glasses and, mindful of the holiday, they gave thanks for successful barley crops in Ireland.

Either Myrna had been waiting for someone else to appear or she smelled the whiskey. She popped out of her apartment toting a pizza—the lone survivor from the previous night, but her kids didn't emerge until Laurie and Judy drove up and turned Stella loose. They also brought a dozen eggs, half a jar of peanuts, and an open bag of blue-corn tortilla chips.

* * *

The sun was reddening in the west as the group reassembled on the portal, sated by their feast of cold pizza, French toast, and chicken sandwiches washed down by enough whiskey to dull memories of holidays past. The talk was low, and Tom poured himself two fingers and walked down the driveway to get a better view of the sunset. He let his mind empty and lost himself in the colors. The sound of footsteps behind him, followed by a whiff of Laurie's perfume, brought him back, and he turned with a smile. It was Judy. "You've been into your aunt's perfume."

She laughed and gave his forearm a squeeze. "You really are a detective, aren't you, Tommy? Most men would never notice. No, it's the same stuff, but I buy my own." She moved beside him as they turned back to the sun. Tom felt her arm press briefly against his. "So, will you come to the opening tomorrow night?"

"Do you need to pack the house? I don't think Orange Marilyn would fit my color scheme."

She laughed a little too loudly and leaned her head back until it rested against Tom's right shoulder. Her eyes rolled up to meet his. "We

have Marilyn in several colors, but don't worry, we're used to browsers."
She gave a left-sided smile and removed her head to take another sip.

Tom glanced back at the porch and saw Laurie watching them.
He thought she looked bemused, but given the dim light, he wasn't
taking chances. "Sure, I'll come. Let's head back. I need a refill." He
shifted his grip down the glass, trying to hide the fact that it still contained at least one finger. As Judy stepped onto the portal ahead of
him, Tom discreetly poured the rest of his whiskey on a dormant
lavender plant.

Laurie was giving Rosanne rapt attention and kept her back to Tom,
thwarting his attempts to steer her to a quiet corner. He gave up and
sat alone on the glider at the far end of the portal enjoying the gentle
sway. After waiting long enough to make her point, Laurie sat down
beside him. "Well?"

"Look, I didn't. . . ." She cut him off with a laugh and a flick of her
hand.

"Judy's lonely and not particularly shy. There aren't enough men to
go around in this town—at least single, straight ones under sixty."

"I'm feeling less flattered by the minute."

"Well."

"I take it she doesn't consider me your turf."

"Should she?"

Tom looked straight ahead and remained silent to avoid stammer-
ing. Laurie smiled and glanced his way. "Don't answer that. So are you
coming to the opening tomorrow night?"

"Yeah. I like to support our local artists."

"Actually, these artists were New Yorkers who died years ago."

"Journalist. You remind me of my dad, the professor."

"Now I'm flattered. But Judy will have a small painting on the wall
too. It isn't part of the show, but it's a big deal for her to have a piece
out where people can see it. The last time they put up one of hers, it
was a tiny still life, and they hung it in the bathroom."

"How long will it last? We could have dinner afterward." His phone
rang, and Laurie waited while he dug it out of his pocket to check the
caller. They both looked at the screen. It was Colleen. Tom hesitated,
but Laurie stood up and moved to a chair next to Rosanne.

"Hi, toots. Happy Thanksgiving."

"Same to you, Tommy. Where are you?"

"Willie's. We just finished dinner."

"Cassidy and I had our turkey with Justin and Mona at a new place on the Upper West Side. Pretty nice, though not very traditional. We should go there next time you're in the city."

Tom noticed he didn't automatically growl at the mention of Justin. ". . . the world ends not with a bang but a whimper." "That would be nice. How's Cassidy? She never called about Thanksgiving."

"Boyfriend problems, as in there isn't one anymore. That might free her up at Christmas, though. Oh, I've got news. Justin is working on a show for me in Santa Fe—the Modern Visions Gallery on Canyon Road. They have some sort of working arrangement with Justin and Mona. Justin wants me to fly out in a week or two to meet them and look the space over."

"Well, I just moved my stuff in yesterday, so you won't have to sit on the floor."

"That's comforting. Gotta run but I'll give you a call after I book the flights."

Tom noticed she didn't ask what dates were good for him. "Sounds good. Tell Cassidy to give me a call." He hung up the phone and looked up to see Laurie's Subaru receding down the driveway with Judy in the passenger seat and Stella's nose glued to the back window. The windows were closed, so he couldn't hear whether the pup was whimpering too.

~ 12 ~

The thick Friday edition of the New Mexican beckoned from the end of Tom's driveway. The sun was smiling like a coy mistress, and there was no sign of life on the street. He sprinted to the end of his driveway in pajama bottoms, T-shirt, and slippers. The illusion of a balmy morning exploded before the front door was fully open, but he charged ahead, snatched the paper, and made it back to the entryway a few seconds ahead of hypothermia.

The shivers stopped exactly as the coffee pot shrieked an electronic two-note whistle at the pitch of a boatswain's pipe. He finished the first cup of high-test brew and the paper in just under four minutes, and was refilling his cup when the doorbell rang. The clock on the coffee pot read five past eight. His attire seemed decent enough for anyone calling at this indecent hour, so he opened the door.

Niece Judy beamed a smile at him from above a black down-filled jacket. Her hair was stuffed into a black watch cap, and a red messenger bag hung against her right hip. "Hi." She forged ahead with a rustle of nylon, causing Tom to retreat to one side. The bag bounced off his arm as she passed.

"Come on in."

Judy unzipped the jacket and tossed it and her bag on his purple stuffed chair. "Hope it's not too early. I'm on my way to finish hanging the show, but I'm not due there till nine. Laurie said you're a coffee fiend, so I thought I'd try my luck begging a cup." She turned to face Tom and flashed him a grin worthy of the Cheshire Cat. She needn't have bothered—his eyes were busy elsewhere. Judy's black spandex workout suit would have fit her perfectly at age twelve. The fabric clung like paint to every curve and fold, and Tom figured she must have pinched her nipples before ringing the bell. There were no lines suggesting underwear—she was pure flesh and fabric.

"Ahem."

He forced himself to raise his eyes to the smile. "How do you take it?"

She laughed. "Strong and straight."

"You're in luck. I made French roast."

Tom poured Judy a mug of his morning lightning, black, and they settled into opposite ends of the sofa. She took a polite sip before setting it on an end table. It was obvious she had little interest in the brew. "So, Tommy."

"So, Judy."

"OK, I confess. I don't much like coffee."

"Didn't think so."

"I'm more interested in you. We had some chemistry going yesterday before you panicked."

"I didn't panic."

"Sure you did. You're not the kind of man who dumps good whiskey on a bush. Surely I'm not that bad." She rested her head on the back of the sofa and rolled her eyes his way.

"No, you're not." Tom tried to avoid squirming. "Look. You're hotter than jalapeños, and I like you. But my life's pretty complicated right now. Did Laurie mention to you that I'm married?"

"She mentioned that and a lot of other things. It didn't seem to slow you two down much. But Laurie said you and she aren't an item now. Is that right? "

Is there nothing women don't talk about? "Yeah."

"Well, let's give it a try sometime. You seem like my kind of guy. And no, I don't think you're too old. Shit, I'm turning thirty next year."

Tom stood up and walked to the window. He clasped his hands behind his back and stared at the unbroken blue sky. "We can talk about it later."

"When?"

He turned back to the room as Judy rose from the sofa and sashayed toward him. She pretended to look at her watch, but her wrist was bare. "I've still got forty-five minutes." She stopped with their noses six inches apart and rested her left hand on his chest. "I presume you're available." He was fumbling to formulate an answer when she slid both arms around his neck, molded her body to his, and leaned up to kiss him. Tom's mind spun with brief flashes of Laurie and Colleen, but his hormones drove them off. He closed his arms around Judy and lost himself in the embrace. If a woman kisses you, it's a cardinal sin not to kiss her back.

When they came up for air, Tom's head cleared and he dropped his arms. Judy smiled, took a small step back, and began to unzip her top. He reached forward and placed his hand over hers to stop it, but he was too late—a slight twitch of her shoulder caused her left breast to pop free. He pulled his hand away. "Not now. But we will talk. In a couple of weeks."

She waited until he stopped staring at her asymmetric bosom and, with some difficulty, tucked herself back inside the straining fabric. She was toying with him now, but he didn't mind. She deserved to get in a few licks. Her true revenge would come on future nights when he'd wake up in a sweat feeling like an idiot for sending her away.

Judy grabbed her bag and disappeared into the upstairs bathroom. Ten minutes later she reappeared in her usual black jeans and sweater. The missing foundation garments were now obviously in place.

Tom watcher her wriggle into her jacket and head for the door. Obvious premeditation—seduction in the first degree. "What time is the show?"

She paused with her hand on the knob but didn't turn around. "Starts at five, but why don't you come a bit early. We might need someone tall to move a painting at the last minute."

Tom waited until the door closed before retrieving his coffee. It had cooled enough to need thirty seconds in the microwave. He was going to need a lot longer to cool off.

* * *

After a tepid shower and two more mugs, Tom ambled down to Staab Street. Myrna was on her phone and nodded as he headed into his office. No sign of Willie. The barrel lead seemed to be stalled, so Tom switched to the missing soup can. He called Internet Art World and asked for Debbie.

"Tommy. I hope you know that you're the only man I'll talk to who isn't sending money my way."

"Charmed, I'm sure. Listen, Deb, I'm spinning my wheels trying to get a lead on the soup can caper. Anything new on that German fellow who was shopping for a tomato?"

"Not much. When he canceled his soup-wanted ad, Mary followed up to see if he'd found one or just changed his mind. He told her he bought one somewhere else, but he didn't say where, and she didn't ask."

"How often do you sell one these days?"

"Not often—not anymore. They used to be a staple of every major print sale from London to Hong Kong, and they were all over the internet. But not now."

"Any idea why they went into hiding?"

"Sure. Andy was a prolific artist and something of a hoarder. He still had 40 percent of all the art he produced in his possession when he died."

"And?"

"He left almost all the art to his foundation. After the lawsuits subsided, the foundation began selling off the art to finance operations. They sold scads of the prints through a select set of galleries."

"So what happened?"

"They ran out of prints. In the late '90s there was a last call issued by the foundation. Galleries snapped up the final sets, but the supply petered out in a hurry. You still see a soup can now and then. I could get you a cream of mushroom, or a chicken 'n' dumplings, but not many folks want to part with a tomato."

"Seems kind of odd that the German found one so quickly."

"Yeah, assuming he really did. He might have said that just to put Mary off."

"Thanks, babe."

* * *

Tom spent the next four hours checking auction results and online databases for Tomato Soup sales. Two prints were currently for sale by galleries in the U.S., and one had sold in a London auction six months ago. No other transactions showed up in the databases, but a recent sale might not have been entered. The FBI could know more, so he called Kate.

After ten rings he heard the familiar voice of his former partner. "You again."

"Your lucky day. How the hell are you?"

"Pretty good, thanks. I'm hoping to get it down to eight rings next week. What can I do for you?"

Tom filled her in on his soup search. "Could you check for a recent sale? In particular, did one move to a German buyer within the last week or so?"

"German? Warhol isn't exactly the kind of artist Nazis collect."

"War's been over awhile, Kate. Sorry to bother you, but it's my only lead right now."

"Call you back in half an hour, Tommy."

As usual, Kate beat her own deadline and called back in fifteen minutes. "Can't find anything new, but our list will be updated Monday afternoon. The report could be sitting on someone's desk. I'm the only one in the office today. Everyone else must be at Black Friday sales. I'll make some calls. Are Colleen and Cassidy out there?"

"No. Long story."

"Sounds more like a short one, but I'll leave it. See ya."

*   *   *

At four-thirty Judy finally tapped the last nail into the plaster and moved the Chicken Noodle Soup can two inches higher. Bryce and Tracy Lee squabbled constantly over placement, but show time was half an hour away. Fortunately, the prints were large and covered the worst of the damage. Judy grabbed her bag and headed for the basement bathroom to change into her show clothes. She glanced out the window at the empty sidewalks, hoping to see Tom. It was a bit of a long shot, but she liked the big guy, and no one else seemed to want him.

The half bath was tiny, and the little black dress was tight. The struggle took a while. As she finished her contortions, she heard someone coming down the stairs. She didn't want to emerge without final adjustments, so she waited in silence. The footsteps continued past her to the far end of the narrow hall. She pressed her ear to the door and heard a faint whirring sound followed by a large click. After a few seconds she cracked the door and peered down the empty hall. The door to the walk-in vault was open.

Bryce treated the gallery vault like it held the Air Force missile launch codes. No employee had ever been inside. Even Tracy Lee didn't have the combination—she made do with the matching vault in their home. Judy smoothed out a few wrinkles, adjusted her cleavage, and walked down the hall to take a casual peek. Bryce was standing at a small worktable in the center of the vault with his back to the door, so she had a few seconds to check out the contents. The room was at least twelve feet square. Two walls were lined with floor-to-ceiling shelves packed with paintings and framed prints. Stacks of oversized map cases, presumably for unframed prints and other works on paper, took up most of a third. Judy felt slightly disappointed there wasn't anything more exotic in view. Bryce appeared to be wrapping a framed Warhol print for shipping.

She gave a slight sniff to announce her presence. Bryce started and turned around. His surprise morphed into leering appreciation as he scanned what there was of her outfit. She struck a pose. "Like it?"

Bryce looked like he might lapse into serious drooling. "Damned nice. You need to stand next to a front window upstairs. You'll set off a feeding frenzy—we'll sell out."

"Why, thank you, boss." She gave him a coy hint of a curtsy and tripped up the stairs.

From the other side of Canyon Road, Tom and Laurie peered through the front window of the T&B Gallery. The only people in view were Judy and Tracy Lee. Tom grabbed Laurie's elbow and steered her up the street. "Let's prowl around a bit. I'd rather we weren't the first ones in." The Canyon Road sidewalks were devoid of tourists, but most galleries were open. They browsed a few window displays and then turned onto Delgado Street. Tom led the way around the new fortifications and into Southwest Cultures. His main goal was to get warm, but it never hurt to show the flag. The entry room was quiet and unoccupied. As they looked over the merchandise, the aged floor creaked with every step. The front room had been restocked with replacement rugs and pots looking much like the stolen ones. The only trace of the robbery was a slight mismatch of paint color around the repair work.

"Ah, Mr. McNaul."

Tom was startled and turned around. George Hayek had managed to enter the room behind him without a sound. Must know where to step. "Hello, Mr. Hayek. This is my friend, Laurie Kepler. Perhaps I should warn you she's a reporter for the New Mexican, but she's not here for a story. We're just browsing."

Despite the disclaimer, George looked hopeful. "Do you have news regarding my missing wares?"

"Sorry, not yet." Tom made a show of looking around. "Looks like you're back at full steam."

George deflated. "Yes, but we had to borrow a lot of money. Have you made any progress?"

"Some, but I won't kid you, Mr. Hayek. I'm not close yet."

It was a few minutes past five when they returned to the T&B. Though Tom hadn't noticed an increase in foot traffic, a noisy crowd was surging inside the gallery. Two men in tweeds at the far end of the front room were looking closely at a Lichtenstein that resembled a bubble gum cartoon. A stylish young woman stared with rapt admiration at a Warhol print of Ingrid Bergman in her "Bells of St. Mary's" nun's attire. The woman wore sewn-on jeans with sparkling rhinestones on her butt, probably to distract eyes from her limited bust line. The fifty-something man with her, dressed as black as Johnny Cash and sporting a gray ponytail, was staring at her ass. Ingrid appeared to be praying for them. Another twenty or so souls were milling about and chatting up a storm with their backs to the art. Occasionally, someone would turn and point at a print with a wine glass or a paper plate of cheese and olives.

Tom took Laurie's parka and discovered Judy's landscape hanging behind the coat rack. He made sure neither Bryce nor Tracy Lee was looking as he slid the top-heavy rack in front of a small Warhol drawing of a cat done on cheap paper and hand colored blue. He squinted at the tag. It was from a series named "25 Cats Named Sam and One Blue Pussy." Laurie and Judy were sipping wine in front of another print of Ingrid Bergman—this one done from a "Casablanca" publicity still. They glanced his way, leaned their heads close together, and turned to wave at him. Tom escaped into the next room.

He found himself in a stare-down with John Wayne. Bryce must have bought a set of the "Cowboys and Indians" suite, as four of them were clustered about the corner with the refreshment table. Together they formed a type of Warhol Mount Rushmore. In addition to Duke, there were stern portraits of Geronimo, Teddy Roosevelt, and General Custer. Tom grabbed a toothpick and speared two cubes of a cheese-like substance. He expected little and was still disappointed. It took the next twenty minutes to cleanse his palate with four skimpy glasses of bland merlot poured by a grumpy caterer. Ten bucks in the tip jar removed the scowl and resulted in a more-generous fifth glass. He began to feel pretty good and resumed his assessment of Andy's view of the wild west.

As he pondered the inclusion of Custer in the august refreshment table group, he smelled one or the other of the Kepler women approaching but refused to guess. The simultaneous three-point body contact from rear enfilade removed all doubt. "Hi, Judy."

"Glad you showed up, Tommy. And thanks for moving that coat rack. Bryce is such an asshole."

"My pleasure."

"Let me get you another." She grabbed his half-empty glass and was back in seconds with two full ones. They drained them while affecting interest in Custer's profile. Judy tired of the pretense. "Come 'ere a sec. I want to show you something."

Tom ducked his head under a low beam as he followed her into an L-shaped hallway leading to the stairs. He grasped the railing hard as he followed her down to the basement. She stopped in front of the six-foot-high steel door to the vault. "Ever seen one of these? I finally got to see it open today."

"Seen lots of these. FBI, you know."

"Well, then, let me show you something else." She led him a few steps back toward the stairs but opened a small wooden door on the right. She spun around, grabbed Tom by his right wrist, and twisted him into the tiny bathroom, slamming the door. It was pitch black. What the hell? But he knew what. Tom dropped all resistance as she undid his belt, peeled down his pants, and pushed him onto the toilet seat. She didn't have to lift her skirt more than a couple of inches as she straddled him. His memories of what followed were confused, but he later remembered thinking she must have studied some sort of vaginal tai chi. They cooled down with a lingering kiss, interrupted by gasps for air, and shared simultaneous final sighs. Judy deftly hopped off him, made a few perfunctory swipes at her crotch with a yard of toilet paper, and bounced out the door. "We can still talk later if you like."

By the time Tom caught his breath, reassembled, and stepped out into the hallway, he found himself alone. He went back to look at the vault door but couldn't see any significance in it. A few deep breaths failed to return him to sobriety, and he stumbled twice as he ascended the stairs.

Judy and Laurie were back in whisper and giggle mode though they had moved on to a portion of the gallery that wasn't part of the show. They were standing in front of an abstract painting with a lot of yellow in it. Laurie had wanted to leave around six and have dinner somewhere. Tom checked his watch and was embarrassed that it took a couple of seconds for his eyes to focus. Ten past six. He was in no condition to drive, so he took his medicine, apologized to his credit card, and walked Laurie to an above-pay-grade restaurant a couple of blocks up the street. He looked across the table at her and felt considerable twangs of guilt, so he ordered a bottle of expensive cabernet. Later on he tried to order another, but Laurie shook her head at the waiter.

*   *   *

At the T&B, the crowd consumed their fill and dribbled off to home or elsewhere. Bryce and Tracy Lee hung around for a while grousing about the lack of sales before disappearing into the night. They didn't plan to open until ten the next morning. Judy swept up fallen crackers and napkins and filled a couple of small wastebaskets. When the Jacksons were well gone, she turned off the lights and headed for her car. Plenty of time to finish up in the morning. She was parked a block off Canyon Road. It was not quite eight when she turned left onto Garcia Street and pressed the remote's unlock button three car lengths from her red Golf. A second later she sensed movement behind her in the shadows of an arched gateway. Before she could react, she was stunned by a blow to the back of her head. There was no pain, just a spiral into oblivion.

*   *   *

Laurie fished the keys to Tom's truck out of his pocket without being unduly indecent. She drove him home and urged him inside with a slight shove. He was still on his feet as she closed the door and drove herself home.

Tom worked his way to bed, complimenting himself at random intervals on such triumphs as opening a tube of toothpaste and removing his shoes without falling over. He didn't bother to undress and launched himself face down onto the bed. He was gone within seconds.

A couple of hours later the sound of his phone jarred him awake. The caller gave up before he remembered the device was in his left pants pocket. He left it there and continued to lie on the bed, taking deep breaths as he struggled for control. Several minutes later, the phone began singing again. He didn't get it out of his pocket in time, but he saw it was Laurie and called back. She answered immediately.

"Oh, Tommy." Laurie was sobbing. Tom struggled to recall what he might have said earlier but came up short and remained silent.

"She's dead."

"What? Who?"

"Judy. I just got a call from Eddie Romero. Somebody killed her."

"What?" She didn't reply. "Look, I'm … I'll be right over." *What the hell is going on?* He set the phone on the nightstand and struggled to tie his shoes. With a mighty surge, he regained his feet just as the phone rang again. He assumed it was Laurie and didn't look at the number. "Hi."

It was Honest Eddie. "That you, McNaul?"

"Yeah, who else?"

"Don't go anywhere. We'll be there in five minutes."

It took most of the five minutes, or however long it was, for Tom to comb his hair and tuck in his shirt. The doorbell rang to announce Eddie and his partner. They skipped the pleasantries.

"What's up, Eddie?"

Eddie took a whiff of Tom before answering. "You know Judy Kepler, Laurie's niece?"

"Yeah, I know her, and you know I know her. So what's up?"

"Where were you tonight, Tommy?"

"Never mind that, what's this about Judy? Laurie just called."

Eddie shifted gears. "We found her body on Garcia Street."

"Her body? What do you mean?"

"I mean she's dead. Someone bashed in the back of her head. So, like I said—where were you tonight?"

"Can we sit down?"

"Yeah, but let's do it downtown. Get your coat."

*   *   *

As Eddie and his partner drove Tom down the hill, he noticed his truck was missing. The drive to the Santa Fe Police Department took twenty minutes. Nobody talked. The interrogation room was sadly similar to most others. Furniture and paint were a bit below FBI standards, but that hardly mattered. Tom sat in a bolted-down metal chair across a bolted-down metal table from Honest Eddie. The partner leaned against the wall next to the door. He must have had a name, but Tom couldn't recall it as he took a deep breath and started his account of the evening. He cringed when he got to the encounter with Judy in the basement bathroom. Maybe he should have left that part out, but he'd been a lawman for a long time.

Eddie looked disappointed as he gave up and pushed back from the table. His chair wasn't bolted down. "OK, Tommy. I already talked to Laurie, and we know you were with her. You got any ideas that might help us?"

He shook his head. "Not a thing. I don't know much about Judy's personal life. I only met her a couple of days ago."

Eddie rolled his eyes to stare at Tommy. When he'd made his point, he stood up. "You don't see any connection to your soup can case?"

Tom shrugged. "I don't like coincidences any more than you do, but I don't see a link."

"Me neither. OK with you if we take a DNA swab before we drop you off?"

"Sure, but what for? I already told you what you'll find."

Eddie looked hard at Tom while deciding how much to say. "Whoever did this tried to stage the scene. He left Judy's body with her skirt up, and her wallet was gone. The on-site boys didn't think it looked like a rape. And muggers don't usually bash in the back of someone's head. Made a clumsy-ass job of it." He showed a brief smirk. "But if we find two types swimming around in there, it's best to know one of them."

*   *   *

It was after ten when Eddie dropped Tom back at the condo. He downed a glass of ice water and collapsed in the purple stuffed chair. He had to call Laurie. She answered after four rings. "Thanks, Tommy, but let's talk tomorrow."

"OK, toots. I'll call."

Laurie hung up without saying goodbye. Tom was beginning to sober up, and there was no way he could go back to sleep. He fired up the coffee pot. While it was brewing, he changed his phone back to a stock ringtone.

~ 13 ~

Tom flailed at his keyboard for over an hour, pushing back depression by pretending to work. It was futile—he couldn't concentrate. He emptied the last of the coffee into his mug, started another pot, and turned out the lights. A motion to postpone thinking about Judy was tabled. He dragged and hoisted the purple stuffed chair from the living room up the half flight of stairs to a spot in his bedroom where he could see stars in the western sky. Coffee mug in hand, he sank into cushions exuding familiar smells of spilled whiskey and sweat. The clouds were gone along with the wind and most of the dust. He stared at the sparkling stars until thoughts of Judy caused his eyes to lose focus. His mind began to sharpen, driven less by caffeine or heroic work by his liver than by rising anger.

Nothing made sense. Anyone, particularly any woman, could walk down the wrong street at the wrong time. But someone tried to stage a rape-murder scene, and badly. Was the killer really that dumb? Tom bet on genuinely stupid for the time being, and probably male—given the modus. Dumb, violent male covered a lot of ground, though.

He fetched a pad and pen along with an oversized hardcover book of Uncle Scrooge reprints to serve as a lap desk. There weren't any moveable lamps in the bedroom, so he rummaged through his miscellaneous drawer and fished out an LED headlamp before settling back into the chair. A sideways glance at his reflection above the dresser confirmed that he looked like a certified idiot. He grinned at the fool in the mirror and began scratching out notes, drawing boxes around some of them, and connecting the notes and boxes with twisted lines and arrows. He knew the notes themselves were a waste of time—they were two-dimensional sketches and he was a three-dimensional thinker. He'd never refer back to anything he was writing, but the rhythm and pace of the scratching pen worked his subconscious. Over the years his refusal to keep detailed notes had infuriated enough colleagues to form a good-sized lynch mob. He always brushed them off with the self-justification that the FBI attracted too many anal types and he was their antidote. Pretty lame, he knew, but the hell with them.

Despite good intentions, Tom didn't have enough information to get far. He made himself feel better by crumpling the notes into wads and tossing them over the back of the chair. The balls of paper skittered along the tiles like mice. He clicked off his headlamp and expanded into the darkness. It was hopeless—too many possibilities, too few facts. Hell, maybe she really was raped, but the cops would know that by morning. If she was, Tom hoped the guy hadn't used a condom to hide his DNA. Laurie gave him a solid alibi, but still, he'd have left the only sample.

He gave up. There were no more notes on his pad, so he tore off a blank sheet, crushed it into one last ceremonial wad, and tossed it toward the others. It was just after two-thirty when he hit the sheets.

* * *

Four hours later Tom dragged his favorite chair downstairs and staggered into the kitchen. The neglected coffee pot had turned itself off during the night still holding a full load. He stuck the carafe in the microwave, hoping the lid didn't have any metal parts. The kitchen window faced east, and he saw a semicircle of light spreading upward ahead of the rising sun. It reminded him of a scene from an old Saturday matinee mummy movie—heralds carrying torches through the streets of ancient Thebes announcing the arrival of Ra. It seemed odd that civilizations burning in deserts tended to worship the sun, but maybe they were just hedging their bets. Tom grabbed his coat, filled his travel mug, and tried to beat Ra to town.

The Saturday breakfast crowd at Rosie's was slim to none, but the huevos rancheros took their time anyway. They were worth waiting for. Tom always opted for red chile. Rosie's version possessed the menacing darkness of a lava flow and about as much heat. He slathered extra honey on a tortilla and wiped sweat and tears from his face. Fabulous. Rosie was married, but maybe she had a good-looking cousin.

Although most of the citizenry was gearing up for football broadcasts and turkey sandwiches, homicide cops miss a lot of holidays. Tom took a chance and called Eddie's office.

"Lieutenant Romero."

"Eddie, it's me." Tom coughed and a dose of chile escaped as far as his nasal passages, causing a violent sneeze. He grabbed a napkin and tried to wipe snot and chile off his phone without accidentally hanging up.

Eddie just laughed. "Breakfast at Rosie's, eh?"

"Yeah. Anything new you can tell me?"

"Why should I tell a goddamn P.I. anything? You know better than that."

"Come on, Short. For Laurie, at least." Tom resurrected a nickname from their best-friend days before the "Honest Eddie" commercials. Eddie wasn't particularly short, but he played shortstop on the high school team. He and Tom were "Short" and "Left" in those days, since their dour Norwegian coach never learned names well enough to be sure of them. "OK, Left, but only if I'm never going to hear 'Honest Eddie' again. Deal?"

"Deal."

"Judy died pretty quickly from a blow to the head. She wasn't raped. No DNA results in yet, but I'll let you know if ... well."

"You figure robbery?"

"I don't figure anything yet. Her wallet's gone, but it doesn't smell like robbery. Not a place where muggers hang out at any time, especially after the galleries close."

Tom nodded to himself. "She was young and wearing a down coat and jeans. She couldn't have looked rich, but the guy clubbed her from behind. Whatever happened to 'gimme your wallet?' "

"Yeah. Look, I can't really say more about it now. You got any ideas for us? Seems like the town turned into Tombstone the minute you got off the train. How about a connection to your drive-by gunner?"

"No. Even if they sent another guy, he wouldn't go after Judy. I'll think about it, Short, and if I come up with something ...."

"I won't stay up nights." Eddie's brief flirtation with pleasant demeanor vanished as if he'd suddenly realized his mistake. He hung up.

Tom left a good tip and chose a meandering route to the office, hoping the cold walk would shake loose some ideas. Problems were rarely solved during his walks, but by the time they were over, things seemed clearer. He recalled Nietzsche's advice to distrust any idea you had while sitting down. It didn't work that way for Tom. First walk. Then sit and think. He was almost to the sitting stage when he entered the office and found Willie leaning back in his desk chair playing with the Maltese falcon.

Tom tossed his coat on the sofa. "Top of the morning. What you doing here on a Saturday?"

"Chickens."

"That's a falcon."

"Fuckin' chickens." Willie stared at the plastic statue. He looked as forlorn as an Oklahoma Democrat on election day.

"Have it your way. What kind of chickens?" Tom wondered if Willie really had stolen the bird they ate for Thanksgiving dinner.

"Free range. Organic, I think, whatever the hell that means with regards to a chicken." He stood up and put the falcon back on Tom's desk. "Someone stole a pickup load of chickens from a commune up along the high road to Taos. They want me to find them. Can you believe I said yes?" Willie's voice wailed like a coyote arriving at a pack meeting after the rabbit was served. He sat down at his desk and looked up at Tom. "You're looking for a couple of hundred grand worth of old rugs and pots. I'm supposed to find sixty-three chickens and ten dozen eggs. If I don't get a move on, scratch the eggs."

Tom searched in vain for a sympathetic expression. He sat on top of his desk. "So let's talk about murder." Willie shed his self-pity as Tom related the story of Judy's death, this time leaving out the sex in the basement. When he finished they both sat staring out the window. Willie broke the silence. "How's Laurie doing? Judy was the closest family she had."

"I'm not sure. She wouldn't talk last night." Tom slid his butt off the desk and into his chair. "How does it look to you? I don't see it as a random attack, but who'd want to kill her? The way she was left could mean a jealous ex. Laurie said Judy was lonely, but that doesn't rule out some guy who thought she was his."

"Nah. She was pretty tight with her aunt, and Laurie never mentioned any frustrated Don Juans." Willie swiveled in his chair until he could see Tom with both eyes. "For what it's worth, I don't think she was mugged either. And she's not a junkie—I can tell. Your turn."

"The death threats to Laurie? Some sort of final warning?"

"That's so goddamned lame I'm going to put some money against it." Willie leaned forward and pulled a worn leather wallet out of the left-rear pocket of his Wranglers. "Twenty bucks, giving two to one." He made a show of opening the wallet but saw only bare leather and scowled as he slipped it back into his pocket. "Even in New Mexico there isn't anyone dumb enough to murder a woman to send a message and then try to disguise it as a rape."

They sat staring past each other for at least five minutes. Willie spoke first. "Well?"

Tom sighed. "OK. We both figure she was killed by someone who wanted her dead." He arched an eyebrow at Willie, who grunted assent. "And the half-assed coverup—the guy may have been dumb, but anyone who watches TV would do a better job than that. I think the guy was in a hurry—no time to think it through."

Willie grunted again. "Not bad, kid. So, what's left? Let's say it was a hit. Say, she knew something she shouldn't. If you're right about the haste, it means she hadn't known it long. Work backwards."

Tom turned to stare out the window. As far as he knew, Judy had spent the entire day at his apartment and the T&B Gallery. She hadn't seemed particularly excited about anything other than him. But she'd talked to Laurie during the show. He pulled out his phone and hoped Judy hadn't shared the more-lurid details of the evening with her aunt.

Laurie's voice was composed, though the calm was obviously forced. "Hi Tom. Sorry I didn't talk last night, but you know. . . ."

"Yeah. Would you like to go somewhere and talk? I've got plenty of coffee at my place."

Laurie forced a brief laugh. "I'll bet you do. But no, thanks. I'm heading down to Las Cruces in a few minutes to see Judy's parents. I'll be gone a few days. And Tommy, I need a small favor."

"Sure."

"Great. I'll drop her at your office in a few minutes."

"Her?"

"Stella. Judy's mother has asthma and is allergic to anything with fur. I can't take her with me. Bye. "

Tom stared at the wallpaper photo of Humphrey Bogart on his phone and tried to convince himself he hadn't just adopted a dog. His hopes were about gone when Willie cleared his throat. "Well? What did she say?"

"Stella's on her way over."

"Oh, yeah. She told me about that. Congratulations. Figured you wouldn't backpedal fast enough. You FBI types jump to volunteer. Us marines know better. But other than that?"

"Nothing."

"Let's make more coffee."

*　　*　　*

Fifteen minutes later Tom saw Laurie's Subaru pull up in front of the McNaul Brothers Detective Agency. As promised, she opened the rear of the station wagon and lifted out Stella along with a dog bed and a bulging blue shopping bag. The stubby corgi strained at the leash, pulling Laurie and the baggage toward her possible new home.

The cooing, licking, and barking lasted at least ten minutes. Willie said nothing but maintained a smile like a man paying alimony whose ex had just remarried. Tom managed to maneuver Stella and Willie into the back office and closed the door while the little dog worked the seductive magic of her species on his big brother.

Laurie looked at him with apparent appreciation, as if she were awarding him an A in fatherhood skills. "Thanks. I think you'll love her. Here's a key to my place in case you have to drop her off sometime." She handed Tom a key and stared at him until he took the hint and gave her his spare one.

He noticed there was no mention of Stella's relocation as being temporary, but he decided not to ask. "Glad to help out. But before you go, I need to ask you something." Laurie cocked her head to the right. "You talked to Judy several times at the opening last night. Did she mention anything unusual?" Laurie's expression changed to quizzical, but Tom thought he could detect a smile slightly south of the Mona Lisa's. "I mean, did she say she had heard or seen anything odd recently? Like at the gallery? It might be important." The wrinkles flanking Laurie's eyes deepened. He was digging himself in deeper.

"Like what?"

"I don't know, just something out of the ordinary. Maybe something about the show." Her face softened. Maybe he would make it.

"I can't think of anything. She was telling stories about Tracy Lee and Bryce fighting over how to hang the show, but that's par for those two. And she did mention that she got her first peek inside the sacred vault in the basement. She was disappointed, though—nothing exotic. Just Bryce wrapping a print for shipping. Maybe she was hoping for lost Inca gold. She thought it odd he was packing a print a few minutes before show time, but that's about it."

"Did she say which print?"

"No, I don't think so. Just that it was a large one."

"OK, thanks. I hope it goes OK with her folks."

"They're taking it hard. I guess it'll give me a chance to play the good soldier." She headed for the door. "Gotta run. You two have fun."

Tom watched Laurie's car round the corner and then returned to the inner office. Willie and Stella were sitting on the sofa like teenagers caught necking. He was embarrassed to feel a shiver of jealousy.

Willie extracted his hand from Stella's mouth, dried it on his jeans, and rested his feet on the coffee table. "Speak." The command was directed at Tom.

"I saw Judy twice yesterday, at my place and then at the gallery. She didn't mention anything unusual either time."

"Not even in the downstairs crapper?"

Tom jerked his head to face Willie's shit-eating grin. "What?"

"Laurie told me. Never mind, go on."

"No, not even there. So all we've got is Laurie's comment that Judy saw Bryce wrapping an unknown print."

Willie frowned and pinched his beard. "Unknown to Laurie and us maybe. But Judy must have seen what it was."

"Why so?"

"Because she knew it was a print. If she'd only seen a large wrapped package, or the back of a framed piece, she wouldn't have known it was a print. The T&B sells plenty of paintings."

Tom began to pace like a caged lion. After five minutes doing laps around the desks, he stopped with a stomp, wheeled his swivel chair to the coffee table, and sat across from Willie. "This lead is slimmer than your wallet. There's no way we get to square one unless we find out which print she saw."

"Agreed, but the primary witness is deceased. I suppose you could ask Bryce nicely, but I don't fancy your chances."

Tom shook his head. "That would warn him." He stared at the floor for over a minute. "I need to go in."

"In where?"

"The T&B."

Willie's eyebrows rose until they met the swirl of silver hair hanging over his brow. "You mean at night? That won't work. Even if the print didn't ship today, it would be in the vault. You couldn't break into a glass piggy bank."

"Don't have to. I just want a look at their books. With a bit of luck, they'll be in the office. If not, the shipping receipts might still be there."

Willie leaned back and rested one arm on Stella as he eased into a smile of admiration. "My little brother. OK if I come along?"

"Oh, yeah."

"When you want this burglaring done?"

"Tonight."

~ 14 ~

At **a quarter to four, winds began to stir branches along the streets of** Canyon Road as a dark cloud band loomed to the north. Within fifteen minutes the winds were howling like a wolf jamboree, scattering the last of the gallery shoppers and other loose debris. "Shit. Back home they'd call this a blue norther," growled Myrna. She leaned against Willie as they sheltered alee of a squat gallery two doors west of the T&B. "Should have known. The only time in five years anyone brought me to gallery row and it's not fit for man nor beast."

Willie ignored her and peered around the edge of the recessed doorway. All was in readiness. They knew Tracy Lee was in Albuquerque for the evening, and Bryce had never met Myrna. She should be able to make a quick tour and check out the security system. A few other customers would be nice, but none of the browsers fleeing the wind chose to shelter in the T&B. "So much for crowd cover. You'll have to go in naked." He gave Myrna a pat on her ample backside and twitched his head toward the target. "Go get 'em."

Willie eyed her disguise with tenuous satisfaction as she stepped out onto the sidewalk and lowered her head against the wind. The getup probably wasn't necessary, but he didn't want some friend of hers to walk in and make a fuss. Fortunately, Myrna kept a bountiful stable of well-groomed wigs, including one with long black hair that haunted the upper shelf of the office supply closet. It had taken ten minutes to cram her unruly mass of red curls out of sight and smooth the lumps. As a bonus she undid two more blouse buttons than usual to encourage eyes not to linger on other details.

As Myrna entered the gallery, she spotted Bryce sitting behind a desktop computer in a room to her left. He leaned out from behind the monitor and glanced up to show her a practiced smile designed to minimize strain on the facial muscles. "Welcome. Let me know if I can answer any questions." He started to lean back to his work but stopped for a second look as Myrna opened her coat. "Anything in particular you'd like to see?"

Myrna could see there was no point in asking Bryce the same question. "Just looking around, thanks." She turned to a print on the wall opposite Bryce and watched his reflection in the Plexiglas. When his head disappeared behind the screen, she moved on to admire work in rooms closer to the back door of the gallery. As she turned the first corner, she slipped a tiny camera from her coat pocket and took silent shots of each window, the back door, any sensors attached to walls, and the alarm control box. She buttoned her coat as she strode back to the front door. Bryce peeked around the screen but no longer saw anything of interest. He returned to mouse clicking. "Thanks for coming in."

*   *   *

Willie was partial to midnight, but Tom convinced him it was safer to go earlier when their presence on empty streets would be less suspicious. At nine-thirty they climbed out of Tom's truck and walked in opposite directions. Ten minutes later they rendezvoused at the back door of the T&B Gallery and donned tight latex gloves. Willie's perusal of Myrna's recon photos had revealed a primitive defense system. There were no motion detectors, at least upstairs, and the point-of-entry sensors were wired to a control box only fifteen feet inside the back door. There might be something special on the vault, but that wasn't the target.

Willie handed Tom the tool kit and made a selection from his set of lock picks. It took him three minutes to spring the door. "Getting old, I guess." The alarm timer began rhythmic beeping as he grabbed the tool kit from Tom and hurried down the back hall. There wasn't time to pick the small lock on the control box, so Willie jammed a slim pry bar between the door and frame just above the lock. The box popped open on the first try, and Willie disabled the power and phone line within five seconds. Tom eased the back door shut as the beeping stopped. They switched on red penlights. Willie moved to the small office off the room with the Warhol portraits and found the door unlocked.

Tom hurried to the computer facing the front door. He started by searching desk drawers with his penlight. The gallery was cold but he began to sweat, hoping that Willie hadn't made any slips with the alarm.

The center drawer and the top one on the right contained jumbles of office supplies, several dozen stickies annotated with assorted scrawling, and some stacks of advertising fliers for the gallery's better-known artists. The bottom drawers on each side were larger and contained racks of files. He flipped through folders looking for signs of receipts or log books but came up empty. Soft clanks came from down the hall as Willie worked his way through a metal file cabinet. Tom hurried to the office and found Willie kneeling as he closed the bottom drawer of an olive-green cabinet that might have been salvaged from the Manhattan Project, though it had no lock. "Any luck?" He tried to whisper but his vocal cords kept cutting in.

"Nah." Willie's voice was barely audible but smooth—a genuine prison-yard whisper. "They've got lots of photos and catalogs in here, but nothing that looks like correspondence or sales records. I'll have a look in that closet. You try this desk. Willie stood up and opened the closet door but found only more office supplies and pieces of computer equipment waiting for their final ride to the recycling center.

Tom blitzed the office desk and found it a near clone of the one in the front of the gallery, save for the fifth of Glenmorangie scotch behind some files in the right lower drawer. He considered taking a pull but didn't want to leave a DNA sample. He sighed as he closed the final drawer and looked up to see Willie watching him.

Tom shook his head. "The records must be on the computer. Either that or he totes the ledgers downstairs to the vault every night like Ebenezer Scrooge."

"You're the one to crack computers, little brother. I'm too slow."

"Yeah. Let's go."

Tom handed Willie a black cloth purchased from a fabric store that afternoon. Willie scanned the empty street and spread the makeshift blackout curtain over the glass. The plan was to tape the cloth to the frame, but his masking tape wouldn't stick to the fabric, and he ended up pressing the top corners of the cloth against the frame with his hands. As Willie stood there, arms stretched upward and nose mashed against the shrouded window, Tom powered on the computer. It needed a password. He shuffled through the sticky notes in the center drawer, mostly names and numbers. As he flipped through them, one little yellow square had only a number. It jarred Tom's thoughts, and he stopped to scan his memory banks. Pilar! The number on her cell phone in Albuquerque. He filed the fact and jumped back to his search, stopping at a short list of character strings that were obviously what he wanted: proper names with a few numbers added. The first string worked, so he logged on and began scanning files. The keyboard clattered like driving rain on a skylight. There were no secondary security features until Tom worked his way to the financial software, which wanted a different password. It turned out to be the last one on the sticky: tracybitch101, all lowercase. He showed it to Willie, and they shared nervous grins.

The T&B was fifteen years old, and it did a lot of business. Tom scanned some of the more-recent files, but it was clearly going to take too long. He stuck a memory stick into an empty USB port and copied all the folders with names suggesting sales, budgets, or shipping. Willie was beginning to grumble about the pain in his arms, and Tom's nerves were twitching, so he added the address folder to his stick and shut down the system. Willie shook his arms and stowed the black cloth.

It was almost ten. As Tom repositioned the desk chair and mouse, they heard a car approaching. He ducked low behind the desk, and Willie stepped to the left side of the window as light flowed in and swept across the far wall. The car slowed in front of the gallery. Tom tensed and began to construct a battle plan. The back door was unlocked, and they could make it if they started as soon as they heard a car door close. They had to get past the front entry before anyone got to the door. He scurried around the desk and tugged on Willie's pants leg, but the car turned right onto Garcia Street and disappeared. Tom struggled to his feet and waited for the trembling to subside.

Willie developed a tic in his neck, his head making sudden jerks to the right. "How much did you get?"

"Can't tell yet, but it looked like I got most of the relevant business files. If Bryce keeps secret ones somewhere else, we're out of luck. Let's go."

"Maybe we should take a look downstairs."

"Not a good idea—Myrna didn't get us any photos down there."

"It'll be OK. The main alarm's disarmed, and we'll stay clear of the vault."

Tom clenched his teeth but gave a single nod and led the way down the worn stairs, flinching at each creak. He scanned the narrow hallway with his red light. There was no sign of a motion detector. The vault was closed, as expected, but there were two other doors. Willie recovered enough to suppress the twitchy neck. He looked at Tom and bobbed his head toward the open bathroom door between the vault and the stairs. Tom shook his head and ignored Willie's grin. They turned to the remaining door behind the stairway.

Willie tapped his chest twice and reached for the knob. It was unlocked. Both hinges squeaked as he eased the door open. He scanned the room with his light, revealing floor-to-ceiling shelves surrounding a long, narrow workbench with a sink. Sparkles of red like angry fireflies twinkled along the walls as the beam reflected off rolls of bubble wrap. The shelves were stuffed with cleaning supplies and packing materials. Willie stepped into the room and moved to his right along the length of the bench.

"Shit."

"What?"

Willie inhaled a deep breath and expelled it with a whinny. "Feet."

"What the hell are you talking about?"

"There are two feet sticking out from behind the bench. Got to be women's feet."

Tom leaned against the wall next to the door. "Another one? I mean … how can you be sure they're women's feet?"

"The shoes. High heels, and they sparkle. Sequins, maybe."

Tom clawed for control. "Sequins? What color?"

"Who the fuck cares? In this light they look like the ruby slippers."

Tom recovered and joined Willie, edging around the other side of the workbench. They peered around its back corners at the same time. Both broke into snorting giggles. The mannequin was bald and nude except for the shoes.

Willie knelt beside the fallen dummy and lifted one arm a few inches, holding the wrist like he was feeling for a pulse. He looked up at Tom with a sad expression and shook his head. "We're too late. Say, you sure it was Judy you did on the john? This one looks pretty damn good."

"Your mother."

"Nah, she's too young."

"It's probably for shows with a weaver."

There was nothing else of interest, and they ascended the stairs. Willie used his lock picks to close the door to the security box. "They'll just figure they had a power failure." There were fresh scratches on the door, so he wiped dust from the top of a doorframe onto his handkerchief and rubbed until they matched the older marks. They slipped out the back door and returned to Tom's truck via different routes.

*   *   *

Tom pulled in behind Willie's Ford half a block from their office. They sat in silence, staring straight ahead. Willie tugged at his left ear. "You think Bryce has another computer for the shady stuff? A laptop maybe?"

Tom thought for a moment. "Maybe for a backup. But I'm thinking that computer is for his use only. No way Tracy could be using it given the password. We'll soon see."

"Getting late. Guess I'll go home and see if it all makes more sense in the morning."

"See ya." Tom watched his brother make his way to his own truck. Willie waved back without looking as he drove off. His motions looked tired, almost painful. Willie's getting on. He won't be doing this much longer. Tom felt a pang of loss. His mind ran to the time he'd visited Uncle Claire in Kansas and found the faithful farm dog worn out and resting away his final days in the shade. He shook it off. As soon as Willie's truck disappeared around the corner, Tom slid out of his and headed for the office. Portions of the hopscotch court remained visible in the streetlight. He took three hops on the sidewalk to reassure himself. Intense yapping was coming from the other side of the door.

After being pawed from the knees down and having his hands licked enough, Tom hitched up Stella and walked her around the tiny yard. He kicked her poop under a scrawny chamisa, figuring the local soil needed help. The coffee pot smiled at him, but he bypassed it in the hope of getting a few hours' sleep later.

The computer woke with a whir as Tom plugged in the memory stick. While the data were loading, he turned off all the lights except his desk lamp. The falcon looked on unimpressed from beyond the bright circle as he familiarized himself with the organization of the filing system. There was a separate folder for each year. Tom guessed from the file sizes that the T&B's business had peaked around 2008 and been slow to recover. He would analyze that later. Best to start with the sales records for the past two years. If there was anything suspicious, he could follow the trail backward.

Tom made three passes through the transactions files. His handwriting, never artful to begin with, began to slur around midnight, but he had eight pages of notes by one-thirty. The ache in his butt drove him from the hard chair, so he stretched and began a slow circuit of the room.

The monthly totals sheets confirmed that the T&B Gallery was having a weak year. It was in the red for every month except July and August, the peak tourist time. With a good Christmas season, it might break even. That didn't seem so bad in the current economy. The owners probably subsisted on Tracy's inheritance. Still, Bryce lived like a man who could print his own lottery tickets, and he was only drawing a token twenty-five thousand in salary. There had to be problems at home. Perhaps that explains tracybitch101.

The primary income for the T&B came from selling paintings and the odd piece of sculpture, mostly works by artists from New Mexico and adjoining states. For the current year those sales were covering only about 60 percent of the overhead. The rest was coming from sales of art that Bryce purchased from collectors or other galleries and sold to both local and internet buyers. Most of them were prints by famous artists, though two were paintings. He seemed to have a knack for turning good profits on each piece. The Warhol prints displayed in the previous night's show were from two sets of ten purchased from a private seller. The Lichtenstein prints came from Lillian Contemporary Art, a respected Philadelphia gallery.

Some of the works sold were described with all the relevant identifiers, but a few were simply labeled "Warhol print." Tom did not see any records of prints sold during the past two weeks, but it was possible that Bryce hadn't yet entered the sale of the print Judy saw.

The gallery's expenses seemed high but ordinary. There was no rent since Tracy Lee owned the building. The only unusually large item was listed simply as "printing costs." During the past two years, the T&B had paid $20,000 to High Road Fine Arts, a printing firm with a Taos address. Seemed like a lot of cash for brochures and artist's statements. Tom also found a note showing that the Warhol prints had been delivered by High Road Fine Art. That was odd, but perhaps the seller was local.

Fatigue, abetted by hypo-caffeineism, overwhelmed him. Enlightenment would have to wait. He joined Stella on the sofa and was asleep in seconds.

*   *   *

Tom woke in the dark with a humming on his chest. His phone was set to vibrate and was still in his shirt pocket. When his left eye achieved focus, he extracted the phone and saw that it was 5:50 a.m. The caller gave up. Tom rolled on his side, causing Stella to bail, and managed to sit up. His shoes were still on. The phone rumbled again and he answered.

"Yeah?"

"Tommy?"

"Kate?"

"Got one, partner."

"Jesus, it's not even six. Got what?"

"Almost eight back here, and I've been in since six-thirty. Get a move on—you're burning daylight."

Tom took another look at the black window. "Not exactly. Hey, isn't this Sunday?"

"Your tax dollars at work. You can get a lot done on Sunday mornings."

"Impressive, but I repeat, got what?"

"A soup can sale. Jason Stone had the updated international sales list and emailed me a copy. You're getting an exclusive—it won't go on the website until tomorrow afternoon."

"Gee, that's swell of you. I'll repay the favor the next time I get up before sunrise." Tom was fully awake now and forced himself not to squeeze the phone. "Any details?"

"It was sold to a private buyer in Hamburg. Anonymous, of course. The sales agent in Germany reported the sale last Wednesday. I'll have someone pay him a visit soon. The report means that the money has changed hands, but I can't tell if the print's been shipped yet."

"What flavor?"

Kate paused, a tease to the end. "Let me see, I must have that somewhere. Ah, yes. Tomato."

Tom kissed the phone with a loud smacking sound.

"Same to you, handsome."

"By any chance, was the print number in the report? A number nine would be nice."

"Don't press your luck. No number reported. But are you ready for this? The seller is in Santa Fe. It's a place called the T&B Gallery. You know it?"

~ 15 ~

There were hints of dawn toward the mountains as Tom loaded Stella and her trousseau into his pickup and made it home in three minutes. Dog and belongings pretty much filled the area behind the seat of the extended cab. Fresh clothes were in order, but he failed to make it past the coffee pot. He'd be taking a travel mug somewhere. The can of French roast made him flinch—less than forty-eight hours ago, he'd handed a cup to Judy. Organic Sumatran it was.

Tom opened his underwear drawer to bare wood and two handkerchiefs. An exchange of prisoners was arranged with the laundry hamper, and the freshest available were left to air on the bed while he savored a brief shower and endured an encounter with his razor. The coffee pot chimed itself off as he donned the limp attire and headed for the purple chair. His new roommate was occupying the preferred seating, so he settled on the sofa and drained the first cup. As he poured another, he stared at Stella. "You know, sweets, I'm pretty damned lucky this town is no higher than it is."

She opened her one visible eye, so he continued. "We're at seven thousand feet here. Water boils at 195 degrees Fahrenheit, and that just happens to be the optimum brewing temperature for coffee. Civilization is impossible at higher elevations." The eye closed. He felt a bit stupid, but at least she was someone to talk to.

Tom opened his laptop and looked up the website for High Road Fine Arts. It was indeed a printing company, though it focused on fine-art printing rather than personal or business products. High Road worked with artists to produce etchings and woodcuts, all works that could be printed using standard presses with steel drums and moving beds. It also advertised itself as a silkscreen specialist that would produce multiples based on original paintings. The contact information listed an address a few miles south of Taos near the village of Talpa and an owner named Gary Martin. Tom closed the laptop and put his feet on the coffee table. Just what was this print shop providing to the T&B Gallery for twenty grand? Seemed like time for a road trip.

*   *   *

Tom wasn't sure of Stella's bladder capacity, so he loaded her into his truck. He found an open bakery selling fresh pastries and a seasonal special—pueblo revival gingerbread houses lavished with frosting and candies. They headed north with a bag of bear claws, a pocketful of dog cookies, and his mug of coffee. It was quarter to nine when he turned off U.S 285. onto the high road to Taos. He hadn't taken the famous scenic route for at least ten years, and there was no hurry. Tom preferred to case the closed print shop around midday when there would be other traffic. Scattered but growing clouds dusted his windshield with dry snow crystals every few minutes. A particularly brisk squall dropped the visibility and caused him to slow as he entered the village of Chimayó. The low-slung adobe houses seemed to huddle like cattle against the wind. The tops of mud-plastered walls surrounding front yards were splotched with white, reminding him of the gingerbread houses but with less frosting. There were no pedestrians about. He made a short detour to drive past the Santuario de Chimayó where a lone photographer was shielding his camera from the snow. Tom was getting hungry and pressed on.

Several villages later hunger intensified its attack, so he turned left at a stop sign into Picuris Pueblo and pulled off where he could watch a few buffalo browsing. An heirloom pickup entered the pasture, and a man in the back tossed armloads of hay to the small herd. Long time since he'd seen buffalo. Tom always felt things were simpler in New Mexico, several layers closer to the essence than life in his adopted city homes. Bucolic romanticism? He couldn't tell. He liked it here but was nagged by a feeling that he didn't really belong anymore—like a ram going home to his flock and discovering he'd become a wolf while he was away. But no, that was arrogant of him. There were plenty of wolves here too. They were just leaner and hungrier than the predators of Boston and New York.

*   *   *

As Tom approached Talpa, a small sign on the left marked the turnoff to the print shop. The rough dirt driveway twisted around a stand of cottonwoods before arriving at a rectangular building with a peaked red roof above brown stucco walls. It looked deserted, but one

Review Copy -
not final

never knew. He drove back to the highway and backtracked a few hundred yards to a ranch road. It didn't look popular, so he found a spot behind two junipers and left truck and dog. Five minutes later he was at the front door of the print shop. A white panel truck was parked next to a closed rollup metal door halfway down the front wall. Patches of snow were growing around the van, and he saw no traces of tire tracks. Tom knocked on the door. There was no response inside, but his blows on the rough wooden door roused a raven that abandoned a piñon tree for the relative safety of a roiling sky. Tom moved on to window peeping.

The window nearest the front door was caked with dust on the outside. He didn't want to wipe it clean, so he proceeded down the long wall to a smaller but clearer window sheltered from the prevailing winds by the raven's piñon. Most of the interior consisted of open space. The lights were off, but the rear wall had six windows, each about four by six feet. They clearly weren't there for the view. The windows were clean but they faced a windowless outbuilding the size of a three-car garage. Tom stepped back to get his bearings and realized that the windowed wall faced north for the best light. It was shining on three floor-model etching presses. The largest had a bed at least five feet wide and ten long. The visible walls were lined with workbenches, two containing large sinks with chemical traps on the drains. A small office with glass windows faced the work area from one corner. Assorted worktables were scattered about.

The snow remained light, but it was steadier now and coating the ground. Tom would leave footprints if he explored farther. The snow might end, letting the sun melt the prints, or it might continue long enough to fill them. Partially filled would be unfortunate, but two out of three wasn't bad, so he began a quiet circuit of the building. When he reached a rear window, he could see that the inside of the front wall was lined with drying racks. Most were empty, but one was loaded with a couple of dozen vivid prints. A lone print with similar colors lay on a workbench close to his window. It arguably resembled a longhorn cow viewed during an LSD trip. He assumed the others were similar. Nothing within view suggested that High Road Fine Arts was anything other than advertised.

He turned to the block outbuilding. It wasn't visible from the road and had been decorated accordingly with peeling remnants of a single coat of green paint. It was obviously the neglected stepchild of the pair.

Tom circled the building and found no windows. The only door faced the main shop building and was painted the same brooding green as the walls. It looked heavy enough to withstand a charge by one of the Picuris buffalo. Should have brought Willie and his lock picks. Damn.

Tom looked back at the main building and noticed four low-slung ventilator fans on the rear side of the pitched roof. The outbuilding roof was flat with a low parapet, but he'd bet it had similar fans for the highly toxic inks printers often used. He hurried back to his truck, retrieved a small bag of tools and rope, and tossed a couple of dog treats Stella's way. Neither cookie struck leather.

The rear of the outbuilding sported a tangle of pipes and conduits resembling a Hong Kong construction scaffold. Tom worked his way to the roof without difficulty and could hear the crunch of rotting wood as he eased toward the first of the three roof fans. Abandoning subtlety, he went for his crowbar. The nails held out about as long as a ten-dollar hooker as he pried the flashing off one side of the fan and tilted it upward. The opening was large enough to slide through, so he propped the fan up with the crowbar and looked inside. His penlight illuminated several floor-to-ceiling racks of what looked like individual framed paintings standing upright. Two tables held short stacks of square and rectangular cardboard boxes from two to four feet on a side and a few inches deep. Most of the long back wall was lined with a broad worktable. A six-foot sink was centered on one side wall. It was a couple of feet deep and surrounded on three sides by splashguards at least five feet high. A shower curtain on the front was bunched at the left side of a crossbar. The sink had a chemical trap and was equipped with a power spray head attached to a flexible hose. Tom smiled. Classic silkscreen operation.

The penlight in his mouth stabbed randomly into the darkness as he lowered himself through the opening and hung by his fingers. It was only a short drop, and he landed on his feet. The first target was one of the vertical storage racks loaded with frames. As he thought, each one held an individual screen. He turned the light on a print lying horizontally atop a drying rack. It was a Southwestern landscape with a broad color palette. He didn't recognize the artist. Tom stopped counting the colors after two dozen.

He turned his attention to a stack of the thin cardboard boxes. The top one was unsealed. He opened two large flaps. The box contained a short stack of prints roughly two by three feet, each separated by a sheet of glassine to protect the image. Tom carefully lifted the paper from the top print. He stood motionless, staring for at least ten seconds. It was a red and white can of Campbell's Chicken Noodle soup. He checked the next two and came up with Tomato and Cream of Mushroom. There were two other flavors below.

The dim light coming through the opening under the roof fan began to pulse red and blue. Police lights were reflecting off the falling snow. Tom froze. There wasn't time to climb up and pull the fan back into place—he'd have to hope the parapet would hide it. He closed the box of prints and sat on the cold concrete behind a drying rack. His hands began to shake, so he searched his memory for a soothing mantra to recite. None came to mind.

He heard car doors slam, closely followed by two voices. Someone must have reported a prowler. The voices got louder—they had to be circling the main building. They'd be able to see that it was empty from the array of north windows. Hopefully, that would satisfy them. Hope was short-lived. He heard a slight crunching of snow as at least one of the men came over to try the fortress-like door of the outbuilding. The handle rattled but stood its ground. He heard footsteps circling the building. Tom thanked himself for hiding his truck up the side road as he practiced silent breathing. The voices and footsteps receded. Car doors slammed again, but the lights kept flashing. Tom checked his watch. They were probably radioing in their report. After a few minutes the light through the roof opening returned to a dull gray. He waited another five minutes before beginning his egress.

Fortunately, the building had a standard eight-foot ceiling. He moved a wooden chair under the opening and hung his boots around his neck by the laces. The position of the chair might not cause suspicion, but boot prints on the seat could. He pulled himself up, wriggled through the narrow opening, and put on his boots. The fan creaked as he lowered it into place and bent the flashing almost back into position. Most of the nails slipped easily into their former holes, but one needed encouragement from a small hammer. The job wouldn't pass much of an inspection, but unless someone took the trouble to make a winter visit to the roof, he should be fine.

Tom started down the pipe tangle on the rear wall. He sighed with relief as he reached firm ground. As he started toward the larger building, the sound of car doors slamming stopped him in midstride. The cops were still there. Probably taking a leak, but they might come back for a final check. He scrambled back to his rooftop lair. Sounds of muttering voices and crunching snow approached and circled the building. He lay on his back watching snowflakes stream past his eyes. The snow beneath him melted and seeped though his jeans and thin windbreaker. Rivulets of icy water tickled his cheeks. He fought to suppress a sneeze as the voices once again receded. After five minutes, he heard the engine start and the sound of tires slipping on snow.

There were no dry clothes in the truck, so he peeled off his wet shirt and undershirt and wrapped himself in Stella's blanket. She might have fleas, but this was not the time to check. Tom tossed the wet shirts and sopping coat in the back, flushing the corgi into the front passenger seat. The heater blasted hot air on his legs. When he reached the main road, he turned toward Ranchos de Taos. The faster low road would do just fine under the circumstances.

*   *   *

By two, Tom was largely submerged in a clawfoot tub of water about two degrees short of parboiling. Perfect. If he ever bought his own place, the first thing he'd install would be a Japanese bath. No better place to think. The folding chair next to the tub held a tumbler of ice and an open bottle of Bushmills. He had arrived home shivering and fully confused, but now he felt like the heat was distilling truth from the mash.

Was High Road printing counterfeit Warhols? Tom hadn't actually seen any Warhol-like screens there, so it was possible the print shop was just an intermediary. But why ship the prints through Taos? Ah, because they needed something to copy.

Tom clambered to his feet and almost passed out. He grabbed the shower nozzle and held on while his head cleared. A few towel swipes later, he was on the sofa with the cold metal of his laptop chilling his naked thighs. He drummed his fingers on the frame while he waited for the T&B's financial files to load. When he'd worked his way to the records for the three most recent years, he scanned them looking for transactions involving Warhol prints. The numbers didn't seem to add up, so he retrieved pen and paper, pulled on a sweatsuit, and began making lists.

An hour later he set the computer on the coffee table and leaned back to compare sales with purchases. The lists didn't match. Bryce had purchased two sets of ten Warhol prints each during the past two years: Campbell's Soup I from 1968 and a Cowboys and Indians suite from 1986. Each purchased print was identified by name and edition number. All twenty were recorded as sold and carried identical descriptions, but there were fifteen other sales for which the only description was "Warhol print." These could have been bought in previous years, but the difference in notation seemed suspicious. Tom expanded his search to previous years but found no further records of Warhol purchases.

He began to pace the room. There wasn't any doubt. Twenty prints in, thirty-five out. There was an unrecorded source in the supply chain, and it was located in the grungy, green outbuilding of High Road Fine Arts. He walked to the upstairs window and faced the setting sun at parade rest. "Not a bad day's work," he said to the empty room. A blunt object nudged his calf from behind, followed by a low growl. "Yeah, kid, I'm hungry too, but hold on a bit."

Tom retrieved the whiskey from the chair by the tub but poured himself only a single finger. He settled into the purple chair, noting the fresh coat of dog hair. The forged Warhols had to be connected to the theft of Tracy Lee's print, but it wasn't clear how. Why swipe your wife's print if you could just print another? And how could this connect with Judy's murder? The T&B had been selling Warhols for more than two years. Why would it matter if Judy saw one in the vault?

Tom decided to let the case simmer overnight. He was feeling chuffed about his first true success as a P.I.—might as well enjoy the mood while he could. Reality would probably shoot him down in the morning. Despite his good mood, he thrashed about the bed for an hour before he reached sleep.

~ 16 ~

Shadows were getting short as Willie's pickup passed Tom's office window and pulled to the curb. Myrna struggled out of the passenger door, and the two waddled up the sidewalk like repeat offenders at a breakfast buffet. That might explain the nine-thirty arrival. Tom met them at the door and pried them out of their coats. He left Stella with Myrna and steered Willie into the inner office where fresh coffee waited. Aroma and temperature were within Willie's bounds, so he leaned back and rested his feet in the customary drawer. "OK, Tommy. Spill it."

Tom raced through a well-rehearsed summary of his trip to Taos, the discovery of the silkscreen operation, and his analysis of the T&B Gallery's books. When he came up for air, he watched Willie nodding his head with dilated eyes. Tom was afraid his brother was dozing off. "Give me some help here. Any of this make sense to you?"

Willie's eyes focused and rolled toward Tom. "Nice work, kid. But you didn't actually see any silkscreens with soup can images on them, right? Those would prove the prints were made onsite."

"Yeah. I should have looked around more, but the cops scared me off."

Willie went back to nodding. "And you figure they won't know you've been inside the building?"

"Sure as I can be, but you never can tell."

"Well, first off, you need to make sure the ink man in Taos is really printing bogus Warhols. Seems easy enough. You could track down the buyers of the excess prints—see if you can find out what they really bought. Or you—make that we—could pay the shop a visit when it's open. If you're right, the printer is just the hired help, a small timer who gets peanuts while Bryce pockets the real money. He'll cave like a sandcastle at high tide."

"Which one first, wise one?"

"Start with the buyers. I'm stuffed right now, but I'd love to catch a late lunch at Julie's Diner in Taos. How about we leave around noon?"

Tom started Myrna searching for names and phone numbers associated with the shipping addresses of Warhol prints. She issued a ceremonial growl as he left to rejoin Willie in the back office. After five minutes of watching Willie check the sports news on his computer, the steam pressure in Tom's head was tickling the safety valve. Patience. Gotta have Willie along this time.

"Hey, what's up with the chickens?"

Willie kicked back. "Case solved. They was et."

"Elaborate."

"Kid driving the truck stopped at the Blue Horse Tavern on the way to the Santa Fe farmer's market. Seems his folks are teetotalers, and it was his chance to sneak a few. Kid thought it was funny that the place served 'Chicken Killer.' " Willie laughed, followed by a couple of coughs. His eyes teared. "Kid should have checked the alcohol content—that barley wine is over 9 percent. Anyway, he passed out and fell off his stool. An unknown hungry man lifted the keys while the barkeep and other patrons were all mysteriously picking lint from their navels. Nobody saw a thing. The hungry guy left the truck on a back road and locked it. One of boys at the Blue Horse seemed to know where I might look for it. It was there. No chickens or eggs, though."

"You get paid?"

"Yeah, the commune was happy to get the truck back. They don't believe in insurance, or I don't believe they would have given me a cent. I badgered them up to two hundred bucks and five bushels of zucchini."

Tom was about to make fun of his brother but swallowed it. Willie hadn't shared his client list, but it was obviously short. When the silence became awkward, Willie broke it. "The hell with lunch. Let's hit the road."

* * *

Ninety minutes later Tom pulled up to High Road Fine Arts and set the brake. From habit they took positions on each side of the door and made eye contact. Tom rapped on the door. No response. He shifted his weight from foot to foot twice and tried again. The second attempt triggered a muffled string of inaudible words inside. Ten seconds later the door was opened by a tall, shaggy scarecrow of a man with a four-inch beard. The brothers were enveloped in a warm surge of air reeking of solvents and other chemicals. A shop apron splattered with multicolored inks covered the scarecrow's front. It looked like a

Technicolor Rorschach test. The apron looked wet and seemed to be the source of the gas attack.

The printer looked at Tom and Willie as if he wasn't used to gentlemen callers. "May I help you?" trilled out at a surprisingly high pitch.

Tom made a show of looking around. "Are you Gary Martin?"

"Yes."

"And this is your place?" Without waiting for an answer, he strode into the shop, forcing Martin back and to one side. Willie followed them and stopped a step inside the doorway.

The splattered man frowned at Tom. "Yes. But what do you want?" He eyed Willie but seemed to feel safer shifting his gaze back to Tom.

"We're here to take a look at some silkscreens."

"Silkscreens?" The man began blinking at an alarming rate. "Do you want me to make you prints? Are you artists?"

Willie shook his head. "Not hardly."

Tom let Gary stew for a few seconds before turning to make eye contact. "I'm not going to beat around the bush. We're here to have a look at your collection of Warhol prints, and you're going to show them to us. Now. Let's go." He stuck out his thumb like a hitchhiker and aimed it through the north windows. "Back there."

Tom saw rising terror in the printer's eyes, but the man tried to rally and make a show of resistance. "You guys can't just come in here like this. You need a warrant or something."

The fellow was being brave—Tom gave him credit for that as he stared into the blinking eyes and assumed a one-sided grin.

The front latch clicked as Willie eased the door shut. He moved beside Tom and blinked back at the printer. "You must have us confused with somebody else. Police need warrants. But we don't."

"Who . . . no, just get out of here. I'm calling the police."

Willie stepped forward and grabbed a fistful of quivering beard. He leaned in close enough to smell garlic breath that outdid the solvent fumes, then backed off a few inches until his eyes focused. "You're not calling anyone. You've been printing counterfeit Warhols in that green blockhouse out back, and you've been selling them to Bryce Jackson down in Santa Fe. Nice little side business, eh?"

The printer tried to pull his head back without success. His blinking hit the pace of a telegraph operator's speed key but he said nothing. Willie slid his fingers out of the beard and wiped them on his pants as he took a step back. Tom moved in for the kill. "Listen, Gary. Maybe you thought you weren't doing any real harm. Bunch of fat-ass rich folks want some soup cans for their dining room wall. Who cares if they don't get the real thing? And what the hell? Even if you get caught, the penalties aren't too stiff."

Tom paused just long enough for Gary's expression to regain an aura of hope. "Only it didn't work out that way. A pretty young woman named Judy—a friend of ours—got killed Friday night. Because of your soup cans. It was murder, Gary. And if you call those cops, they'll be coming for you."

Gary's knees buckled, and he toppled backward. Willie grabbed his shirt to keep the man's head from denting the floor. Tom took one arm, and they wrestled the limp printer onto a short stool. They each held a shoulder to keep him sitting upright until his breathing rate slowed to only two or three times normal. He looked up at Tom. "I didn't hurt anybody."

"You're at least an accessory." It was a stretch, but Tom figured the man was through, and it was time to finish him. "We're not looking to put you away for that. That's not our job, and anyway, you don't seem like the killing type."

A glint of hope returned to Gary's eyes. "No. Of course not. I didn't hurt anybody; I just did some prints for Mr. Jackson. I didn't ask why he wanted them."

Willie growled like a Rottweiler. "Cut the crap, bud. You got paid plenty for those prints, and you didn't think he was using them for wrapping paper."

Tom put a hand on his brother's arm and made a show of calling off the dog. "Gary, you're a small timer. We know you got paid twenty grand in the last two years for at least fifteen prints, probably twenty including the five in the box next door. That may seem like paydirt to you, but Bryce is selling them for ten times what he pays you. You're just the chump."

Gary's forehead wrinkled as surprise appeared to overcome fear. "Uh, forty."

Tom angled his head to the right. "Forty? Forty what?"

"Forty prints. You said twenty."

"Forty?" It was Tom's turn to blink.

"Yes. Bryce bought two sets. One was ten soup cans, the other was a bunch of Western pictures, mostly portraits. He had me make two copies of each set. He offered me five hundred per print.

"Did you sign and number them?"

"Yes. The soups on the back in ballpoint with stamped numbers. The cowboys on the front in pencil. He had me use the same numbers as the originals. The soup cans were all nine—a pretty early set. The Western ones were numbered higher: one twenty-seven, I think."

Tom knelt beside Gary and locked the broken printer's eyes into his stare. "Don't take the fall for this, Gary. We've got you cold—we've seen the prints in the shop out back. What we want is to nail Bryce for the murder, and we need your help for that. Work with us and maybe you'll get off easy."

"Like what?"

"Like we look at the prints out back, and we go away. Then we hold off awhile before we tell Santa Fe's finest what we figured out. Maybe you could call them yourself before we get around to it. Lay on some remorse and cut yourself a deal. Sound good?"

The stricken printer sat staring at nothing of interest on the floor. He eventually stood up, still staring at the floor, and peeled off the apron. His hands were shaking, and it took him most of the trip to the green silkscreen shop to find the right key on the ring. The keys stopped jingling as the lock clicked open.

The printer flipped on the lights, pointed to the stack of cardboard boxes, and stepped aside. Willie stayed with him as Tom walked to the table and folded back the flaps of the top box. He removed the top sheet of glassine. Chicken Noodle was still on top. "My favorite soup as a kid." He checked to make sure the other four flavors remained in place. The other boxes contained blank sheets of print paper and museum board of the types used to print the soup and cowboy counterfeits. Tom moved them to another table and returned to the box containing the bogus soup cans. "When were you supposed to deliver these?"

"Thursday."

"Thursday when?"

"Around six."

"You usually call first?"

"No."

Tom picked up the box of prints and thought for a moment. "We're taking these. You're not going to talk to Bryce, cops, or anyone else until you hear from us. Understood?"

Gary nodded.

"Louder."

"Understood."

Willie leaned close to Gary's left ear. "Not my business, I suppose, but it wouldn't be a bad time for you to take a short road trip."

*   *   *

The drive back to Santa Fe invigorated Willie's appetite, so Tom veered off to a burrito stand on Cerrillos. Despite a respectable coat of dust and dried mud, his late-model Toyota stood out from the surrounding pickups like a tux at a barn dance. The air inside the truck became saturated with essence of red chile as they stared through the windshield at fellow patrons with Monday faces. Tom cracked his window. The box of prints was wrapped in a tarp and secured to the bed of the pickup with bungee cords.

Tom plucked an ample chunk of fallen pork off a fold in his yellow shirt, wishing he'd worn a darker color. "I figure that printer will already be on the road."

"Yep. Won't be back anytime soon. So what the hell was going on back there with the 'forty prints' talk?"

"For starters, the printer is getting a worse deal than I thought. But more important, the T&B bought two sets of Warhol prints—twenty in all. They showed sales of thirty-five. I figured they sold twenty real and fifteen bogus ones. The five in the back would make twenty fakes. But the ink man said he printed forty."

"Meaning?"

"I got it wrong. I think all thirty-five sales were counterfeits."

"And the twenty real ones?"

"All in the vault. I'm thinking that Bryce couldn't bear to sell original Warhols when he found out he could get the same money for fakes. So he made a nice little addition to his private collection."

Willie finished his burrito first, as usual, and wadded up the tinfoil. "Not bad, little brother. Got a plan?"

"Beginnings of one. Those crook prints in the back aren't much use as evidence. We can't explain how we got them. But when it comes time to tell Honest Eddie, the cops may find the images still on the silkscreens. That'd be enough to prove the forgery. That and tracking down some of the buyers."

"Yep, but it won't make us any dough. And it still doesn't explain Judy's murder. Even if she saw a bogus print in Bryce's vault, she wouldn't have known it wasn't real. So why would that get her killed?"

Tom sighed. "True, and I don't know."

Willie stared out the window during the drive back to their office. As they climbed out of the cab, Tom made the connection and slammed his hand on the hood. The reverberating thud caused two dogs to bark and Willie to burp. "Because she didn't see a counterfeit. She saw a real one—Tracy Lee's real one." He slapped the hood again, renewing the ire of the local dogs. "Judy said the print in the vault was framed. But she saw that framed Tomato Soup print hanging in Tracy Lee's kitchen during a Christmas party, and Bryce knew it."

"Ah. And if she said something, counterfeiting art would be the least of his problems. Tracy Lee would give him the boot—goodbye checkbook."

"Exactly."

They leaned their elbows on opposite sides of the hood and faced off. Willie broke the stare down. "It's a good motive, but how can you prove it?"

"I'm not sure, but we need to get inside the vault. My guess is that Tracy Lee's soup can is still there. If we can get our hands on it, we'll have Bryce by the balls. I think we could crack him on the theft and forgeries."

"Maybe. He's not going to cop to murder, though. Bryce may be an artsy man, but he's a lot harder case than the printer." Willie stood up straight and buried his hands in his pockets. "And while we're at it, how did he pull off the murder? Judy saw the print, did you on the downstairs pot, and apparently stayed to clean up the place while Bryce went home with Tracy Lee. Then someone clubbed her on Garcia Street."

Tom gouged his thumb into one side of his chin and began tattooing the opposite cheek with his fingers. "Do we know Bryce went home with Tracy?"

"No, but we can check, and I'll bet he did. Tracy Lee tries to keep that tomcat on a pretty tight leash. No way she'd leave him running around town on a Friday night."

Tom stopped the finger rolls and switched to heavy scratching. "How long between the time Judy saw the print and the time she was killed?"

"Mmmm. She saw it in the late afternoon while they were still hanging. Got killed around eight or nine, I think. I'd say four or five hours."

"Time enough to call someone."

"Maybe. It'd have to be someone he was tight with—you don't exactly look under M in the yellow pages."

"Any ideas?"

"Nope." Willie led the way to the office door. As he reached the porch, he stopped and turned around.

"You really think you can crack that little Fort Knox Bryce has in the basement?"

"Maybe he'll crack it for us. It looks like Bryce used the printer as his shipping guy. Tracy's soup can is probably sitting there waiting for Gary to pick it up Thursday night. That's when he's supposed to deliver the last five cans. Since we chased the poor guy off, the least we can do is finish the delivery for him."

Myrna could smell the burritos on Willie's breath and quickly spotted the red stain on Tom's shirt. "You walk pretty well for a man with a belly wound. Didn't bring one home for me, I take it?" They made their apologies and headed for the inner office. Tom was closing the door when Myrna looked up. "Oh, Tommy—just a second. You had a call." She retrieved a small pink note from the otherwise-empty in-basket. "A Mr. Thornton. He's in Flagstaff. I think he's some sort of rug collector, and he wanted to ask you about a Navajo rug he's eyeing. He said Lieutenant Eddie Romero told him to give you a call. For some reason the guy is worried the rug is hot."

17

Tom spent an hour losing a game of phone tag with Honest Eddie and listening to Myrna's learned assessment of men in general, and Bryce Jackson in particular. Stella was whining at the door, providing an excuse to escape the lecture. Once clear of Myrna, he decided to give Stella the run of what passed for the office yard. He stuffed the leash in his coat pocket and sat on the front step watching the cars. Staab Street was hardly a main artery, but four-thirty was the beginning of what passed for a rush hour in Santa Fe. An irregular flow of Mercedes sedans, Smart cars, and pickups of all ages fought a few brave or insane bicyclists for possession of the narrow lanes. A man who looked like he was still drawing a Civil War pension wobbled by on a tricycle. His handlebar basket contained a terrier the size of a poorly fed squirrel. Tom heard the front door open and shut. Myrna settled down beside him.

"You really think Judy was killed over a phony print? That seems like a bullshit excuse, even for an asshole like Bryce."

"More likely a real print. Tell me, you've known Tracy Lee and Bryce a long time. Has he always flashed money around like a drunken sailor?"

"Not really. He used to be the quiet man, kind of standing around in the background watching Tracy Lee strut her stuff. Chased the odd young honey when the wife was out of town. But that changed about five years ago when he got some serious hots for his current item. You may know her—the blonde who owns that gallery three or four doors up Canyon from the T&B.—Muffy, or Mitzi, or something. She got the gallery as the settlement from her, shall I say, somewhat-older husband. The babe likes to spend money, and Bryce obliges. Nice boost for the local economy."

"And Tracy Lee knows about them?"

"Must know something. Everyone else does. Bryce and the doll are pretty cagey, though. Tracy may not be sure, or maybe she's just putting up with him. God knows why she'd bother."

Tom leaned back against the crumbling stucco. "Tracy Lee may not care that much about where Bryce gets his kicks, but there'd be hell to pay if she caught him dipping his hand in the till. I think that's it."

"Say again?"

"Bryce is scamming Tracy Lee. He's buying himself art with her money and selling fakes."

"Hoo, I like to think what'd happen if she knew that."

Tom couldn't manage a smile. "But it's just art, Myrna. Bunch of goddamned images on paper. Printed with ink and paid for with blood. Why?" He was still shaking his head when Laurie's aged Subaru rounded the corner and pulled to the curb. She looked road weary as she unfolded herself from the driver's seat. "Hey, Tommy. Myrna."

He leaped to his feet but slowed to more-deliberate movements, hoping to appear less excited. Myrna pursed her lips. Laurie didn't react to either, and he met her halfway up the sidewalk. They hugged tightly but with faces averted. After a few seconds of rocking, they stepped apart. "How are Judy's folks taking it?"

Laurie grimaced. "As well as folks do, I guess." She looked up at Tom and tossed her hair back. "How are things here?"

Tom gave a Gaelic shrug but then remembered Stella. His eyes scanned the sidewalks. "Damn, she's gone."

Laurie spotted the end of the leash dangling from Tom's pocket. "You mean you let her loose out here? Shit. We've got to find her before she gets run over."

Tom helped Myrna to her feet, and they headed down Staab Street in opposite directions. Laurie followed Tom.

"There." Tom spotted the rear end of a golden retriever disappearing up a driveway two buildings down. He jogged to the driveway, hoping to find Stella at play, but there was no trace of her. He began calling Stella's name. No response.

"Hurry, Tommy. She isn't street-wise."

Tom's yells rose in a rapid crescendo. "Stella! Stella!" He hurried down the sidewalk and stopped in front of a sprawling adobe carved into doghouse-sized rentals.

A man in a tweed coat that may never have been new opened the door of Apartment C as Tom's voice reached its maximum decibel level. "Stella!"

"What the hell? Is this some sort of performance art crap?"

"You see a little brown dog with big ears?"

"No, and I haven't seen Blanche DuBois, either. Beat it." He slammed the door. Stella emerged from beneath a truck-shaped pile of rust with round fenders and ran to Laurie.

As Tom watched the woman-and-dog reunion, he began to feel like he'd been set up. He glared at Laurie, who tried in vain to hide her grin behind a demure hand. "I named her. She tends to wander off, and I figured Niece Judy would end up running around town looking for her. I didn't know she'd end up living with you."

"As my old man used to say, I may be dumb, but I'm not stupid. Your point."

Laurie picked up Stella and received a severe licking. Myrna arrived short of breath from her brief scurry up the sidewalk. As they moved inside, Tom's phone rang. "Must be Eddie."

"Hello, Tommy." It was Colleen.

"Oh. What's up?"

"Change of plans—I had to move the trip up. Cassidy and I are flying to Albuquerque tomorrow night. I'm going to meet with the owners of Modern Visions on Wednesday. Is that OK? I'm sorry for the short notice."

"Tomorrow?"

"Yes. Justin and I have to be in Washington late next week about a possible show in the spring. Cassidy said she was free. Is it OK? We could stay in a hotel."

It occurred to Tom that the art business in Boston must be doing pretty well if they didn't mind the cost of last-minute airline tickets. "Sure, it's OK. And you can stay with me. What time do you get in?"

"Around seven, I think. I'll email the info. And if you can't meet the plane, we could take a shuttle."

"I think I can pick you up, but I'll get back to you. Hey, toots. It'll be good to see you. How long will you be here?"

"Just one night. Can you believe it? I actually booked us on a red-eye back to New York Wednesday night. I have a lunch meeting Thursday, and Cassidy has school."

"Oh. Well, tell Cassidy I'm happy she can make it." Tom felt like nobody's priority.

"Will do. Gotta run. Bye."

Tom turned around and faced Laurie's annoyed stare. "Does your wife have some sort of sensor on your phone? Every time I'm with you, she calls."

"Maybe so." Tom pretended to examine the phone. He was giving it a shake next to his ear when it rang again. The screen said Eddie.

"Only got a minute, Tom. A guy named Adam Thornton called me. He's connected with Northern Arizona University—an archeologist, I think. Collects Navajo rugs on the side. He saw an ad for a couple of Germantowns on some website. The dealer was in Phoenix, so he drove down from Flagstaff for a look. The guy didn't show him the actual rugs—just pictures. He liked what he saw, and the price was right, but he got worried. He started calling around to see if there were any stories he should know about."

"And he called you?"

"Not directly. He called the Phoenix police. They had seen our report of the Southwest Cultures robbery, so they called me. Four Germantowns were part of the haul, as I recall."

"Well, I appreciate the referral, Eddie, but why me? Isn't this police business?"

"Nah. We haven't got the resources to go chasing stolen property. The Phoenix cops know the fence. He's been around, and he won't have any hot goods on him. Even if the pictures are of your stolen rugs, we press him and he'll just say some anonymous seller gave him some photos. Then what? We'd do a lot of heavy lifting and find nothing under the rock. So I told him to call my good friend, Tommy Mc-Naul—a genuine private investigator."

"Thanks. I'll look into it."

Adam Thornton was still in his office and answered on the second ring. His account of the visit to the Phoenix dealer jibed with Eddie's. "Fellow's name was Sam Epstein. He showed me photos of two Germantowns in very good to excellent condition. He said his source might have two more. I got suspicious in a hurry—they're just too rare to show up in a cluster like that. What do you think?"

"Could be ones stolen from my client, but I'd have to see them. Did he give you copies of the photos?"

"No, and that worried me too. What sort of art dealer won't let you have a picture to go home and drool over?"

"Too bad."

"I did get a photo, though. The guy turned his back for a minute to look up a price on a Two Grey Hills, and I snapped a quickie with my phone. Just got the one on top, though."

Tom's posture improved with a jerk. "Can you email me a copy?"

Five minutes later Tom was showing Thornton's photo to Laurie and Myrna and comparing it to the file pictures provided by George Hayek. Myrna squinted. "A little blurry. The bugger should get a newer phone."

"Yeah, but it's good enough. That's definitely one of the Hayek rugs from the Southwest Cultures job."

Laurie looked puzzled. "For the record, what's a Germantown?"

"Late eighteen hundreds, after the Navajos went home from Bosque Redondo. Some of the rugs from that era were woven with finer and brighter yarns from Pennsylvania mills—mostly in Germantown. They're pretty distinctive—don't look much like traditional home-spuns." Tom handed the photos to Myrna and began to pace. Eddie was right. The dealer would hardly have the rugs hanging on his office walls, and he'd run for cover if the cops showed up. But maybe he'd cut a small deal if the soles of his feet got hot enough. A bit of info for some peace of mind.

"Something of a long shot, ladies, but I need to generate a little cash flow. I think I'll hop the next flight to Phoenix."

Laurie looked thoughtful. "Mind if I come along?"

"What for?"

"Could be a good story. I'm bogged down on the oil scandal. This is a local theft—a big one. I might get a Page 1 if you can close it."

It seemed unlikely to Tom, but he hadn't been having much luck saying no to women since he got to Santa Fe. He decided not to try again. Besides, the idea of Laurie's company appealed. "I suppose it wouldn't hurt."

Myrna called George Hayek at Southwest Cultures and gave him the hard sell. He was skeptical about Tom's need to take an assistant but reluctantly approved the expense. Laurie decided she'd call in sick the next day and left to pack. Tom asked Myrna to book their flight and set up a rendezvous with Colleen and Cassidy at the Albuquerque airport.

*   *   *

By seven Tom and Laurie were sitting by a gate at the Albuquerque International Sunport en route to separate rooms—her request—at a weary chain motel in Scottsdale. By nine they were on final descent into Phoenix. Tom slouched in a window seat near the tail. He pressed his forehead against the cold plastic. The Valley of the Sun was ablaze from the millions of lights below, but from the plane, the stars still sparkled. He wondered just why there was a city of Phoenix. Laurie's seat was near the front, and she was waiting for him at the gate. "Why did you check a bag anyway? We're only going to be here a few hours."

"Professional considerations." He received the silent treatment. "My gun—I have to check it." Laurie grunted and took a seat on the rail of a dormant carousel.

They rode a shuttle halfway to nowhere to reach the Phoenix tower of car rentals. Laurie knew the city better, so she took the helm. As they wound toward the exit ramp, their level began to fill with smoke. Tom saw a lone car engulfed in flames fifty yards to the right. There was nobody in or near it. "The driver must be off filing a complaint," he said. The woman who checked their paperwork at the exit was watching the blaze but acted as if it were a routine nightly sacrifice. A few blocks from the garage, Laurie stopped at an intersection where three fire trucks were heading in three directions. The only one seemingly on course to the parking garage fire lost heart and hung a U-turn to follow one heading west.

Laurie glanced at Tom. "At this rate the city will be down to ashes by dawn."

"We'll get to see if it lives up to its name."

When they arrived at the motel, another fire truck and an ambulance with lights flashing were parked outside the attached restaurant. Firemen were standing by while an emergency team wrestled a loaded gurney into the back of the ambulance.

The young clerk inside could barely see over the front desk. She craned her neck sideways to peer around Tom at the flashing lights. "Poker tournament in the bar," she said. "I'll bet one of the old geezers couldn't stand the excitement."

The motel was lightly populated, and they got adjoining rooms. Laurie unlocked her door and didn't look Tom's way as she said good-night. He waited until her door clicked shut before opening his own.

*   *   *

Tom was four cups into the morning when Laurie appeared in the breakfast area. Half an hour later they were sitting in their rental outside a small strip mall with cracked brown stucco and a shallow portal. A cardboard sign in one window read: "Sam's Native American Arts."

Behind the window was a small office with a counter and a door to a back room. Sam didn't appear to be there. The adjoining businesses were a payday loan shop and a tattoo parlor with a black hog chained to a post supporting the portal roof. The motorcycle had a black helmet with an SS death's head insignia hanging from the handlebars. The helmet wasn't chained to anything.

After half an hour of impromptu stakeout, Tom was down to his last cinnamon donut from the breakfast bar. Laurie appeared to be made of sterner stuff—she ate nothing. An ancient Cadillac with fins like a great white shark pulled into two spaces in front of the sign. A short man with a monk's fringe of hair and a shape like an overripe papaya rolled out of the driver's seat while a young tidbit in a two-inch black skirt and probably something on top hopped out the other door. They went in and brought Sam's emporium to life, and the saggy man disappeared behind the inner door. The girl sat cross-legged on a stool, removing all evidence of the skirt. Tom watched her through the window as she settled in. "Best if you stay here."

"Best for you, maybe. I'm going in too."

The leggy girl looked up as Tom pushed open the door and forced himself to look her in the eyes. There were purple speckles in her long black hair and stuck to her skin in strategic spots ranging from cheekbones to her plenty-of-nonsense cleavage. He wondered if they were glued on or just remnants of an all-night rave. "Hi. We're here to see Mr. Epstein." Laurie smiled and stayed by the door.

"Is he expecting you?"

"No, but we were referred by one of your clients."

The girl slid off the stool and disappeared into the back room. Tom kept his back to Laurie. "Glued on, you reckon?"

"You want me to find out?"

Tom perceived enough snarl to warrant silence. The girl soon returned with Sam, who regarded Tom and Laurie with a look most people reserve for Jehovah's Witnesses. "What can I do for you?"

"We've been looking for a good Germantown rug for some time now. It's not easy to find one. A friend of ours in Flagstaff said you had some available. Is that right?"

"Who is this friend?"

"Adam Thornton. He's an archeologist at Northern Arizona. He called us last night and seemed pretty excited. We don't want to cut in line if he's buying one, but he said you might have at least two."

"I don't have any in stock. I do know a guy who may be willing to sell some, though. He's a bit touchy about taxes, so he keeps a low profile."

"Well, this is Arizona."

"Indeed. Just who are you anyway?"

"We like to keep a low profile too, Mr. Epstein. But our names are Tom and Laurie. Can you describe the rugs, or do you have pictures?"

"Just a sec." Sam disappeared into the back room and closed the door. Tom could hear the clicks and grunts of a printer working.

The tidbit resumed her pose on the stool, and Laurie sauntered around Tom to get a closer look at the sparkling cleavage. The girl arched her back to provide a better view. Tom was beginning to wonder about both women. Laurie had only one functional fingernail, the rest having been chewed to stubs while racing deadlines. She extended the one claw and slowly flicked at a sparkle halfway down the girl's left breast. It held fast. "That's great. What do you use?"

"Just standard glitter glue. You want to try some?"

"No thanks, but it gives me ideas."

"You give me some ideas too." The girl arched her eyebrows, causing Laurie to retreat to her spot behind Tom.

Sam opened the door to the back room and waved Tom and Laurie inside. He handed Tom two photos of Germantown rugs. Tom nodded approval as Laurie leaned around his left arm for a better look. "Very nice. Look to be in very good condition." He shifted his eyes to Sam.

"Very good to excellent, Tom. I handle only the best."

"When can we see them?"

"I can set up an appointment for you. It would take me a couple of days to pick them up from the seller. I need to see some identification and verification of funds from you first. Nothing personal, you understand, but my seller doesn't want to be bothered with buyers who aren't serious."

"I understand fully."

Sam sat down at his desk and picked up a pen. Tom retrieved four pieces of paper from his inner coat pocket and unfolded them. He selected two pictures and laid them on the keyboard of Sam's computer. "Your rugs look a lot like these."

Sam stared intently at the photos. "These are interesting pictures. Where did you get them?" As he leaned his head closer to the photos, his hand crept toward the top right drawer of the desk.

Tom leaned across the desk and placed his left hand on the drawer, holding it shut. "Let's have a look, eh?" He waited until Sam's hand slipped off the handle before easing the drawer open. A thirty-eight special was lying on a pad of paper. Tom closed the drawer, stood up, and unbuttoned his coat to give Sam a view of the Glock in his shoulder holster. "Don't, Sam. I'm better at this sort of thing."

Sam pushed back from his desk. The chair wheels rattled on tiles as they moved off the plastic mat. "Who the hell are you?"

"I'm a private investigator hired by a gallery in Santa Fe. That would be the gallery that owns these two rugs. Also a lot more stuff taken in the same robbery. Tom braced his foot against Sam's chair and shoved. Sam and the chair rolled four feet and banged against a table. Tom dragged a small side chair to the computer and sat down. One of the Germantowns was still on the screen. He located the open folder on the computer desktop and clicked through a few more image files—an assortment of rugs and pots. After a few more keystrokes, the printer burped to life.

"Those aren't my goods." Sam collected himself and started on his cover story. "A guy came in here a couple of days ago and left the photos on a memory stick. Said he was selling his late mother's collection."

"You can do better than that, Sam. Where's the memory stick?" Tom feigned a sudden urge to scratch the armpit with the pistol.

"Center drawer. The green one."

Tom found it in the pencil tray. "Let's talk, Sam."

"Let's not. I want my lawyer."

"No you don't. There's enough here to put you out of business at minimum. A nice prison term is a real possibility."

"Get real. You can't pin anything on me, and the cops aren't going to give a damn."

"But I do. And the lady by the door is a newspaper reporter."

"Shit. I'm sayin' nothing."

"Think it through, Sam. You can't sell any of this stuff now, and when the story hits the papers, goodbye business. That would be the good scenario. I'd bet on something worse."

"Go on." Sam was a cooler customer than the terrified Taos printer, but he didn't have much bargaining room.

"My clients want their goods back. We aren't talking some backdoor insurance deal here. They didn't have much insurance. I just want to get their wares back to them so I can get paid." Tom pulled his chair closer to Sam's. "And one other thing. I want some names."

"You get names, I get cops on my ass. No dice."

Tom rocked back onto the rear legs of his chair and thought. He's right. There has to be more protection in it for him. Tom banged the chair back to a four-point stance. "OK. I want some names. Not for the cops, and not for Laurie's story. I want to find out who paid for this heist. Personal reasons. I won't give up the names to the cops, and we'll can the story. But I want the names."

Laurie's glare of fury would have shamed Scarlett O'Hara. Tom held up a hand. "Stow it, toots. I didn't have to bring you along, and I need this." Laurie spun and stomped out of the room, the sound effects muted by her soft-soled running shoes.

"Come on, Sam. I'm as honest as you deserve. Who's behind this?"

"Nothing in the papers?"

Tom looked at the empty doorway and then back at Sam. "I'll keep a lid on it."

Sam nodded. "OK. Anyway, I don't like to handle stuff this hot. I don't know a lot. I got a phone call from a guy I know in Santa Fe. Name of Bryce. Bryce Jackson. He runs a gallery there, and I've done some business with him. He said there was a collector there—old guy—who wanted to thin out his collection before he croaked. Nice stuff. Didn't want to attract attention."

"You lay hands on any of the stuff?"

"Nah. Bryce just emailed me some pictures, and I saved them on that green stick. Maybe half a dozen rugs and some nice pots. Big pots, and they looked old. Asked if I was interested. I said I was." Sam shrugged and sat up a bit straighter, but he stared at the wall. "I've never seen the pieces. Didn't know they were stolen." He faced Tom. "That's it. Really."

"Sure?"

"Yeah, really."

"You said you've worked with Jackson before. You actually sell some of his pieces?"

"Yeah, but it was all legit. I can prove it."

"OK, but when you sold the stuff, who delivered it?"

"I don't remember their names. Couple of rough-looking guys in a black pickup with a cap. Had a goddamn pit bull in the back with the rugs. I'm surprised he didn't piss on them. I had to clean the hair off before I could sell them."

"Last thing, Sam. When I get home, I may email you pictures of a couple of guys. I want to know if they're the delivery boys. That OK with you?"

"Yeah, but that's all. Deal?"

"Deal."

Laurie was fuming in the car as he slid into the passenger seat. "You gave away my story, you asshole."

"You didn't have one, toots. We didn't have a thing we could prove. Sit tight—I can smell something bigger in the wind."

*   *   *

Laurie leveraged him into picking up the check at an upscale steak-house on the way to the airport. As he was signing the charge slip, Myrna called. "Yo, big boy. Your rendezvous is arranged. Colleen and Cassidy get in just after seven—about an hour before you. How are you going to cram them into that pickup?"

"Not a problem. We drove down in Laurie's Subaru."

"That sounds like a bigger problem to me. Wish I had a seat on that ride."

Laurie was buttoning her coat. "Who was that?"

"Myrna. We're giving Colleen and Cassidy a ride to Santa Fe. They'll be waiting for us in Albuquerque."

"You might have told me."

"I thought I did." Tom stared out the window the rest of the way to the rental car drop. He didn't see any traces of the Monday night fire, but he figured there might be a hotter one in Albuquerque.

18

Tom could see the top of Laurie's head six seats forward of his spot in Row 24. Southwest must have downsized the seats again; his squeezed like a boa constrictor. Wedged between a left tackle and a poster lady for an anti-obesity campaign, he longed for his private compartment on the Southwest Chief. Despite the cramped quarters, he felt thankful for the separation. Laurie had stopped bitching about her lost story sometime between the steaks and dessert, but her demeanor was like the eye of a typhoon—warm and breezy with more hell on the way. A sailor once told him that during World War II, the aerologists of the Pacific fleet named typhoons after poisonous snakes. After the war they switched to naming them after their girlfriends.

As Tom approached the end of the jetway, he slowed his pace and moved to one side, letting more-eager passengers scurry past. Colleen had never met Laurie, but she'd quizzed Tom relentlessly about past girlfriends, even back to high school days. Nowhere to hide, though. He squinted as he stepped into the brighter lights of the terminal.

Colleen stood out like a bride in black, seeming to have more clear space around her than anyone else, as if people sensed menace. She eased into a come-hither smile and stood her ground. Tom walked slowly, making unnecessary adjustments to the shoulder strap on his briefcase while he scanned the gate area for Laurie. He spotted her standing by the boarding counter. Her eyes followed his as he approached Colleen. "Hi, toots."

"Hi." Colleen leaned up, kissed him with as much tenderness as she could spare, and stepped back to look him over. Her lipstick was still perfect. "Not bad, Tommy. You look like you've lost some weight. Eating OK?"

"When I can afford to." He looked around. "Where's Cassidy?"

"Getting a coffee back toward the exit. Ready?"

"Yeah." Tom turned and waved for Laurie to join them. He took a step away from Colleen. "This is Laurie Kepler—longtime friend. She flew in with me and is giving us a ride to Santa Fe." He should have said more but was afraid of sounding even more awkward than he felt.

"Oh?" Colleen gave Laurie her smile for greeting hotel maids. "That's very kind of you. I hope it's not an inconvenience."

"None at all. I live there too." Laurie's face was relaxed. The women locked eyes for a second and exchanged data faster than a FireWire stream. Tom felt the hair on his arms rise. Was there really electricity? Surely not.

Colleen was wearing more money than Laurie made in a month, and was proud of it. Laurie was in jeans, a navy blue sweater that might have been real navy issue, and her runners, but she showed no signs of being cowed. They shook hands. As best Tom could tell, neither one tried to squeeze too hard.

"Weren't you two high school sweethearts?" The lines of Colleen's face seemed to soften.

"Oh, well, yes. For a little while." Laurie glanced at Tom and then back at Colleen. "We dated for the last couple of years, but we lost touch during college. Tommy went east, and I stayed here. How long have you two been married?"

"What is it, Tom. Twenty-five years now?" Colleen moved closer to Tom and slid an arm around his waist to emphasize her right of possession. Point made, she let go of him. "How did you two happen to be on the same plane?"

"Laurie traveled with me to interview a suspect in a major art theft. She's a reporter for the Santa Fe paper and wanted to do a story on it."

Colleen held the smile as her face turned to steel and her pupils shrank to pinpoints. Tom turned away from the death stare but then recoiled from Laurie's mask of fury. Oh shit. He shouldn't have mentioned the damned story.

Laurie ignored him and faced Colleen. "I was going to do a story. But this so-called detective bargained it away for some shaky info and a chance to earn himself a paycheck. I lost my story and wasted most of two days for nothing but a steak and a night in a hotel room with mildew." She spun around and disappeared into the ladies room.

"Was there really mildew, or were you too busy to notice?" Colleen sounded like an executioner asking if the accused had any last words.

"Not in my room. I can't say about hers."

They circled each other without moving their feet for a few moments before calling a truce. Colleen looked down the concourse and began waving one hand above her head. "There's Cassidy."

Tom spotted a slender arm waving back above the stream of moving heads. It disappeared for a second before Cassidy skipped sideways out of the herd and into the clear. She approached with short, rapid steps and only limited success at keeping coffee inside the cup.

His eyes teared. At first impression, Cassidy didn't appear to be related to either parent. Her flaming red hair and freckled nose were unmistakably Irish but bore little resemblance to the long black hair and clear ivory skin of her mother. Nor did she share Tom's range of browns. Cassidy's teen-aged version of Colleen's flawless figure had all of the sex appeal but lacked the finish. She stood a couple of inches shorter than her mother, and the top of her head tucked in easily beneath Tom's chin as she squeezed him. She made several joyful noises without forming words. Tom felt scalding coffee on his left arm and pulled back. Cassidy tried to soak it up with a token paper napkin, but he waved her off. "Doesn't matter."

After a few minutes of polite airport inanities, Laurie reappeared, her face betraying no trace of anger. She extended a paw. "Hi. You must be Cassidy. I'm Laurie, the old high school friend and your ride to Santa Fe."

Laurie led the way to baggage claim, and grinned as Colleen chided Tom for checking a bag. Even women who didn't like each other seemed to gang up on him. There was a brief folk dance in the parking garage as they sorted out the seating in Laurie's car without anyone actually expressing a preference. As they rolled north, Cassidy was riding shotgun next to Laurie while Tom and Colleen wedged into opposite corners of the back seat. Laurie made a token effort to describe landmarks, but it was pitch black outside. Conversation between the front and rear seats was all but impossible once Laurie goaded the trembling Subaru up to eighty-five. Tom's auditory diagnosis was that the whining bearings were older than God's dog, while the exhaust system was missing altogether. He and Colleen soon tired of leaning across the seat to yell into ears and settled into silence.

They reached Tom's condo just past nine thirty. He was surprised when Laurie climbed out of the car and followed the group to the door. Enthusiastic barking, sounding like a large dog with an attitude, erupted inside. Tom smiled over his shoulder as he unlocked the door. "That's just Stella."

As he pushed the door open, Colleen and Cassidy peered in, then lowered their gaze to meet the smile beneath the jaunty ears. "Quite a set of pipes for such a short dog," sniffed Colleen.

"Think of her as a subwoofer."

As they moved inside, Cassidy dropped to one knee and found herself rubbing necks with Stella. "I didn't know you had a dog."

Laurie broke in before he could answer. "He doesn't, actually. She's mine. Tom was taking care of her while I was on a trip to Las Cruces. I left her with Myrna when we flew to Phoenix, and she said she'd drop Stella off tonight after work."

Colleen looked like she was having trouble deciding which eyebrow to arch first. "I'll bite, who's Myrna? I take it she has a key."

Laurie again beat Tom to the punch. "She's Tom's assistant. And yes, she does have a key. I offered her mine so she could drop off Stella, but she said she didn't need one. It's a friendly town." Laurie scooped up Stella and lugged her toward the door. As she opened it, she smiled at Cassidy. "Nice to meet you. Enjoy Santa Fe." She turned and headed up the driveway without closing the door.

Tom's chest sank as he watched Laurie load Stella into her car. Blowing off her story was a serious mistake, and now he'd lost her. And Stella—he'd miss them both.

"Anyone not have a key to this place?" Colleen was trying to appear amused.

"Just Honest Eddie. You don't know him, but he's another old friend and a local cop. I make it a rule never to give a key to a cop."

"How about a drink?" Tom moved into the tiny kitchen and got out glasses. Cassidy was only seventeen, but she'd spent the past summer in France and was now allowed to indulge in a bit of wine with her folks. No doubt she indulged in more without them. Tom opened a decent Cabernet and poured two whiskies. He put both bottles on the coffee table next to the glasses and settled into a corner of the sofa. Colleen and Cassidy blitzed the condo, sniffing his lair like dogs at a barbeque. At least he didn't hear drawers slamming. Tom watched Cassidy sprawl across the other corner of the sofa. He felt a twinge of sorrow as he pictured young Judy sitting in that spot and not drinking her coffee on the day she died.

Colleen dropped into the purple stuffed chair, and the women began to bombard him with competing versions of Cassidy's dreams for college and life ever after. Most of the schools mentioned were crawling with ivy and development officers. Tom's mind numbed well before he reached the bottom of his glass. He bit his lower lip and managed to refrain from backing the first shot with a double. The ladies clearly didn't expect him to contribute much. They were not disappointed.

At midnight a massive bell began to toll. Colleen craned her neck looking in vain for a clock. Her eyes settled on the living-room window. "I know this is Santa Fe, but what kind of cathedral chimes the witching hour?"

"It's Big Ben, actually." Tom's laptop maintained a wireless connection to his stereo. "Maybe we should resume this tomorrow."

Cassidy smiled, grabbed her bag, and hopped down the stairs to the guest bedroom. A belated "good night" ricocheted up the stairway.

Tom could feel Colleen watching him. He turned and offered her his hand. "Shall we?" He helped her to her feet and put the bottles away as she toted her own bag up the half-flight of stairs. No talk seemed necessary, so Tom killed the lights and they settled into a routine performance of don't-scare-the-kid sex. It was cool in the bedroom, and they lay on their backs under the sheet afterward. Eventually, Colleen turned her head his way on the pillow. "So what really happened in that house in Boston? The New York papers covered the story pretty well for two days and then dropped it cold."

"It was in Lexington, actually. The papers got it mostly right. It took about an hour to get from the hotel to the house given the snow and traffic. There were two guys, and the muscle stayed on the porch with me." Tom rolled away from Colleen and stared at the wall. "I screwed up—I let them separate us. Kate can take care of herself, but there should have been two of us in the room." He rolled a one-eighty until he was facing Colleen. The curtains were open, and there was just enough ambient light to see the folds of the sheet clinging to her figure. Her face was in shadow except for a faint point of green light in one eye—a reflection from the LED on his radio. The sheets rustled as Colleen gave his arm a squeeze.

"Anyway, I hesitated, and she went in alone. We figured they were just there to size us up, but the guy inside opened up on Kate before she could get her gun out. I outshot the one on the porch and ran inside. Kate was lying on the floor, and it looked like the inside man was aiming to finish her off." He rolled on his back. "You know the rest—the papers I saw were right on. No gun in his hand, and yes, I shot him in the back."

"How's Kate doing?"

"Better. She's back at work with enough humor to be bitching about how the scar will look. She's damned lucky to be alive, though."

"She deserved some luck. That was a bad break having that asshole get the phone call when she was alone with him."

"Yeah." Tom stared at the ceiling and said nothing. His breathing slowed, but he was no longer sleepy.

Colleen began plumping her pillow. "What are you going to do with Cassidy tomorrow morning?"

"I'll leave it up to her. We'll grab some early huevos and talk. The weather's supposed to be good. Maybe I should stick her on a horse for an hour or two. Or we could go up to Bandelier—I don't think she's been there."

"Mmmm, the cliff dwellings seem safer than a horse, but you two have fun." She made a show of settling in for the night. Tom continued to stare at the ceiling until well past two.

*   *   *

Cassidy's usual choice from one of Tom's activity lists was none of the above, so he was surprised when she showed enthusiasm for Bandelier. After her critical review of Tom's new pickup, he wedged her in the rear jump seat for the short drive to Modern Visions. The owner emerged, adjusted his ascot, and escorted Colleen inside with enough flamboyant gestures to allow him plenty of body contact. Neither Tom nor Cassidy waved as they drove off.

They talked of all and nothing for more than three hours. Cassidy seemed to enjoy the scenic drive and the trail among the ruins. She climbed all available ladders and posed for the mandatory photos. They had the place almost to themselves on a winter Wednesday. The air was cold, but the sun warmed the rocks. When they returned to the visitor center, they found an empty picnic table in the sun beside Frijoles Creek and rested. Cassidy's smile disappeared. "Things aren't going so well with you and Mom, are they?"

Tom resisted the urge to spout platitudes. "No, not really."

"Want to talk about it?"

"In truth, no, but I suppose you're entitled to ask." He shifted his position, but the rough bench remained too hard for comfort. "It's tough on a marriage when you have to live apart. I thought we'd all be able to live together in Washington, but your mom needed to stay in New York. Her art was finally taking off, and she deserved a turn in the sun. Lord knows she followed me to plenty of backwater towns." Cassidy just looked sadder. He couldn't lie to her. "I don't think we're going to make it. I did, but not anymore. Sorry."

She looked away, staring down the canyon toward the brightly lit cliffs. "I'm OK, Dad. I just feel bad for you." When she turned back to him, there were no tears in her eyes.

They grabbed a late lunch in Los Alamos on the way home. It was almost three when Tom pulled up in front of the Staab Street office. "I need to make a call or two. Why don't you give some business to the vendors on the palace portal? We'll need to leave in about an hour for the airport. He slipped Cassidy some spending money. She looked uncomfortable but took it anyway. Tom headed inside.

Myrna's eyes remained on her e-reader as Tom hung up his coat. "I dropped Colleen off at your condo. She made some comment about being the only woman in town without a key, but I hung onto mine anyway."

"Atta girl." Tom moved to the inner office and closed the door. He called Kate's cell number and slid the Maltese falcon closer to the lamp while he counted the rings. She answered after three.

"Hey, Tommy."

"Hey, partner. Gotta be quick. What's the latest you've got on the stolen Vermeer?"

"I'm not sure where we left off. The Irish boys had it for a long time. I figure they still had it when we drove out to Lexington. An occasionally reliable informant thinks it was moved right after that—got too hot to keep around after our night of glory. He could be right, but he had no clue where it went. If it went anywhere."

"I think I might be able to help, Katie." Tom swallowed a couple of times as his mind replayed Colleen's words. "I'll call you soon. Might be at an odd hour."

*   *   *

Tom and family reached the Albuquerque airport ninety minutes before flight time. Security lines were short, so they grabbed coffees and made a slow circuit of the shopping area. Tom steered them to a spot out of the main traffic lanes and looked Cassidy in the eye. "I need to talk to your mother for a few minutes." She gave a faint nod, glanced at Colleen, and took off toward the newsstand.

"What's this about?" Colleen looked more annoyed than curious.

He moved in close enough to smell her perfume and watched her eyes. She began to glare at him. She usually won the stare-down contests, but not this one. "It was you."

"What?"

"It was you, Colleen."

"What in hell are you talking about?"

"The phone call, toots. How did you know about the phone call to the house in Lexington?"

Tom could sense her fear. Her mind was racing, but she was a good bluffer. "From the papers, I suppose. I read a bunch of them. Probably was in the Times—that's the one I read every day."

"The phone call was a holdback. The papers didn't know about it."

Her lower jaw began to advance. Always a fighter. "Well, then you must have told me. You weren't all that coherent the first couple of days after you got shot. What difference does it make?"

Tom shook his head. "It was you. You made the call. You knew the sting was set for six, but you weren't sure how long it would take us to get to the site. So you waited an hour to call. Lucky guess on the timing, but it didn't need to be exact. You just didn't want to tip the boys off too early. If you did, they'd split before our team got there."

"Are you feeling OK, Tommy? This is just nuts. Why would I do anything like that?"

"Because you figured I'd be the one dealing with the mob boys. You didn't know Kate was playing the buyer."

Cassidy had crept within earshot. Colleen spotted her first. "Leave us alone for a few minutes. Your dad and I are just having a spat."

Tom interrupted. "How much did you hear?"

"Enough." Cassidy's voice was hushed but didn't waver. "I'm staying for the rest."

Colleen's expression was approaching hatred. "How dare you insinuate this bullshit in front of our daughter?"

"I figure you, and maybe your man Justin, had some sort of stake in the deal. You didn't want the small-time hoods messing up the main event with their little side game. So you tipped them off. But the timing was the sweet part. You had a shot to get rid of another little problem while you were at it—me. Almost worked, but you bagged Kate instead."

Colleen's expression softened to concern. "You need help, Tommy. Have you got an infection or something from the wound? You're delirious."

"The devil take the women—they always lie so easy." Tom spun on his heel and began walking toward the exit.

Colleen's pitch rose an octave. "Tommy! We've been married for twenty-five years. That must mean something to you."

He stopped for a moment and looked back over his shoulder. "Yeah. It means I'll give you two hours from the time your plane lands before I call Kate." He resumed walking.

Colleen clutched Cassidy's forearm. "I feel awful you had to see your father this way. He's gone through a lot these past weeks, and he's just lost it. We've got to go now, but I think he'll be OK. I'll find him a good doctor once we get home."

Cassidy pulled her arm away and ran after Tom.

~ 19 ~

As he slipped his key into the condo lock, Tom half expected to hear Stella barking up a storm. The only sound was the click of the deadbolt. Cassidy followed him inside. She hadn't said a word since she grabbed his arm at the airport door. Her coat spun onto the floor as she hurled herself backward onto the sofa. After staring at the ceiling for a few minutes, she broke with a wail that trailed into heaving sobs as she turned and buried her face in a pillow.

Tom let her be. He rinsed out the previous night's glasses, poured two whiskeys, and settled into the purple chair with a glass in each hand. It was a short wait. Cassidy blew a lungful of air into the cushions and rolled onto her back. Her eyes roamed the dark wooden patterns of the beam and latilla ceiling. Tom could see red around her eyes, but they looked dry. When she rolled them his way and spotted the glasses, he extended his right arm. "I really shouldn't corrupt my daughter with the juice of the barley, but wine doesn't cut it at a time like this."

"I've been around, Dad. Thanks." Cassidy grinned as she swung toward an upright direction. For a moment Tom thought she'd make it, but she stopped at the angle of a teen-aged daughter slouch. She closed one eye and stared at the extended glass. "Looks to me like there's a bit more in the other."

"My kind of daughter." Tom switched the glasses. "Easy now. You're not used to the altitude." He watched Cassidy hoist her glass and swirl the amber fluid. It looked like she was planning to down it in one shot, but she made do with a sip and a wince. Not a hard drinker, not yet anyway. He raised his own glass and took an honest belt.

Three or four sips later, Cassidy realized Tom wasn't going to speak first. She squeezed her glass with both hands. "You know about Mom and Justin, don't you?"

Tom thought for a moment before nodding. "I guessed, anyway. You like to think you're wrong." He took a longer pull. "When did you find out?"

"At least a year ago. They aren't exactly careful. God, I actually saw them at it once when I came home early. I slipped back out before they noticed me." Her eyes flicked to Tom. "I'm sorry. Maybe I should have told you sooner, but. . . ."

"Thanks, but it's better you didn't."

Cassidy slithered into a more-erect pose, and they clicked glasses. This time they drained them. Tom hesitated but then poured her another. "Last one, sweets. I still have some sense of propriety."

She gave an amiable smirk. "Liar."

"Well."

When Cassidy's glass reached one finger, she laid her head against the tall back of the sofa and stared at him. "Do you really think she . . . well, what you were talking about?"

"Not now. I'll tell you when it's wrapped up, when I'm sure of everything, but not now."

"What will happen to Mom?"

"Don't really know." Tom looked at his watch. "Her plane gets in just before five. I'll check that it's on time and then. . . ."

"Spare me the details. I mean what happens in the long run?"

"Same answer. I don't really know. Your mom's a survivor, though, and I'll bet she's got some sort of cover. She knew the FBI was hot after the stolen Vermeer. If she's in on that deal, she'll have a seat near the exit."

Cassidy leaned back, fingering her glass. "What you said to Mom. Do you really think women are better liars than men?"

"It's a line from an old Irish song. She knows it."

Tom stood up and collected Cassidy's glass. It wasn't quite empty, but she didn't protest. "You'd best get some sleep, toots. We've got a lot to talk about tomorrow."

"You used to call Mom 'toots.' "

"True, but I call most women toots."

"Doesn't it make some of them mad?"

"Yeah."

Cassidy looked annoyed, but Tom waited until she was headed down the stairs with her back to him before he smiled.

*   *   *

After rolling over for the sixty-third time, Tom gave up and turned on the light. The alarm was set for four, but his internal clock was running fast. He clicked off the alarm, pulled on a dark blue sweatsuit, and carried his shoes down the stairs to the kitchen. Best not to wake Cassidy before he called Kate. The laptop woke up after a few minutes of worrisome grinding noises. Colleen's plane was on the ground in New York. Tom turned the purple chair toward the window and collapsed while the coffee pot did its duty, belching enough steam to make sure he knew it.

Something didn't add up. Tom's subconscious had battled the whiskey all through the short night, leaving him groggy and unenlightened. He stared out the window at the only visible frame—the neighborhood fire hydrant, splendidly lit within the cone of a streetlight. Erratic snowflakes spiraled down through the beam of light. The scene lacked only a couple of dogs wearing fedoras and drinking coffee.

What was it? Colleen had to have made the call to the house in Lexington. That was solid, but was she really trying to get him shot? If so, what the hell for? It's not hard to get a divorce these days—she didn't need to play Henrietta the Eighth.

The second cup of coffee failed to lift the fog but thinned it a little. Tom checked his watch—ten till four. Bit more than an hour before he'd call Kate, but what would he say? His phone rang. He lurched to his feet and grabbed it off the kitchen counter. It was Colleen.

"Hi . . . toots." He dropped back into the chair and stared out the window at the snow. It seemed to be picking up.

"Listen, Tommy. You can believe me or you can go to hell, but I didn't try to get you snuffed." She waited for a reply but got none. "It's true, damn it. Can't you believe me?"

"No. Why are you calling?"

"Time's short, so let's cut the shit. We need to make a deal."

"That's rich. I can't wait to hear it."

"Oh, shut up. Look, Tommy, someday you'll realize you're wrong. Or at least partially wrong. Are you recording this?"

"Hell no, I'm not that smart, particularly at this time of the morning."

"OK, then. Here's what happened. Justin brokered a deal for the Vermeer taken in the Gardner theft—The Concert. He didn't have it, but he knew who did, and they were ready to sell. I don't know names, just that the painting was in Boston and the folks were Irish, if that's any help. Justin also knew someone who'd pay for it. Pay a lot. The commission could have been a couple of million."

"What a surprise. Go on."

"Those two junior mob clowns you gunned down in Lexington didn't have the painting—just some photos they'd copied. They were pulling a con of their own. Figured a greedy rich lady wouldn't have any way to come after them when they ran off with her cash. Their boss didn't know about their little swindle, and the punks figured he'd never be the wiser. It was a stupid risk, but I guess it might have worked if your team hadn't answered their ad."

"Yeah?"

"But that afternoon in Boston, just before you and I ripped up the sheets, you told me about your sting. If your team got a look at those pictures, sooner or later, you'd find out Justin was involved in the sale. I couldn't let that happen to him, Tommy, but I didn't mean for anyone to get hurt."

"Oh, please. Nobody gets hurt? Then why did you hold off calling until we were in the middle of our mission?"

"I didn't have the kid's goddamned number. His cell number. Justin had to track down someone who knew it, and my opening was going on. Jesus, Tommy. I'll admit I've, well, been with Justin. And I did know about his plan to sell the Vermeer. But I swear on St. Paddy's tomb I didn't set you up to get killed."

Tom wavered. Colleen was an accomplished liar as long as you couldn't get close enough to look her in the eyes. But what she was saying made some sense. She and Justin had nothing to gain by triggering a Boston massacre with full press coverage. Their best move was to get the young punks to run for it. "Why are you telling me this? You made the call, and you know the result. You'll go down for this, maybe not as hard as your rich gallery man, but you'll do time."

"For what, Tommy?" Colleen's voice turned to ice. "You've got no proof I made that call. It's not traceable, and nobody but you heard me mention it. It was just you and me in that bed."

Colleen was no fool. Tom couldn't think of any way he could pin the shootout on her, and maybe she wasn't part of the deal for the Vermeer—just an interested party. One who hoped to profit big time if her sex appeal held out. Still, she couldn't be sure the FBI wouldn't make it hot for her.

Tom changed gears. "What do you have in mind?"

"A deal. Your part is to keep me out of it."

"Is that all? Two men dead, Kate and me shot. And you don't want your name sullied? Sounds like a hell of a favor. What am I supposed to get?"

"The Vermeer."

"Oh, come on."

"I'm serious. Once your sting blew up, the owner got really hot to move it. I can give you the name of the guy who bought it. I overheard Justin talking to someone on his phone about delivering it."

Amazing. A few seconds ago she was only trying to save her lover, and now she's offering him up to save her ass. "That's it?"

"That's plenty. Besides. We're talking about a cultural treasure. It doesn't belong in some rich guy's playroom. What if you could send it back to the Gardner?"

"Maybe I could get my old job back?"

"Don't joke, Tommy. We have a chance to do something good here. Deal?"

Tom chewed one side of his tongue. Colleen was impressive. She could change direction like a point guard. "Make it more explicit. What exactly do you want?"

"I give you the name. You don't tell Kate, or anyone else, about me making the phone call or about the sale of the painting. You can go after it yourself, but if you get it, it was from an anonymous tip."

"Why do you think you can trust me, toots?"

"Unlike me, you're a straight-up guy. And besides, it wouldn't look too good for you if they found out you were the leak that spoiled the operation."

It smelled bad, but the chance at the Vermeer seemed real. If Colleen was bullshitting him, he could renege later and take the heat. "OK, deal, but only if your info checks out. Who bought it?"

"A billionaire oilman. From Texas, naturally. His name is James Kinkaid. You can look him up. If he's the Kinkaid I think, he's a pretty big wheel in Dallas. I heard the painting was shipped to a Dallas address two days after your sting."

"Shipped how?"

"I don't know. I'd guess a special art courier, or maybe one of the boys just drove it down in his car."

They listened to each other breathing for at least five seconds before Colleen spoke.

"What's going on with Cassidy? She can't just stay in New Mexico. She has school to finish."

"We'll work out a plan. I'll leave it to her to tell you about it." They went back to heavy breathing, but there wasn't anything left to say. "See you in hell, toots."

"Not if I see you first." She hung up.

Tom stood and turned to wrestle his chair back to the coffee table. He found himself in the gaze of a ghostly apparition staring at him from behind the sofa. Cassidy. His daughter was draped in a sheer white gown, fortunately not backlit. He grabbed a throw blanket from a basket on the floor and tossed it to her. "I keep it cold in here. Look, kid, I know this is your life too, but you've got to stop eavesdropping like this."

She wrapped herself in a wool cocoon and eased onto the sofa. "Sorry, Dad. You're right. But don't worry, I didn't hear much this time."

"Want some coffee? We might as well talk a bit about what we're going to do with you once the sun comes up."

"Sure. Bit of milk in it." While Tom was filling the mugs, Cassidy disappeared downstairs. She returned in her travel clothes, showing no evidence of time spent in front of a mirror. Tom watched with fatherly pride as she dove into the coffee. Eventually, she came up for air. "Will it cost a lot to get me a new ticket home?"

"Probably, but more to the point, where's home?"

They both sat stirring minds and coffees for several seconds. "I can't go back to Mom's place."

"I agree, but you've got a term of high school to go. Bad time to be moving."

"I've got a good friend who graduated last year. You don't know her, but she comes from a pretty posh family with a place in the Hamptons. She's going to Columbia, and her folks got her an apartment on the Upper West Side. I'm pretty sure I could live with her until June."

"You did say 'her'?"

Cassidy feigned annoyance. "Yes, Dad. I'll call her a bit later, but I've spent some weekend nights at her place already. I think it'll work." She shifted gears. "So what's going to happen with you and Mom?"

"We'll see. The marriage isn't long for this world, but the rest is still to be determined. If it's any consolation, I don't think you'll have to visit your mom in a women's slammer."

Cassidy shivered. "Guess that's something."

"One problem. You'll probably have to downgrade your college expectations unless you can get a pretty hefty scholarship. I'm not generating much cash flow yet, and there's a chance your mom's galleries won't be in business much longer."

She shrugged. "Harvard was Mom's idea, not mine. I've applied to some state schools she doesn't know about. Don't worry—I'll be fine." She perked up. "How's the detective business going anyway?"

Tom gave a grim nod. "Not too bad, actually. Willie solved a stolen chicken caper, though he didn't actually find the birds. I haven't brought in a big one like that yet, but I'm working on a couple of cases."

*   *   *

Cassidy's face and waving hand disappeared as the two o'clock airport shuttle turned left onto Sandoval Street and headed south toward Albuquerque. Tom drove back to the office and found Willie deep within one of the saggy leather chairs opposite Myrna's desk. He wrapped up a rambling monologue as Tom sank into the other.

Myrna pretended to be looking over Tom's shoulder? "Where's the family? I've been looking forward to learning why a woman would stay married to you? Wanted to meet Cassidy, too."

"Apparently, there is no reason, and Cassidy just left on the shuttle. I'll explain later." He pointed his chin at the door to the inner office. "Come on, big brother. Time is short." He eased the door closed behind them, cutting off Myrna's glare. He heard her desk drawer slam shut as he wheeled his chair next to Willie's desk. "We're supposed to deliver the bogus Warhol prints to the T&B Gallery at six, and we have no plan."

"Plenty of time, but before you hatch one, I want to hear what's been going on with your women. And Myrna has to hear it, or she'll be a pain in the ass for weeks."

Tom lurched to his feet and retrieved Myrna, who strutted into the room like a banished field marshal just recalled to the front. She nabbed Tom's chair before he could, so he told the tale while making his customary laps of the room. When he finished, he faced them with legs spread and arms folded, daring them to speak.

Myrna gave a multi-pitched hum. "You lead a more interesting life than I thought, Tommy. I only divorced my man and thought that was pretty big stuff. Never thought of shooting him." She looked him up and down with exaggerated head movements. "Now that you're back on the market, maybe I should lose a bit of weight." She stood, threw Tom a wink, and strutted toward the door, her backside swinging like a wrecking ball. The walls were still standing as the door clicked shut.

"Ah, Myrna." Willie swung his feet onto his desk and smiled at the ceiling. "As I recall, you figure Bryce will be so happy to see us, he'll open his sacred vault and let us take inventory. That about it?"

"Sadly, yes. Suppose we park where Bryce can't see the truck from the window in the back office. You stay flat to the wall, and I'll knock and hope they don't have some Boy Scout secret code knock. He may take a peek out the window, but I'll hold the print box so he can't see my face. I'm about the same height as the printer, and it'll be dark. When he opens the door, you take over."

"Sounds risky. What if the vault door isn't open?"

"I think it will be. Guys with that kind of lockbox don't like someone standing around while they work the combination. They worry someone will see, and then they forget how many times you have to spin left past eighty-four."

"But if it's not?"

"Maybe you can persuade him. Make sure you carry your forty-four magnum. Even if he never saw 'Dirty Harry,' it's big enough to get his attention."

"You must be new to this sort of thing, Tommy. Two problems. First, we don't know the damned soup can print is still in the vault. If we go busting in Bryce's back door, beat the crap out of him, and it isn't, we're the ones who'll end up in the pen."

"Maybe. What's the other?"

"Say the vault's actually open. Bryce's back door has a cheap lock but a good frame. If he doesn't like what he sees from the window— tall, dark man hiding behind a cardboard box—he'll run downstairs and slam the steel door. We wouldn't be able to kick our way inside fast enough to stop him."

Tom sagged onto the sofa. "Got any ideas?"

Willie's chair emitted a range of short squeaks as he fidgeted, laced his fingers behind his head, and leaned back to the edge of disaster. "First, I need to oil this damned chair. But yes, we can improve our chances if we go in both doors at once. You keep him busy in front while I pick the lock in the back and slip down the stairs. Now that I've done it once, it shouldn't take more than thirty seconds to get past the door. Can you keep up your act that long?"

"Yeah. But if the alarm goes off, I'll have to grab him while you beat him to the vault." Tom managed to escape from the depths of the sofa and disappeared into the supply closet. He emerged with the cardboard box containing the counterfeit prints. "We need to take these along, not just the box. If we show them to Bryce, he'll know what they mean."

~ 20 ~

At 6:05 p.m. the McNaul brothers set out for the T&B Gallery in two trucks, a precaution in the event they became separated on the way out. They thought it best to reach the doors about twenty minutes past six, when Bryce should be getting impatient. Both were dressed for a dark alley: jeans, black shoes, and dark ski parkas. Black watch caps concealed their hair. Tom pulled onto the shoulder of Garcia Street near the spot where Judy was murdered. He estimated Willie would need five minutes to park somewhere and work his way to the back door of the gallery. One of the bungee cords snapped free with a clang as he removed the tarp and box of prints from the truck bed. As he wrestled the bogus Warhols to the sidewalk, his phone vibrated. It was Willie.

"Bryce's car is in a single space off their rear driveway. I blocked him in with my truck and locked it. No way he can get far if he makes a run for it. I'm at the door now."

The snow flurries had tapered off around five-thirty, but they left a couple of inches of fresh powder. As Tom began to walk, his lonely footprints seemed to stand out like the yellow brick road. He tried to appear nonchalant as he carried the large box two blocks to the T&B. The acting was wasted—not a soul in sight. Yellow light flowed from the gallery windows onto empty ceramic flowerpots still manning their positions along the front wall. Tom raised the box to shield his face, his feet slipping as he shuffled up the icy sidewalk.

The porch was visible from windows on each side of the door. The room with the computer desk was to Tom's left, so he kept the box on that side of his face and his back toward the right window. He knocked lightly but heard no sound inside. After two more tries, he pounded the door with his right hand. That produced a rattle of chair wheels on pine flooring followed by footsteps that stopped short of the door. Bryce must be looking out one of the windows. More steps. After four or five eternal seconds, the door opened.

"Why are you carrying that box upright? That's no way to treat prints." Bryce was clearly peeved, but he backed into the entry and stepped to Tom's right. With the box no longer shielding his face, Tom took two quick steps inside, shoved the box into Bryce's hands, and closed the door.

"What the hell?" Bryce's face shifted from shock to anger in less than a second. "Get out of here." The box slid from his hands and landed flat with a hollow thud.

"Special delivery, Bryce. Your regular boy couldn't make it tonight."

"This is outrageous. I'm calling the cops." As Bryce strode toward the room with the computer, Tom heard the sound of footsteps from the back hall. Evidently, Bryce heard them too—he bolted toward the basement stairs.

When Tom reached the top of the stairway, Bryce was halfway down, taking two steps at a time. Sounds of scuffling feet were coming from the downstairs hallway. Willie must have won the race. Bryce hit the basement floor with both feet, bounced off a side wall, and disappeared toward the vault. By the time Tom made it to the basement, Bryce was standing outside the vault screaming obscenities through the open door. The language wasn't much by Willie's Marine Corps standards, but the volume of the echoes in the cramped hallway made up for the modest vocabulary. Bryce's face was the hue of red enchilada sauce as Tom peered over his shoulder to see his brother inspecting a large package wrapped in brown paper and several miles of tape. Willie lifted the parcel and gave it a playful shake. "What do you suppose is inside?"

Tom clamped his hands on Bryce's shoulders, but the startled gallery owner recovered and twisted free. The three men exchanged silent glares for several seconds. Tom ended the stare-down. "We have some things to talk about."

"Like what? What the hell are you guys doing, breaking into my gallery like this?" Bryce's color had eased off to a shade closer to medium rare.

"That box upstairs isn't empty. It has five flavors of soup, all fresh silkscreen prints made by Gary—your printer man up near Taos. The inks are barely dry." Bryce's eyes flickered between Tom and Willie as he strained to understand the situation. "The man gave you up, Bryce, and he's split for parts unknown. But he's not important. Just a poor artist trying to pay his rent. It's you we want."

"Want for what? Why are a couple of private dicks sticking their nose in my business?"

Tom nodded to Willie. "Open that."

Willie picked at the overlapping strands of tape but soon gave up and extracted a black combat knife from inside his parka. He held the blade near the tip to keep it from damaging the contents of the package as he sliced. The paper and tape gave way to a box made of dense cardboard. When one end of it was unsealed, Willie laid it flat on the central table and eased out a large wad of layered bubble wrap held in place by yet more tape. Tom kept a close watch on Bryce, who seemed fixated on Willie's knife as it popped plastic bubbles and severed tape. The core of the package lay beneath another layer of brown paper, this one held together by masking tape. Willie gently peeled it open to reveal a black metal frame with a loose slab of cardboard covering the image. He glanced at Tom and Bryce before lifting it. "Any bets?" Seeing none, he flipped the cardboard cover to the floor. The brilliant red and white soup can print sported the word "TOMATO" in red block capitals. "Bingo."

Tom kept his eyes on Bryce and was surprised to see the gallery owner relax as he pointed at the print. "Is that all this is about? For Christ's sake. I bought that print, and I've got receipts. I needed some cash, so I decided to sell it. End of story. That's my business—I buy and sell high-end art. You boys get the hell out of here while I call the cops."

"Not a bad try, Bryce, but nobody's buying it." Tom stepped back slightly to cut off Bryce's only line of retreat. "That's Tracy Lee's print. The one she hired me to find."

"So what? Yeah, it's the one I gave her for her birthday, but I needed the dough, so I repossessed it. I admit I shouldn't have told the cops it was stolen, but the insurance claim hasn't been paid, so no harm done. This is just between Tracy and me. Look, if you're worried about your little finder's fee, I'll see you get paid."

"We're not here for Tracy Lee's print. You've been running a counterfeiting operation, buying real prints and selling fakes in their place. We've got five samples of the bogus soups upstairs, and you sold a hell of a lot more than that. I'm betting those flat boxes in the corner still have all the originals in them."

"That's just plain stupid." Bryce stuck out his jaw in a vain attempt to look outraged. "Sure, I've got some originals in there, but I paid good money for all of them. And I've got no idea what's in that box upstairs. Gary used to make some prints to sell to low-budget types who wanted something one grade up from a poster to hang in their living room. But we never represented his stuff as anything but copies. It's all in our books. Not that I'm going to show my business records to a couple of two-bit bums like you. What a pair. Like I said before, get out."

Tom smiled as he fished a computer memory stick out of a front jeans pocket and held it between his left thumb and forefinger. "Your books are right in here, asshole, and they show nothing of the kind. You're selling counterfeits as the real McCoy—I can tell by the prices." Bryce looked like he was considering a lunge for the memory stick, so Tom returned it to his pocket. "One thing puzzles me, though. Why are you selling Tracy's real one when you could have one made to order?"

"We don't forge prints, dammit." Bryce looked at Willie. "Go on. Have a look in those boxes. You won't find a single bogus print, not anywhere. You guys are blowing smoke."

Willie stepped to the right-rear corner of the vault and picked up one of the boxes. Tom took his eyes off Bryce for a second to watch. In his peripheral vision, he saw sudden movement as Bryce leaped to his right and grabbed the side of the vault door with both hands. Tom lunged too late as Bryce threw his full weight into a heave. The door slammed shut, and Bryce flipped the locking lever closed before Tom took him down.

"How does it open?" Tom pressed his knee harder against Bryce's spine, pinning the gallery owner to the concrete floor.

Bryce winced and gasped for breath. "Only from the combination lock. It's an old vault, and there's no safety lever on the inside."

"OK. You're going to stand up and open it now. Nice and easy." Tom slid his knee off Bryce's back and stood up. Bryce took time to recover what composure he could muster before struggling to his feet. "No."

Tom stepped closer to Bryce, but the emboldened gallery owner stood his ground. "Stop fooling around, and open the damned door." He heard muffled thumping from inside the vault.

"Why? What's in it for me? You tough guys come busting in here and rough me up. What the hell for?" Bryce seemed to be gaining courage by the second, and his voice rose half an octave. "You can't prove a damned thing. If there are any forged prints in this gallery, they'd have to be the ones you carried in yourself. Assuming there are prints in that box. If a printer in Taos is screwing around with forgeries, he's the one the cops should want. And don't give me any crap about my books. You don't have them on that gadget in your pocket, and you couldn't read them if you did."

Tom figured it was time to interrupt the adrenaline rush before Bryce announced a run for Congress. "Tracybitch."

"What?"

"You heard me. Tracybitch one-oh-one. Your password. A choice that will probably cost you extra in the divorce settlement."

Bryce's bluster crashed like the Hindenburg. His voice dropped to gravel and hiss. "What the hell do you want? You can't really be here just because of Tracy's goddamn soup can."

"Open the door. Then we'll talk."

"No. You talk first. That vault is airtight, and it's not all that big. Not my fault if some burglar trapped himself inside. You'll never get him out of there before he suffocates, so lay off." Bryce rallied. "I don't know what you think you've got on me, but my business is none of yours. I'm going home now."

"Not until you unlock the door."

"I'm not going to open it with wild man Willie inside. I'll give you the combination, but you let me get the hell out of here before you let him out."

"Oh, sure. You'll write down a bum combination and split."

"What good would that do me?"

Tom hesitated. There should be plenty of air in the vault, though no telling how long it would take to break in. But the deal seemed good enough with Bryce's car blocked in by Willie's truck. Besides, the bastard didn't know they were after him for Judy's murder. He wouldn't run very far. "Deal."

Bryce fumbled in his coat pocket and retrieved a pen, but he had no paper. Tom backed a few steps down the hall and opened the door to the tiny bathroom, grabbing a paper hand towel without losing sight of Bryce. The sharp ballpoint shook in Bryce's hand, tearing the paper, but the number was legible.

Tom nodded, and Bryce sprinted for the stairs as Tom began twirling the dial. He forced himself to breath slowly to avoid mistakes. The combination finished with a right turn passing nineteen once before stopping there. He grabbed the lever and pushed down. It didn't budge. He could hear a faint yell and continued soft thumping from inside the thick steel.

Tom raced up the stairs. He heard cursing followed by breaking glass as he ran out the back door of the gallery. Bryce reached inside the broken driver's window of Willie's truck and fumbled for the lock, but

Tom grabbed Bryce's hair and jerked him away. Bryce stumbled and was trying to stay on his feet as Tom let go and landed a right hook to the jaw.

When Bryce's eyes focused, Tom grabbed him by the shirt collar, dragged him inside the building, and bounced him downstairs to the vault. "Open it."

There was no fight left in Bryce as he began turning the large dial. Tom noted that the next-to-last number was different from the combination on the paper towel. The dial stopped at nineteen, and this time the lever moved downward with a tight click. The door swung open under the force of Willie's charge.

Tom stepped between his enraged brother and the ashen gallery owner. "Let's not lapse into carnage." He turned to Bryce and backed him into the vault. "You want a turn in here?"

Bryce kept glancing sideways at Willie, who was popping bubble wrap with the tip of his combat knife. "I wasn't going to leave him in here. I would have called you once I got my car going. Given you the right number."

"Sure."

"Look, I'm sorry. I didn't trust you guys. No harm, eh?"

Willie increased his rate of bubble popping, and Bryce began to panic. "I don't get it. Why are you guys doing this? Why do you care so much about a few lousy prints?"

Tom's voice was barely above a whisper. "We didn't come here for your prints. We're here for Judy."

"Who's Judy? You mean that little babe who worked for me? Hey, is she the one who gave you my books?"

"That's her, but no, I got into your computer myself."

"So what the hell's your interest in the girl? You have the hots for her or something? I mean, I feel bad she got killed, but what's that got to do with my prints?"

Tom clenched both fists and controlled his breathing until the flash of hatred faded. He cleared his mind to combat mode. "Which phone did you use, Bryce? Your cell or the one in the office upstairs? Either one is traceable."

"Now what are you talking about?"

"When you called Langston and set up the hit on Judy, which phone did you use? You didn't have time to run out and find a disposable."

"You're nuts. I have no idea what you're talking about."

"You're done, Bryce. That phone call. Hiring a murder is a capital crime. Why'd you do it, Bryce? Surely, even you wouldn't murder somebody for the price of a Tomato Soup print. That's only about thirty grand." Tom began to shout. "But you knew Tracy Lee would ditch you if she found out, didn't you? She'd look deeper and see how you've been playing her. No more Tracy Lee and no more Tracy Lee's money. Which was the clincher, Bryce? Love or money?" Willie placed a hand on Tom's shoulder to cool him down.

Bryce ran out of ideas, hope, and courage all at the same time. He collapsed against the wall of the vault and slid to the floor. Willie looked down at him with more disgust than anger. "I'll take him in, Tommy. Give Honest Eddie a call to let him know we're coming. If he's not still in the office, he'll come in for this one."

The brothers hoisted Bryce to his feet and worked him up the stairs and out the back door. "Shit. Look what this yo-yo did to my window." Willie let go of Bryce and opened the driver's door. Shards of glass tinkled to the asphalt. Willie grabbed a baseball cap from the back of the cab and used it to sweep more glass off the seat. He retrieved the guilty brick and tossed it at a lidless garbage can overflowing with bulging plastic bags. The brick ripped the top bag, spilling its reeking contents. "You got any cuffs?"

Tom produced a pair, and Willie used them to fasten one of Bryce's arms to a corner tie-down ring in the bed of his pickup. He dug some short lengths of rope out of the cab, and when he was finished, Bryce was securely spread-eagled on his back. Willie climbed into the truck. "Reckon I'll try out a couple of streets with speed bumps on my way to the station."

As Tom watched the lights of Willie's truck disappear around a corner, he felt empty. He wasn't sure the evidence against Bryce would stand up. They hadn't exactly followed police procedures. But what did it matter? Judy was dead one way or the other. He made a quick call to the police station, left a message for Eddie Romero, and headed into the gallery, locking the back door from the inside. The box of counterfeit prints was still lying on the floor just inside the front door. Tom carried it down to the vault and set it on the worktable. He opened it and carefully removed the prints, shifting Tomato Soup to the top of the pile. It was printed on relatively lightweight paper, and he was careful not to dimple the image. The forgery appeared to be a perfect copy of Tracy Lee's framed print. He removed Tracy Lee's original from the frame and compared the signatures on the backs. Close enough. Each was labeled #9/250.

What was the difference anyway? The artist's vision remained the same. Tom's eye could see no difference between the prints. Presumably, Andy Warhol had pulled the screens on Tracy Lee's, but maybe not, since he'd worked on them with at least one assistant. Tom couldn't escape the feeling that Judy had died for the difference, though he knew there was more to it than that. Tom spotted a three-foot stepladder in the vault and pulled it open. He sat on it, staring at the two prints. Tracy Lee's original had been poorly mounted. The framer had matted the print rather than floating it with rice-paper hinges. Not quite a sacrilege but a break with tradition. Tom couldn't see any discoloration between the exposed portions of the paper and the areas covered by the mat. Evidently, it hadn't been hanging too long on Tracy Lee's sunny kitchen wall.

There didn't seem to be any point in trying to remove fingerprints, but perhaps a bit of staging was in order. Tom let the debris from Willie's unwrapping job lie where it fell. He refilled Tracy Lee's frame and set it on a shelf along the back wall next to some of the prints from the previous Friday's opening. It seemed best to leave the new counterfeit prints on the table in the vault. The police would have no reason to suspect the forgeries were delivered less than an hour ago. Tom put one print back in the cardboard box, ferried it to his truck, and secured the box to the truck bed under a tarp. The street was still empty, with no new footprints in the snow. He returned to the vault for a final inspection. Satisfied, he headed upstairs, settled into the chair facing Bryce's computer, and searched its list of applications. There was a chess program, so Tom chose white and pushed his queen's pawn. The computer steered him into the Albin Countergambit, but Tom knew it well and was a pawn up when his phone rang. It was Eddie.

"Don't you McNauls ever take a day off? Your brother just showed up in his pickup with Bryce Jackson loaded in the back like a bale of hay."

"More like a load of manure, but go on."

"I haven't heard everyone's story yet, but when I have, I want to talk to you at the scene. Are you still there?"

"Yeah."

"It's a little late to say don't touch anything, but try to hold down the damage until I get there. I'll send a car ahead to keep you company while I talk to Willie and Bryce."

"Anything you say, lieutenant."

Eddie hung up. Within five minutes a patrol car pulled up and discharged two cops. The driver was young and had the well-pressed look of a man freshly minted at the academy. His partner had veteran's wrinkles around eyes that overlooked a nose redder than Rudolph's. The older cop's belly sagged over his belt, but he looked to be in good shape otherwise. He started the kid stringing yellow crime-scene tape for no obvious reason and then banged on the door. It was unlocked, so he let himself in and sauntered over to where Tom sat staring at the computer screen. Like Eddie, he told Tom not to go anywhere and set off on the mandatory prowl. Tom waited until the senior cop was downstairs inspecting the vault before phoning in an order for a large pizza. It was going to be a long night.

~ 21 ~

The pizza arrived an hour before Lieutenant Romero, but three slices remained as his car coasted to a stop outside the gallery. Tom had taken the precaution of ordering double anchovies to minimize foraging by the cops babysitting the scene. Eddie stopped just inside the front door and began a series of exaggerated sniffs. He bent over to examine the unchosen remnants of Tom's dinner, now congealed to the texture of latex. "You planning to eat this, or did you?"

"Have a slice and find out."

"Better not. Anchovy breath would mean a night on the sofa." Eddie followed the two patrolmen down to the vault.

Tom shrugged and reached for another slice. Twenty minutes later he heard the thudding tread of three policemen ascending wooden stairs. Eddie sent the other two back on the road and dragged a chair next to Tom's. "Want to tell me your version?"

"Sure. A client hired me to find a stolen print. While hot on its trail, I uncovered a neat little counterfeiting scheme Bryce had going with a printer up near Taos. I had reason to believe my client's stolen print was in the vault downstairs, so Willie and I came over here after hours, hoping Bryce would have the vault door open. He did. Bryce showed us around, and we found the stolen print along with four counterfeit ones."

"Uh huh. Just who is this client? And while you're at it, how did you get on to this alleged counterfeiting?"

"Can't say, and likewise. I have to respect my client's confidentiality. She's not a suspect in any crime."

"Oh, spare me. Half the people in Santa Fe know Tracy Lee hired you to find her damned soup can. She's told that story all over town. My wife asked me if I'd heard about it."

"She can say what she wants, but I can't. Tracy's still my client. Look, Eddie. I was tracking down a stolen print, and I went through some records at Tracy's gallery. I can't talk about what I found as long as I'm working for her. You'll need to ask her yourself or get a subpoena."

Tom's right leg was asleep, so he crossed his legs in the other direction. "What are you charging Bryce with?"

"Nothing. I had to let him go."

"No! What for?"

"Think it through. As far as I know, everything in Bryce's vault belonged to him and was paid for. There are some prints you say are forgeries, but how do I know that? They look real enough to me, and it would take weeks to have them authenticated. Even if they are phony, it's no crime to own them. They aren't contraband, like meth or homemade c-notes." Eddie's calm demeanor disappeared. "Damn it, Tommy. Why didn't you just come to me first? I haven't got probable cause to search Bryce's records. I don't even have evidence of a crime. Just a livid gallery owner delivered to my office hog-tied in the back of your brother's pickup. What could I charge him with? Breaking Willie's truck window?"

Tom stared at the floor. "What about the rug and pot heist from Southwest Cultures? Could you finger him for that?"

Eddie's head snapped toward Tom, his face scrunched into undisguised suspicion. "What's going on with that one? I got a call this morning from Laurie asking a bunch of questions. She said there was some sort of break in the case. Asked if I'd trace some phone calls for her. Did the Hayek brothers hire you?"

"Once again, can't say. But I assume you remember you referred them to me."

"Yeah, but what's Bryce got to do with it?"

"He hired the boys who did the job. But no, don't ask. I don't have hard evidence to show you yet."

"Shit, it's getting late. One more question. You said Bryce showed you around the vault. I don't buy that for a minute, but how the hell did he end up in Willie's truck?"

"As I recall, Willie lifted his shoulders, and I grabbed his feet."

"Always a wise-ass. Get out of here." Eddie glared as Tom donned his parka and headed out the front door carrying the last two slices of pizza.

The powder squeaked under Tom's feet as he made his way back to Garcia Street. Five minutes later he was at the condo. He stashed the pizza in the fridge, fetched the print from his truck, and slid the cardboard box under his bed.

Peace at last. Tom collapsed into the purple chair and slid down until his head rested on its back and his eyes lost focus. Now what? He had no idea what to do next, and no muse was knocking at his door. Maybe he should have let the cops handle it. But dammit, he wanted to do something for Judy. Meanwhile, the weekend loomed and he had no plans. Maybe he could make peace with Laurie and take her to dinner somewhere. He sought solace in the cabinet to the left of his refrigerator. Two glasses of Bushmills finished the bottle.

* * *

By six-thirty the sun was skipping off the snow and through Tom's windows. He could hear the wind playing a dirge with branches and utility wires. A full pot of coffee was brewing to brace him for the trip up the driveway. The leftover pizza slices looked like discarded boot soles, but he wolfed them down cold.

After two cups of morning stimulant, Tom was legally awake. A wind gust stung his face with dry snow as he opened the door. He flushed the newspaper from its hiding place between a chamisa bush and a faux adobe wall and skidded back to warmth. When his mug was filled for the third time, he settled into the purple chair and unrolled the paper. He checked the lead headline to see if Congress had declared war on anyone overnight. It hadn't.

Halfway down the front page, he saw it. A smaller headline read: "Major Breakthrough in Canyon Road Robbery." The byline attributed the story to Laurie Kepler. Tom blitzed through the article and saw it was about the Southwest Cultures burglary. I'll be damned. She did it. He couldn't help smiling. After all, she hadn't made the deal with the shyster in Phoenix. This was going to cause problems, but good for Laurie.

The article sported a photo of one of the stolen Germantown rugs on Page 1 and was continued inside on Page 4. It was clear Laurie had interviewed the Hayek brothers. No doubt they'd given her the picture. Tom read on. A Phoenix dealer was offering items from the robbery in private sales. The dealer, speaking to "this reporter," denied knowing the goods were stolen. He claimed they were obtained from a notable art dealer in Santa Fe and had been delivered by two men in a black pickup truck. The deliverymen were being sought, police had been notified, etc., etc.

What a mess. Laurie must have talked to the police, probably Eddie Romero. That explained the wary look from Eddie the night before when Tom asked about the case. No doubt Laurie's story would piss off Honest Eddie more than Tom. It would alert the Langstons before the cops could get their ducks in a row. The Langstons were unpredictable, and they were dangerous. Not a good combination.

Tom called Laurie. No answer. He left a voicemail asking her to call him. No doubt she was relishing his discomfort. He called again and left a second message advising her to be careful. It was useless advice—she wouldn't know how.

The coffee was still hot and seemed more alluring than Lieutenant Romero. Once he called Eddie, there was no telling how the day would play out. The mug was half empty when his phone rang. He hoped for Laurie but got Eddie.

"Seen the paper, Tommy?"

"Yep. I see you've been talking to Laurie yourself. Holding out on me?"

"It's my job to hold out on guys like you. We agreed she wouldn't publish anything until we finish our investigation. You have anything to do with it coming out today? Please say yes—I'd like to bust your ass a bit."

"Nope. Came as a complete surprise."

"So why'd she do it? It must have something to do with you."

"I'm flattered, but I don't know. I've tried to call her. She's not picking up. No surprise, I guess."

"I've got to move fast now that she's blown the cover. You got anything for me?"

"The phones. You need to trace all the calls to or from Ike Langston's phone, and any belonging to his kids. And while you're at it, same for Bryce Jackson's phone over the last two weeks, maybe longer. If you find any calls between those guys, I've got to know ASAP. And I'll give you everything I've got. Want me to come by the station?"

"Not yet. I don't know where I'll be. Keep your phone on, and I'll track you down sometime today. But don't get your hopes up. I'm not handing you any details unless you've got something good to trade."

"Fair enough."

Two more calls to Laurie went straight to voicemail. Tom decided to drive to her house south of the capitol. He pictured her with a fire going and feet up as she drank spiked hot chocolate and listened to her phone ring. The temperature was stalled in the twenties, and the Tacoma fishtailed on an icy patch as he turned onto Laurie's street. He eased to the curb in front of her house. The veteran Subaru stood alone in the driveway under a thin shroud of undisturbed snow. Tom hopped out of his truck and hurried up the sidewalk. He was planning his opening line and taking long strides when his left heel hit black ice. The foot shot forward while the other splayed to his right. His hands jerked down to break the fall before he could overrule them, and he hit the ice in a sitting position. Pain flashed up his left arm as he rolled onto his right side. He lay on the sheet of glare ice and took inventory. Left hand and wrist hurt like hell, all other body parts reporting as functional. Dignity was another matter. He blew gently on the snow, sending the treacherous dusting of powder swirling off the ice. Not the first time he'd seen nature pull this trick.

Tom squirmed off the sidewalk onto the snow-covered grass where he could get enough traction to stand. His left wrist ached, but he could move his fingers. He pressed the arm lightly against his side and kept to the grass as he inched toward the porch. The door burst open before he got there. Laurie must have watched the whole show from her living room window. She dusted snow off his clothes while streaming a litany of concern and derision. Tom wasn't listening.

Laurie didn't look sure of a safe place to grab him, but she finally opted for his good arm and led him up the steps, out of his jacket, and onto her sofa. Tom worked the glove off his left hand and let her undo the cuff button of his shirt. There wasn't much swelling yet, and at least his arm didn't exhibit any acute angles. She gently stroked and poked, asking, "Does this hurt?" It did. She scolded and prodded him into her Subaru and headed for the emergency room at St. Vincent.

*   *   *

Four hours later Tom was back on Laurie's sofa with his fractured left arm in a sling and a short aluminum splint lightly taped to his forearm and hand. The coffee table sported a large manila envelope containing unread instructions and payment papers beneath an empty foam box with the remnants of take-out enchiladas. Laurie wiped the last of the red chile sauce from her lips and fingers and slapped the napkin on the tabletop. "Say something, damn it. We've been running around patching you up for hours and you haven't said a word about my story. That's why you're here, so you could at least admit it."

"I admit it. Good story, too, though I thought you might have waited a couple of days until Eddie got the phone traces."

"I might have lost the story. You already threw it away once, and besides, it's Friday. Fat paper day." She stood up and moved to the window.

Tom bought some time testing the fingers inside his sling. "Look, cowgirl, I'm sorry about trying to steamroller your story. I'm not here to be mad. I'm worried about you."

Laurie turned and cocked her head to the right, sticking both hands in the back pockets of her jeans. Tom was surprised they fit. She began to rock her hips from side to side as she considered his peace offering. "Worried why? Don't tell me some crap about losing my job. I didn't make anything up."

"Assuming at least one of the relevant rednecks can read—not a sure thing—you're about to make some really bad people really angry. And they aren't the kind of people who will sit around feeling depressed."

"Who are you talking about?"

"The Langstons. You remember—the boys who lived next door to Willie and torched his dog."

Laurie shuddered and folded her arms tightly against her ribs. "That was horrible. But what do they have to do with my story?"

"I think they were Bryce's, shall I say, facilitators. The guys he hires for side enterprises. The guys who knocked over Southwest Cultures and delivered the Germantowns to that fence in Phoenix."

Lights flared in Laurie's eyes, but she still looked skeptical. "How can you know that?"

"Call it a wise bet for now, but once Eddie gets the traces on Bryce's phone, they're going to show he had a habit of calling some guys who don't collect much art. What they do collect are arrest records. They started that way back in high school—stole a car. But Willie says their recent busts have been for dealing meth and arranging the odd dogfight. Not many convictions. I think one of the twins did a couple of years once."

"Oh shit." Laurie hunched over and squeezed her ribs so hard he could see the tendons swelling in her arms. "You think they'd come after me? For writing a story in the paper?" She straightened up a little. "That doesn't sound right, Tommy. It was just a burglary. Small time compared to hard drugs."

"Yeah, but you pitched your story as an ongoing investigation, with you up for best supporting actress." Tom wavered as he pondered how much more he should tell her. "Well, anyway, you need to take some precautions with these guys." He held back his theory about Bryce using the Langstons to eliminate Judy. She was scared enough.

Laurie was breathing normally again. "Thanks, but I'll be OK. I'll keep the doors locked."

"Better if you took a short vacation."

"Can't do that, Tommy. I've got to finish my story."

He'd expected nothing less, but he knew her locks wouldn't be enough if Ike and his boys decided to teach her a lesson. She might be OK if they didn't think she was closing in on Judy's murder. Hell, with luck, Eddie might put the pieces together before Ike's clan learned about the story. Not good odds, though.

Tom stood up to leave. "While you're wrapping it up, do you think you could find any archive photos of the Langstons? They've been arrested enough—they must have made the papers. I'd like to email some to the dealer in Phoenix."

"I'll look. Like me to drive you home?"

"No thanks. My truck has an automatic."

"Wuss."

"Nah. I just need one hand free to shoot."

The one-armed drive home proved simple enough, but Tom spent fifteen minutes trying to figure out how to take a shower without getting his left arm wet. He gave up. What the hell, nobody would be close enough to smell him before Monday. Seemed like time for a ceremonial nip. The doctor had ruled out booze because of the painkillers, but a bit of rum would hit the spot.

A mug of Irish coffee, minus the whipped cream, accompanied Tom to his chair as he settled in to give the case some penetrating analysis. The room was dark when he woke up. The nearest lamp was to the left of the chair, and when he contorted his frame to reach the switch with his right hand, he kicked the half-full mug off the coffee table. He checked his phone. No messages. All his joints were complaining as if trying to compete for attention with his throbbing wrist. He stretched them out with a few laps of the room and tossed a frozen box of lasagna in the microwave.

Honest Eddie was tracing phones. Laurie was poised to search photo archives for Langston mug shots. Time enough to work on the Gardner Museum case. Tom wasn't confident the Texas oilman fingered by Colleen really had the stolen Vermeer, but he needed to start there. No sense waiting till Monday to sic Myrna on the guy. She was always complaining of dull weekends at home with the kids.

"Hey, toots."

"Tommy, my man. What's up?"

"You got some time this weekend? I'd like you to dig up some info on an oilman in Texas."

"I've got time to burn right now, big boy. The kids are on a sleepover in town tonight. Want me to come into town to work? Ooh, I could stand a sleepover myself."

"I'm not at my best right now—only got one arm working. See what you can find out about a James Kinkaid of Dallas. He's allegedly a billionaire with too much of a taste for fine art. Heard of him?"

"Everyone here knows about Big Jim Kinkaid, honey. You've been gone too long. He has some kind of estate in the hills just south of town. I don't know what the house looks like—you can't see it from the road. I hear there's a guard at his gate dressed like a Texas Ranger, only without a badge."

"Could be the guy. Does he come to Santa Fe often?"

"All the time. He and his wife keep horses up here, but the wife likes to winter in Dallas for the social life. Big Jim says he comes north to get away from all that. Word is, he really comes to ride the horse trainer, but I never gossip about such things."

"Uh huh."

"I'll see what I can find out for you. Computer at work runs faster, though, so I'll drive into town. Why don't you meet me at the office? And don't you worry none about that bad arm—Myrna can handle everything just fine."

~ 22 ~

Myrna arrived at the Staab Street office just after seven and seemed surprised to see Tom at his desk. He wasn't anxious to spend the night fending her off, but the search for the art-loving oilman would go faster with both of them on the job. She lured Tom onto the sofa, ostensibly to examine his lame limb. Once the bandage was off, her expression changed from amorous to disgust. "That looks like something I'd throw out from my meat drawer."

"Told you."

She helped him rewrap the arm and disappeared into the front room. An hour later she returned in triumph. "Has to be the right James Kinkaid. He's not the only rich man in Dallas with that name, but the other one isn't in the oil business. Besides, he and his wife are major patrons of the Dallas Museum of Art. There was an article in the Dallas News about them donating a Rembrandt a couple of years ago."

"Nice. I wonder if it was stolen?"

"Probably, one way or another." Myrna sounded tired, and she let the Mae West routine lapse. "What next?"

"I don't know how you can find this out, but I'd like to know where Kinkaid's going to be for the next few days. I think he and I need to have some face time."

Myrna feigned a yawn. "That's no trouble. I'm friends with the horse trainer. Nice lady, but she's fooling herself if she thinks she'll pry Big Jim away from his wife."

"Anyone you don't know in this town?"

"There was a guy with braids and a cowboy hat walking around the plaza last week. Didn't look familiar, but he might have been a tourist."

Myrna disappeared into the front room to call the equine woman while Tom again tried to contact Eddie Romero. No luck. Myrna swaggered in looking as smug as a hound sneaking out the back door of a butcher shop. "Telluride. He's been there the last week or so. The wife went Christmas shopping in Italy, and Big Jim flew Sally—she's the horse trainer—up to his ski chalet. Sally says she's making some progress. Dream on, girl."

"I'll be damned. Thanks. Why don't you take the rest of the week off?"

"Big spender. Well, I'll be heading home. Not much action for a Friday night, but I think I'll at least wait until you get a cast on that arm."

Tom was about to follow her out the door when Eddie Romero called back. "What's up, Tommy?"

"Have you got the phone traces on Bryce?"

"Not yet, and I'm not talking about them anyway until you cough up some trade goods. In the meantime, he's disappeared. You got any ideas where?"

"What do you know? I never figured he'd run. No, I don't know him well enough to guess. You sure he's gone, or did Tracy Lee just say he's late for dinner?"

"I'll fill you in some other time. Maybe."

*   *   *

Saturday morning didn't have much to recommend it. An unusually low overcast muted colors and softened shadows. The damp air was just warm enough to melt what was left of the snow. Tom frowned at the brown slush. Might as well be in Philadelphia. The morning paper was soaked through and required peeling to read.

Tom couldn't find any follow-up to Laurie's story. He decided to walk to the office via an order of huevos rancheros and felt like company, but Laurie's phone was off. He tried Willie and was surprised to catch his brother en route to town. "Getting two new tires for the truck. Rosie's in an hour?"

As Tom slalomed down the hill avoiding ice patches, he recalled the concern in Laurie's eyes when she examined his arm. At least she cared. That was something.

Willie was waiting in a booth. They sat staring at each other for a moment and silently agreed not to talk shop. After an hour of jokes about Tom's arm and the dangers of strong-armed women, Willie drove them to the office. Neither seemed to have much appetite for work. Two hours later Tom was hanging a paperclip chain around the Maltese falcon's neck when Laurie called. He snatched the phone from his pocket and let it ring three more times before answering.

"Hi, toots. How's your morning?"

His mood crashed in an instant. She was sobbing and speaking in gasps. "Tommy, could you come over? I . . . could you just come now? Hurry."

"What's wrong?"

"Just get over here. Please."

"Hang tough, we'll be there in five minutes." He turned to Willie. "Laurie's in trouble. Her place—ASAP."

Tom had one arm in his parka while he struggled into the passenger seat of Willie's truck. The coat was still dangling from his right arm as he hurried across the lawn next to Laurie's sidewalk. Willie raced up the walk and pulled ahead of him. The door was an inch ajar, and he pushed his way inside with Tom a few seconds behind.

The living room was in shambles. Lamps and framed pictures were smashed. The sofa and chair cushions were slashed, and books lay scattered on the floor with pages ripped out. Laurie was sitting on a dining room chair staring at the floor. Willie drew his pistol, his eyes quick as he scanned the room and doorways.

Tom pulled the Glock from the pocket of his parka. "Anyone else here?" She shook her head. "Are you hurt?"

"No."

Tom and Willie made a quick tour of the house and cleared all the rooms. The kitchen door had been forced. Counters and floor were littered with remnants of dishes swept from cupboards. The bedroom dresser drawers were strewn on top of their former contents, and the closets contained only a few empty hangers. Foam bulged through deep gashes in Laurie's mattress. Tom stepped into water in the bathroom and found the toilet stuffed with underwear and brown water. He returned to the living room while Willie checked the back yard. Laurie sat looking broken in the hard wooden chair, but there was no good place to move her.

"Were you here?"

She tried to answer but choked. After several slow breaths, she tried again. "No. I was out of coffee and drove over to Trader Joe's. It was like this when I got back." Her head suddenly jerked toward him. "Where's Stella?"

"I didn't see her. Could be hiding."

"Where is she!" Laurie jumped to her feet and began racing around the living room.

"Maybe she wandered out the front door. It was open a bit when we got here."

"No, it was closed when I got home, and so was the one in the kitchen. But she wasn't here. How could I not have noticed?"

"You had other things to think about. Did you see anyone?"

"No. They must have come for me. I wasn't here, so they did this." She flailed an arm at the devastation. "And they took Stella."

"What about Stella?" Willie emerged from the kitchen.

Laurie grasped at faint hope. "Did you see her out back?"

"No." Willie's face turned dark as death. Tom could see muscles bulging in his brother's neck and jaw; his grinding teeth sounded like pack ice breaking in the spring. He didn't look like he intended to say anything, so Tom stepped away and called the police. Willie went into the kitchen, and Tom heard the back door slam. Ten minutes later Willie returned just as the first patrol car arrived and discharged two uniforms, both young and short. The heavier of the two was a woman with straight black hair and shoulders suggesting an hour a day in the weight room. Maybe two. Her expression was as hard as her muscles. She shooed Tom and Willie out onto the front porch with her male partner while she questioned Laurie. The partner seemed like a nice kid and nodded a lot as the brothers told their versions of the story.

After two or three laps around the truth, Tom got tired of shifting from one foot to the other trying to avoid the cold. He pointed his good arm at Willie's truck. "Mind if we go sit in there?" The young cop figured it would be OK and looked stern as he told them to hang around. Tom hoped the kid would learn to be a little less trusting somewhere down the road.

When the smaller cop disappeared into Laurie's house, Willie looked at Tom sideways. "What you reckon, little brother?"

"Has to be a response to her story."

"Sherlock." Willie slid his seat all the way back and stretched his legs. "You like Ike and his boys?"

"That's my guess. This had to be done by the guys Bryce was using as infantry, but I don't have any hard evidence it was the Langstons. I wish Eddie would hurry up with the damned phone traces."

"There isn't time for that."

Tom was suddenly on his guard. "Why not?"

"Because of the dog."

"Stella?" Tom started to ask for an explanation but stopped when he saw the male cop waving them toward the porch. Another cruiser pulled up as they entered the living room.

Laurie was standing next to the sturdy policewoman and was looking almost coherent. The lady cop flexed her arms and verified everyone's contact data. "Stay in touch. We'll need a statement." She nodded them out into the cold.

Tom looked at the porch from Willie's truck. "I'd like to go back and make sure Laurie's OK."

"Forget it. They'll just toss you out again." He started the engine. "I'll drop you at the office. Got to get a move on."

They rode in silence until Willie hung a left onto Staab Street and parked next to the ruins of their sidewalk. He was staring a long way down the short street. Tom opened his door but made no move to climb out. "Good thing Laurie wasn't home. I'd hate to think what they might have done to her."

"Then don't." Willie bit off the words, and Tom flinched as he felt the cold rage.

"Let's get back to the dog. Are you sure the bastards took her? She might have run off when they were trashing the place."

"They took her. When I went out Laurie's back door, I talked to the lady in the next yard over. She was looking out her window when two guys in ski masks climbed into an old white pickup in Laurie's driveway. They tossed a black garbage bag in the back and drove off. She said it looked like the bag was moving on its own. For all that, she didn't bother to call the cops."

"White pickup? I thought the Langston boys drove a black one."

"One of 'em does, but they probably aren't quite dumb enough to pull a daylight raid in their own truck."

"You said there wasn't time to wait for the phone traces. Why not?"

"Leave it, Tommy. This is something I've got to do alone. Just get out, and we'll talk later."

"Cut the shit. Not enough time for what?"

Willie went back to grinding his teeth for a long minute. He took a deep breath and hissed it past tight lips. "Assume it was the Langstons. Why'd they take the dog? Because they raise pit bulls and fight them on Saturday nights over in Lincoln County. Some of the local fuckwits consider it a sport. Blood and gambling. What could be better?" Willie rolled down his window and spat on the pavement. He wasn't chewing anything. "They move the fights around to different barns to stay ahead of the law."

"What's that got to do with Stella? Nobody would bet on a corgi."

"No, but they like to throw a dog to their pack now and then to rip up as a treat. Keeps their dogs' blood up. And what would be better than Laurie's dog?"

"And you figure on going after them by yourself? Fat chance. Look, Laurie told me what they did to your dog back in Albuquerque. Long time ago, though. I know how you feel, but I'm not letting you charge into that lair in a bloodlust. You'd end up dead. Let the cops handle it."

"You don't know shit. Damn it, Tommy. This is my fight, and it's been a lifetime coming. I can take care of myself, and I'm not taking my one-armed little brother out in harm's way." He feigned a smile. "Hell, maybe they just took the dog to scare Laurie. Want to see if I have the guts to come get her."

"I'm going too."

"No way. Get out, or I'll come around your side and drag you out, busted wrist or not."

Tom tried to stare down his brother but lost. "OK, but drop me at home. I don't feel like walking up the hill."

＊　　＊　　＊

As Willie's truck backed out of the driveway, Tom raced up the stairs and dragged the heavy metal traveling case from the back of his closet. He unlocked it, raised the lid, and surveyed the cream of his private arsenal. This was insane. Or Willie was anyway. He was walking into an ambush like a man with a death wish. No way Tom could let him go alone.

A shoulder holster was a liability with his broken arm unset, so he grabbed a clip-on and secured the Glock to his belt. He chose a smaller service revolver for a backup but decided to pass on his small stock of hand grenades. Donning a Kevlar vest, he pulled aside the shirts on the rear closet rail, revealing his gun rack. No telling how this was going to go down. He selected a twelve-gauge with a twenty-four-inch barrel and dug a box of buckshot out of a carton on the floor. He didn't figure he could aim the shotgun with one arm, but if he removed his sling he could cradle the barrel in the crook of his left arm and work at hip level with the right. Only good for one shot, though. He couldn't count on having time to work the pump one handed. Jesus.

Willie would go home to arm himself—he'd want at least his forty-four. That should give Tom some time advantage. He would get there first, but so what? He couldn't just sit there chatting up the Langstons while waiting for Willie to show. No time to think, he'd have to make up a plan as he drove. He switched his shoes for another pair of old sneakers, eased into a pair of leather driving gloves, and headed for his truck.

Tom was almost to the I-25 on-ramp when the gas warning light came on. Shit. He pumped ten gallons and gunned his truck back onto the highway. As he descended La Bajada, the land looked dry. Friday's meager snow must have stayed farther north. He kept his speed below levels exciting to traffic cops, and forty minutes later he veered onto the I-40 east ramp toward Santa Rosa. Willie would be coming down the slower Turquoise Trail route on the other side of the mountains.

It was approaching one-thirty when Tom's truck emerged from Tijeras Canyon. As he crossed NM 14, he looked north but didn't see Willie anywhere. He left the interstate in Edgewood and worked his way down the irregular array of dirt roads and goat tracks until he reached the track into the small valley north of the Langstons. He turned off. A stand of junipers at the first curve provided enough cover to conceal the Toyota, so he turned the truck around to face the main road and waited. A dead branch with no needles gave him a limited view.

Several bad plans were hatched and abandoned. If Tom could outflank Willie and the Langstons, he might be able to prevent them from killing each other. He couldn't repeat last week's ascent of the ridge north of their valley. It was steep and uneven, and he was toting firearms with only one functional arm. He would have to wait for Willie to pass him and then tail his truck through the narrow, winding draw. If he parked one turn from the end, he should be able to slip into the valley, keeping low behind a line of chamisa. There would be some cover as he worked his way behind the barn. He remembered a short stretch where he'd be visible from the house, but hopefully, the Langstons and Willie would be down by the corral. Not good to count on hope, though. Tom began checking his hardware.

He didn't check long. Willie's dusty white pickup came into view through the trees. Tom froze as it slowed to a stop at the turnoff to his outpost, but after a tense moment, the truck moved on and turned toward the Langston place. When Tom saw the back of Willie's truck disappear into the draw, he started his engine and followed. He stayed in first gear as he eased down a rutted track studded with sharp volcanic rocks. When the draw began to widen, he turned the truck around and parked it facing back toward the main road. His boots landed in loose sand. In the distance he heard a car door slam. Tom removed the sling from his left arm and stuffed it in a vest pocket. He rested the barrel of the shotgun in the crook of his left elbow as he crept around the final bend.

~ 23 ~

Acacophony of dog vocals erupted. Tom peered around the boulder guarding the north side of the road where it spilled out into the valley. The din emanated from the Langstons' barn. Outraged barks and howls accompanied sounds of claws raking metal and shrieks sounding like a cat with its tail caught in a fan belt. At least no one was going to hear his approach. Visual cover was another matter.

Tom figured the action would occur in front of the barn near the corral. On his previous visit, the dogs had charged out a door near that spot. He couldn't see the corral from where he was. To the left of the barn, the dilapidated garage and outhouse somehow remained erect. He could see the house, and anyone in it would have a clear view of him crossing the road. Once across, he could take cover behind the buildings, but the open gap in the shrubbery was wider than he remembered, and the chamisa bushes on the far side looked undernourished. He couldn't see anyone outside. Whoever was riling the dogs must be in front of the barn, or perhaps inside. Tom squinted at the house, but sunlight reflected from the windows, obscuring his view of possible sentries. He'd stand out like dog's balls if anyone were watching the road from the house. Nothing to do but go for it. This chicken needs to get to the other side.

Tom bent over as far as he could, aimed for a juniper about fifty yards past the road, and took short, quick steps without looking toward the house. He tried to move steadily and kept the shotgun low to reduce the chance of sun glinting off the metal. There didn't seem to be any change in the canine chorus, but that didn't mean much. No way they could get any louder. As he reached the far side of the road, the shotgun barrel caught on a bush, scorching his left arm with pain. When he reached his target, he waited for the throbbing in his wrist to lessen, then stood up to survey the scene. He was fifty yards from the back of the metal barn. It was at least a hundred feet long. There were no windows in the back wall, and the only door was closed. The deafening dog noises seemed to be confined to the left end of the building. The dogs were probably still penned in their runs. Maybe Stella had already been fed to them.

He advanced at a brisk pace until he reached the rear of the barn. Turning left he moved along the wall, slowing as he approached the corner of the building. Voices began to mix with the barking, but they were indistinct. Tom laid the shotgun on the ground, pressed close to the building, and slowly leaned left until one eye cleared the corner. The back of the outhouse was a couple of steps beyond the end wall and about ten feet closer to the road. It consisted of irregular pieces of drywall, crumbling from years of rain, and scraps of rotten paneling fastened to the frame by the occasional nail. Several holes were big enough to admit a good-sized chicken if it were so inclined. A wind eddy bathed him in odors of mature outhouse and fresh dog crap. He breathed through his mouth as he edged his head another inch to the left, looking down a narrow wedge between the outhouse and the barn and across an expanse of packed dirt to the front of the corral.

Tom froze. A man was sitting on the top rail of the corral fence with his roper boots perched on the lower. A rifle lay across his lap. He looked to be about fifty and fond of old Carhartt work clothes, but not razors unless he kept one in his boot. He also looked pissed off. Fortunately, his head and eyes were tracking something approaching from his left. Tom took him for one of Ike Langston's sons.

No way Tom could move to a spot behind the outhouse, and then the garage, without the rifleman spotting him. His hope of taking command of the situation evaporated. Now he was stuck in response mode. At least the din from inside the barn was ebbing, as if the dogs were also taking a wait-and-see attitude.

A few seconds later Willie walked slowly into view from Tom's right and stopped almost even with the man on the fence. He had a forty-four in his right hand, the barrel pointed at the ground beside his right foot. He was looking straight ahead, seemingly ignoring the fence sitter to his right. "I've come for the dog." His voice was a monotone but loud enough to be heard above the remaining howls. Tom could see no trace of emotion on his brother's face.

"That a fact?" The deep voice, its owner hidden from Tom by the outhouse, rasped with overtones of chain smoking and bad whiskey. An old redneck's voice—had to be Ike. "What dog would that be, Willie?"

"Laurie's. I know she's in there. I heard her."

"Well, maybe she is. We pick up a stray now and then. But we've got plans for that little bitch. You're welcome to watch."

Tom sensed a tensing of Willie's muscles. There wasn't much time. He guessed the speaker was visibly armed, and Willie might try to take both men down. But what if the Langstons were only bluffing? If he stepped into view with the shotgun, it might set off a firefight for no reason.

"Keep your hands away from that pistol, old man. I'm going in the barn, and I'm coming out with Laurie's dog." Willie glanced at the man on the fence. "No big ideas, bub. Which one are you, anyway? Ike Junior? After this many years, you assholes all look alike."

"Big talker, ain't ya?" The high-pitched voice of the man on the fence sounded as tight as his lips. "You ain't going in our barn unless Pa says so."

"That's Seth. Junior's back in Georgia with some little biker bitch." The old man gargled a load of phlegm and spit. "You boys go back a bit. As I recall, Seth and Junior had some fun with your dog a long while ago. That right?"

Seth smirked, his shrill voice almost giggling: "Quite a blaze, wasn't it Willie? The little mutt ran around like Chinese fireworks."

Willie didn't twitch a muscle. "I'm taking the dog now. I'd advise you two not to do anything stupid."

Tom stepped straight back from the barn, picked up the shotgun, and braced the butt against his right hip. Cradling the barrel in his left elbow, he eased to his left until he again could see his brother and the man on the fence. Willie's eyes were darting between Seth on his right and the unseen man to his front, but his body remained still. He seemed reluctant to take a step toward the barn door.

Come on, Willie. Get Stella and let's get the hell out of here. The tableau continued for eternal seconds. Tom detected a slight motion inside the outhouse. Someone moved past one of the gaping holes in the back wall. Tom looked back at his brother and saw a red dot dancing along the left side of Willie's head. Laser sight. Shit.

Tom took two quick strides to his left, braced, and fired his shotgun at a hole in the back wall of the outhouse.

Willie's head jerked left as a body exploded through the outhouse door in a cloud of splinters and gypsum dust. The man landed face down next to the flimsy door, his pistol bouncing off the packed dirt near his right hand. Willie leaped into a diving roll to his right and fired his forty-four just as Seth got the rifle to his shoulder. The shot struck just above the heart and spun Seth off the fence in a nearly perfect three-quarter back flip. He hit the ground face first as a second, sharper shot was heard.

Tom's left arm was in agony. He tossed the shotgun to the ground, fumbled his Glock out of the belt holster, and stumbled past the outhouse to the front of the barn. An old man in overalls and a white beard was holding a revolver. The gun was pointed at Willie, who was in prone position with his forty-four aimed at the old man.

Willie spoke first. "Put it down, Ike. You missed. I won't."

Ike's jaw was quivering, though Tom couldn't tell if it was from anger or despair. "You shot my boys. You bastards."

"Put it down, Ike."

The old man stared hard at Willie for several seconds, then slowly lowered his right arm. He held on to the pistol but pointed it at the ground.

Willie kept the forty-four aimed at Ike as he regained his feet. The man lying face down in front of the outhouse twitched the last of his life away. The body in the corral wasn't moving either. Willie nodded toward the outhouse ambusher. "Who's he?"

Ike tried to snarl, but his voice wavered. "That's Jack. My youngest. You assholes are going to pay for this." He looked at Tom. "You shot first. Shot him in the back. He never had a chance. You'll pay. I've still got Ike Junior. You'll damned well pay for this."

Tom reached down and picked up Jack's pistol. He pointed it at the ground and shook his hand, causing the red dot of the laser sight to dance near his feet. "I saw that on Willie's head. I did what I had to." As he said it, Tom felt a cold tightness grip his belly. For a moment he was back in the house near Lexington. He'd acted on instinct, then and now. But he was wrong back then. Now?

Willie seemed to sense his brother's worry. He lowered his gun but kept it firmly in hand as he turned his back to Ike and walked toward his truck. Tom could see Willie looking at the driver's side window—watching Ike in the reflection?

Tom's eyes snapped back to Ike just as the old man raised his pistol and fired at Willie. The shot went where he'd been, but Willie was a step to the left when he returned fire. Langston went down on his back across a hay bale, his head and shoulders touching the ground. Tom stared at his brother. "You knew he'd do that."

"Figured so, but it was his call."

"So why'd you do it?"

Willie shrugged.

Tom holstered his Glock and walked a short loop surveying the three dead Langstons. "Jesus, Willie. We just killed three men. What are we going to do now?"

"Well, I suggest we go ahead and rescue the dog. That's what I came for. Can't say about you."

"What about the law? This isn't going to be easy to explain."

"So don't explain. Quit yapping. You go get Stella, and I'll take a look around. Need to see if anyone's up in the house." Willie turned and walked up the path to the front door.

Tom retrieved his shotgun and set it next to Willie's truck. The dogs were back at full volume. As he pushed open the barn door, the noise increased by several decibels. He counted eight narrow dog runs in a row to the right. Each had a ten-foot-high chain-link fence with a pile of straw in the back. They were strewn with piles of aging turds in various states of decay. The raging pit bulls were one to a run, mouths foaming as they snarled and hurled themselves against the fencing. Tom drew his pistol in case one of the doors was unlocked.

In the fourth kennel down, he found the little corgi cowering against the back of a run, her ears drooping below horizontal. She was trembling and curled tight. Tom unlatched the door and walked into the four-foot wide space as the dogs in adjoining runs bit and pawed at the chain link trying to get at him. He holstered the gun and knelt next to Stella, trying in vain to ease her fear. As he reached toward her, she uncoiled and lunged at him, sinking her teeth into his right hand. He yelped in pain and fell back against the fence, only to feel a pit bull lunge against his back. He scooted to the center of the cramped run and began talking to Stella with a soothing pitch. Suddenly, she dashed over and crawled onto his lap. He started to edge backward with her, then remembered the piles of dog dung littering the floor. Clutching Stella to his chest with his right arm, he struggled to his feet and slowly backed out of the run. He carried her outside and put her in Willie's truck. She crawled down on the floor in front of the passenger seat. Tom used his teeth to peel the thin driving glove from his right hand and examined the bite. It hurt like hell, but only a couple of teeth had drawn blood.

Willie came out the front door of the house and hurried down to the barn. "We're in luck."

"Are you nuts? Look around."

"Meth, Tommy. They've been at it again. There's a closet full of decongestant pills up there, and the kitchen has some odd-looking hardware. They must have a small lab out in those mountains somewhere."

"And this is good news because ...?"

"The police will figure it's some sort of drug hit. The cops have busted the Langstons several times for suspicion, but the charges never stuck. Hell, no way anyone's going to figure this scene as a dog rescue."

Tom wasn't so sure, but it was all they had. "Let's clean the place up a bit and get the hell out of here. Someone might get curious about all the gunfire."

Willie laughed. "Around here, they'd be more curious if they didn't hear shooting." He began a slow circuit of the area, looking for anything he might have dropped.

Tom walked back into the barn, staying well clear of the kennels. He noticed a door at the end opposite the dogs and tried the handle. It was unlocked. The room was lined with fake wood paneling and contained two bunk beds, a small cast iron stove, and a square table with three chairs. It also contained six heavy-duty fiber barrels. Tom unlatched the lid to one of them and found a bright Ganado red rug, old but in gorgeous condition, wrapped around a large object. When he peeled back the rug, a large Hopi pot emerged. It, too, looked old, but Tom couldn't quite place the design. He repacked the pot and rejoined Willie.

"So guess what else is in the barn."

"The last of the Langstons?"

"Not quite. The goods from the Southwest Cultures robbery."

"Be damned. Well, kid, looks like you'll get your first paycheck."

"My ass, Willie. We're screwed. No way we can tell anyone we were here."

"We could take the stuff with us."

"Too risky. I told Eddie Romero we suspected the Langstons were involved in that robbery. The cops would be all over us." Tom shook his head. "And another thing. What are we going to do about all those damned dogs? We can't just leave them there to starve."

Willie fingered his gun for a moment but seemed to change his mind. "Not their fault how they were raised. They aren't fit to be around people anymore, but I can't bring myself to shoot them. I'll find a hose and make sure they've got water. We can call someone later."

"I've got a couple of disposable phones in my truck. I'll drive off to nowhere and put in an anonymous call to a shelter in Albuquerque, then ditch the phone." He looked at Willie's boots. "Best ditch your footwear too."

Twenty minutes later the brothers turned their trucks onto the interstate. Tom drove east toward Santa Rosa while Willie and Stella headed for Santa Fe. Tom welcomed the drone of the highway, but it didn't ease his mind. The shootout was replaying in an endless loop. He was sure he'd done the right thing, but he was getting the shakes and didn't understand where the fear was coming from. Suddenly, he knew. He pulled off at the next exit and parked a quarter-mile down the frontage road. As he stared down the empty stretch, it became clear. He was afraid of himself. They'd just shot three men dead, and he didn't feel bad. My God, I'm turning into Willie.

After ten minutes of controlled breathing, Tom drove another fifty miles east, looked up the SPCA number for Albuquerque, and reported dog cruelty in progress at the Langston place. He took the battery out of the phone and tossed both phone and battery in a dumpster behind a hamburger joint on the way home.

* * *

Tom sat alone in his purple chair watching the outside light die. He resolved, just this once, to limit himself to a single glass of whiskey. When only fumes remained, he licked the inside of the glass. His phone began tickling his thigh.

Laurie was gushing relief. "Stella's back. She's OK."

He paused for a second while he tried to conjure up a cheerful mood. No luck. "That's great. How did you find her?"

"She was tied to my front door handle. Someone must have found her and dropped her off."

"They didn't knock?"

"No, but who cares? Maybe they didn't want to see me cry or something."

"Yeah, or something. That's great. Nothing worse than losing your dog." He forced a smile, then realized no one could see it. Laurie hung up to feed Stella. Tom sagged deeper into his chair and pondered whether it was worth turning on a light.

When he could no longer see, he stood up and felt his way to a light switch. He shuffled into the kitchen, ran warm water over his right hand, and poured whiskey on the bite marks. The puncture wounds from Stella's teeth stung but had stopped bleeding. He went upstairs and wrapped his hand in a sterile bandage that hid them. It was only six on Saturday night. No sense waiting around to see if the cops knocked on his door. He grabbed his coat, pulled on loose-fitting gloves, and walked downtown to find a bar. Maybe just one more whiskey.

~ 24 ~

Sunday morning sunshine reminded Tom to cut back on late carousing or buy blackout curtains. He stretched and checked his phone. Nothing. Under the circumstances it seemed good to be forgotten. He fired up a full pot of coffee and was halfway through the New York Times crossword when his phone snapped him to attention. Praying to any available deity it wasn't the police, he eased it out of his pocket. Laurie.

"Tommy, it's me. I'm on my way over to your place." She spoke rapidly and sounded short of breath. "I need you to sit Stella for a while. That OK?"

"Sure, why not? I'm not going anywhere. What's up?"

"I'll explain when I get there. Bye. And thanks."

The doorbell sounded two minutes later. Laurie's eyebrows disappeared beneath her bangs as she took stock of him: unshaven, left arm in sling, right hand wrapped in white bandage but holding a coffee mug. She let go of the leash, and Stella bounded onto the purple chair. "What happened to you?"

"The left wrist you know about. I cut my other hand on a kitchen knife." No way he was going to show her the bite marks.

"You actually cooked something?"

He ignored the dig and stepped aside. "Where are you going?"

Laurie walked to his chair and unhooked the leash. "Got a break on my story. Eddie Romero called and said the state police found barrels full of the Hayek brothers' pots and rugs. And guess where?" She stretched to maximum height and thrust her chest forward like a salvo of torpedoes—a tower of utter triumph. Tom felt an urge to whisper "sic transit gloria" in her ear, but discretion trumped valor. He shrugged.

She pressed on. "At the Langston place. Willie's old redneck neighbors from the North Valley. They lived somewhere out in the sage east of the Sandias. And note that I said lived." She waited for the past tense to sink in, but Tom was feeling sunk in other ways.

"Meaning?"

"They're dead. Somebody shot the lot of them. Just left the bodies lying in the open."

"No shit?"

"Jesus, Tommy. Don't you get it? This is going to make my story. Eddie is headed out to the scene, and he's taking me along."

"That's great. Ought to get you the main headline this time."

"Damned straight. Anyway, I'm not sure how long I'll be gone, and I don't want to leave Stella alone just now. She must have been pretty scared to run off yesterday."

"Glad to watch her. I miss having her around."

Laurie switched to an exaggerated frown. "You weren't much help yesterday. The least you could have done was go look for her. You and Willie drove off like a couple of cowboys heading for a saloon and left me. I was worried to death."

"I'm sorry. We had to work on a case. Hey, you got her back, didn't you? All's well, and so on."

"No thanks to you. You don't really deserve her company, but she'll forgive you. Anyway, thanks for looking after her."

"Yeah. Great about the story."

Laurie waved goodbye to Stella without looking his way as she dashed out the door. The pooch remained curled up in the chair. Tom nudged her with his bandaged hand but withdrew it in a hurry when her upper lip curled, showing off white canines. He finished the cross-word on the sofa about the time the coffee ran out. Time to stop stalling. If the cops found anything linking the shootings to the Mc-Naul brothers, he'd know soon enough. He tossed Stella an oversized dog biscuit, zipped up his parka, and headed for Southwest Cultures. By now the Hayek brothers would know the police had their pots and rugs. Might as well face the music.

* * *

Tom turned onto Garcia Street just after eleven. His truck was the only thing moving. The Christmas tourist rush wouldn't begin for another two weeks. He parked on the wide dirt shoulder a few feet from where Judy was murdered. No signs of the crime were visible. The air was crisp and still as he made his way to Canyon Road, squinting against the bright sky. The crowd swelled to two—a short, spherical woman in an olive-green down parka was standing next to an empty ceramic urn. A silver hoop at least three inches in diameter dangled from one ear, giving her the overall appearance of a hand grenade. She tugged at a leash, causing a shaggy white dog to emerge from a hedge. The pair eyed Tom, turned their backs, and headed east.

The windows of the T&B Gallery were dark. A sign in one window had a fake clock face below the words "Back At," but both hands languished in the six position and seemed likely to remain there. He moved on. Several galleries appeared to be open, though Southwest Cultures was the only one with its door ajar. Apparently, the Hayek brothers were willing to boost their gas bill to snare customers. Tom didn't fancy their chances. George Hayek was alone in the front room and did not try to hide his discomfort as Tom entered the shop. "Ah, Mr. McNaul. I was going to call you this afternoon."

"Oh?"

"Yes. You see, the police believe they have located our stolen property."

"That's a surprise. Did they find all of it?"

"They aren't sure yet, but it sounds as if they recovered most of the major pieces. We should know by tomorrow." Hayek shifted his weight from his left foot to his right, then back. "I wanted to tell you we won't be needing your services any longer." He stared intently at Tom. "My understanding is that since you did not recover the pieces yourself, well, we do not owe you a percentage."

"That's right. Just my fifty an hour. Plus expenses. Myrna will send a bill." Tom had known this was coming, but he deflated anyway. Not much to show for case No. 2. He figured the Hayeks' lost wares were worth at least a hundred thousand wholesale. Maybe double that. Twenty percent would have been—well, best not to think about it. George Hayek made an honorable effort to hide his relief. Tom nodded his appreciation. Maybe he'd have better luck with Tracy Lee. The police were still holding onto her soup can print, but at least they might give him credit for finding it. Only worth about thirty grand, but he needed some kind of payday.

Foot traffic was picking up on Canyon Road. The grenade had gone off somewhere, but a family of four stood stranded across the street as a hotel courtesy van sped off. A pair of young lovers in matching knit caps and ski parkas kissed, oblivious to the gaze of a ceramic white rabbit large enough to run Alice out of Wonderland. Two dogs of complicated heritage walked beside a man in a wheelchair as the trio progressed down the middle of the street—the sidewalks looked too rough for vehicles without treads. Tom lingered for a moment to enjoy the ambiance and then headed back to Garcia Street. He clenched his teeth as he passed the spot where Judy was killed and wondered which Langston had done it. Didn't seem to matter anymore.

The Staab Street office was Sunday-morning still. Myrna wouldn't be in, leaving the Maltese falcon as the life of the party. Tom managed to stop playing with the bird and ponder the lost Vermeer. There wasn't much chance the painting was hanging in James Kinkaid's Telluride lodge, but he needed to confront the oilman before he sniffed trouble.

Tom booked a flight from Albuquerque to Durango, Colorado, for one o'clock the next afternoon. His broken left arm was scheduled for a casting call at an orthopedic office at nine. Should be done in time to make his plane. He didn't want to drive the seven hours from Santa Fe to Telluride with one arm in a cast, but he figured he could handle the shorter trip around the mountains from Durango. Anything was better than flying into the Telluride airport. Tom had seen it one summer while hiking along the top of the local ski mountain. From that vantage point, the airstrip resembled an aircraft carrier with a broken keel. The single runway was short, swaybacked, and ended at a cliff. It was the highest commercial strip in the country, and winter weather chased off 20 percent of the incoming flights. The odds of getting to town were better in a rented SUV.

And there was another problem with Telluride travel—getting out. During the winter there was only one long road into the narrow valley squeezed below looming peaks. No telling how things would play out with Mr. James Kinkaid, but if there was trouble, a quick getaway wouldn't go down easy.

Tom had no plan of action and needed a better feel for the terrain. He switched to Google Maps and typed in the address Myrna had provided. Kinkaid's place was located in Mountain Village, an isolated enclave of cathedral-scale homes surrounding a core of upscale condos and posh hotels. They were clustered on the opposite side of the ski mountain from the town itself. The two settlements were seven miles apart by road, and a good deal further apart in culture, but they were connected by a free gondola that shuttled people and dogs over the mountain—no passport required.

Tom switched to aerial photo imagery and found Kinkaid's hulking lodge in a patch of dense forest a mile south of the gondola station. He zoomed the image to maximum resolution. The structure reminded him of a Viking longhouse in both scale and architectural subtlety. It looked like someone had dropped a pitched roof on a log pile. A paved drive wound through trees tall enough to shield the building from gawking passers-by. The forest extended to within a few feet of the building. Kinkaid didn't seem to be a lawn and garden man. The property sloped steeply downward to the north. There was probably a view of the ski slopes from the upstairs windows on that side.

The house didn't seem to be surrounded by any kind of fence, though Tom couldn't determine the date of the aerial photo. Fence or not, there was likely to be a modern security system. He had neither the time nor expertise to defeat one, so there was no way he'd be crawling in a bedroom window. Entrance would have to be through the front door. He printed out some maps and photos and booked a room in an aging lodge on the Telluride side of the mountain. Ski season rates. He might need to switch to cheaper whiskey.

Darkness captured the outdoors before the printer spit out the last of Tom's reservation forms. He heard the door of the outer office open. A few clunking boot steps later, Willie appeared. "Little brother!"

"None other."

"Glad I found you here. I'm going on the road for a while. Not sure how long. Give Rosanne a call now and then, would ya? She'll have Myrna and her kids around, but, you know."

"OK. Where you going?"

"Not sure. I'll be riding my hog. Need to clear my head. Being December, I'll probably keep to more southerly latitudes."

"Even so, you'll freeze your ass on a two-wheeler. Why don't you take your truck?"

"Not the same, Tommy."

"You sure this is a good idea? The cops just found the bodies. Might look a little funny for you to disappear the next day."

"Nah. I thought about that. There isn't anything solid connecting us to the OK Corral. If they'd found anything, Honest Eddie would be all over us by now."

"Maybe, but I think it'd be a damned sight smarter to lay low in plain sight for a few days."

"Nah, gotta go. I'd think too much. Gotta empty my head. Meanwhile, you watch your back. Still one Langston out there. He might stay with the honey down in Georgia, but I'd bet on him coming back someday."

Willie removed what looked like a black address book from his desk, turned toward the door, and stopped. "I'll take my phone. Won't have it on, but I'll check it once a day. If Eddie comes around. . . ."

"Yeah. I'll call. Just don't stray too far from the border."

Willie snorted. "You think I'd take my fine bike into Mexico?"

"Yep."

"Well." Willie grinned and strode out of the inner office. A moment later the front door slammed. Tom listened for the growl of Willie's bike. His brother constantly tuned the exhaust trying for a lion's roar, but this time it blubbered like a flatulent elephant as it carried him into the dark. Tom stared at the falcon and wondered if Willie would ever make it back. His big brother carried some serious loads, and Tom was sure he didn't know the half of them. Come to that, he didn't really know Willie either. Maybe he was one of those men who never can settle the score. You can't change that kind—just have to minimize the collateral damage. He turned out the lights and headed home to feed Stella.

Packing was light for this trip. Two pistols, a bootleg duplicate of his old FBI badge, and a few electronic items joined a suit and tie in his suitcase. Once again he'd need to check the bag with the guns. Winter clothes and waterproof boots would do for the plane. He was ready to go, but it was only six. Hunger steered him to the kitchen. The larder offered up peanut butter and stale bread—no jelly in sight. He collapsed on the sofa and softened the bread to the texture of leather with a bottle of pale ale. Stella's snores emanated from the chair.

Laurie rang the doorbell at eight, causing a brief eruption of barking. She hosed Tom down with a rapid-fire account of her day at the Langston place while he worked hard to vary his expression between interested and ignorant. Evidently she had enough material for Page 1. She joked about a Pulitzer.

Tom finally got a chance. "Great work, cowgirl. Any leads on who did in the Langstons?"

"Nope. Eddie didn't want to speculate at all, but some of the other guys talked when he was out of earshot. They're thinking it was a drug hit. Could be, but whoever did it must have a soft spot for dogs. An animal rescue group found all the bodies. Went out to investigate a phone tip."

"Any idea who called them?"

"No. Eddie said he'd let me know if they got anywhere tracing the call. Said not to hold my breath—those types use disposables."

"Yeah. Want a snort to celebrate?"

"Sure." Laurie was still hyper and skipped into the kitchen. "Got anything to eat around this cave?" She didn't wait for an answer as she slapped cupboards open and closed and spent two seconds taking inventory in the refrigerator. "Jesus, Tommy. Nothing but dog food. You need to toss this." The remnants of the stale bread loaf clunked as she pitched it into the steel trash can. She spun back to face him. "I'll grab something solid on the way home. What are you offering?"

The liquor cabinet contained more options. Laurie would expect the usual double whiskey, but Tom decided to impress her with something more festive. "I make the best mai tai in Santa Fe. Jamaican dark rum, Grand Marnier, fresh lime juice, and genuine orgeat."

"Probably the only mai tai in Santa Fe—this is a margarita town. I don't know what they taste like, but bring 'em on."

Five minutes later they were on the sofa slurping the sweet tropical nectar at an alarming rate. Half a pitcher of reinforcements waited on the coffee table. Laurie slid a little closer and rested her head on Tom's shoulder. She took a long draw, set her glass on the table, and reached across to stroke his broken wrist. Her hair brushed across his right hand without landing in the mai tai, and her breast pressed lightly against his arm. Tom smiled. He could remember a time when he thought girls did such things by accident.

"Can you use this arm at all?"

"Not much, but I'll get the cast in the morning." Tom flexed his fingers. "Should be OK then. I'm not supposed to lift much with it for a few weeks, but I'll be able to drive with two hands again."

Laurie retrieved her glass and settled against the sofa back. She drew her knees up and tilted her head subtly, suggesting the opportunity for a kiss without actually starting one. Tom's hormones were kicking in, but he hesitated. Maybe it's not a good . . . oh, the hell with that! He leaned in to kiss her, but his lips caught only hair as her face turned down and away. Their moment had passed. Laurie made a small twitch as she took a sip of her drink and suddenly smiled at him from a foot farther away. How did she do that?

"I'd best get along home while I can still drive. Lot of work to do tomorrow." She returned her glass to the table and stood to go.

Tom nodded at the glass. "Never seen you do that before." It was half full.

Laurie flashed him a bemused pout. "Yeah, well. Getting old, I guess. Thanks for the mai tai. Better than I expected. You do a tour in Hawaii sometime?"

"No. Just several at Trader Vic's."

Stella strained at the leash as she pulled Laurie out the door. Tom left it open until her car disappeared down the hill. He reclaimed the purple chair and drained Laurie's glass with a single gulp. As the silence closed around him, he missed Stella's snoring. He was very much alone. In the morning he'd saddle up and ride off to Telluride on his white horse. Save another art treasure for civilization, so some billionaire could collect it or donate it to a museum for a tax break. He looked at his small suitcase near the stairs. That was what he had left. Two guns and a fake badge. He refilled both glasses.

~ 25 ~

Tom climbed into the driver's seat of the only SUV in the rental lot and adjusted the mirrors. It smelled of cleaning solvents and stale smoke, but he needed the four-wheel drive. He removed his left arm from its sling and examined the fresh fiberglass cast. A phone number was written in red marker ink, compliments of an Albuquerque nurse with green eyes and lashes like a Venus flytrap. He rolled out of the Durango airport and turned west to begin the dogleg route to Telluride. It was almost five, so it would be dark long before he reached the San Juans. There would be ice.

Three hours later he reached the road leading to Mountain Village. Just west of the village center, he turned south and followed a winding road lined with evergreens and imposing houses. As he rounded a bend to the right, a pair of stone obelisks loomed on either side of a driveway curving into the forest. A spotlight highlighted brass numerals on the left one. Sixty-six—Kinkaid's place. A three-foot-high metal gate, decorated with silhouettes of Rocky Mountain wildlife, blocked the entrance. The key to the castle appeared to be an illuminated keypad with attached speaker on a post to the left of the driveway. He couldn't see a security camera, but one could be hidden in the undergrowth. The house was not visible from the gate.

Tom parked fifty feet beyond the entrance and slipped back through the trees. The narrow beam from his flashlight revealed an inward-pointing sensor behind the right gate pillar. It looked like a motion detector—probably to open the gate automatically if an outbound car approached. Overall, a surprisingly low-tech system for such an expensive home. Tom hurried back to his car. He drove a couple of minutes to a group of condos near the base of a chair lift and found a parking spot shielded from view by an empty panel truck. One of the well-lit homes a mile to the south must be the Kinkaid place. He consulted his map and pulled a small but powerful pair of binoculars from a bag on the passenger seat. The third light show from the left featured a cluster of floodlights surrounding a hot tub on a second-story deck.

He activated the image stabilization and was able to discern two heads protruding from the tub. He couldn't identify them at this distance, and they seemed in no hurry to exit the tub. Time to call it a day.

Luck was with him—Tom found the last parking spot in southeast Telluride. The Marmot Lodge turned out to be a small converted condo on the banks of the San Miguel River. There was no night clerk and no parking lot, so Tom punched in the provided code numbers and found himself in a dated but comfortable room. The place had the typical mildew scent of a low-budget ski hostel. The rugs probably wouldn't be fully dry before May. He retrieved the room's treasured parking pass, unpacked, and headed into town. Instinct steered him to Smuggler's Brewpub where he wedged into a spot between tables of unabashed ski bums and washed down his burger with several house ales. As he started the final pint, he dialed Myrna. It was after ten, but even on a Monday, there was no chance she was asleep.

"Tommy? I thought you left town. And what the hell is going on there with all that noise?"

"I did, toots. I'm in Telluride having a go at dinner. Got a favor to ask."

"What a surprise. Shoot."

"If you get a phone call from horse-trainer Sally tomorrow, tell her I'm still working for the FBI. OK?"

"Damn, Tommy, she's a friend of mine. You want me to lie to her? What for?"

"Tell you later, but I may need this. Chances are she won't call, but if she does, cover for me. What's her last name, anyway?"

"Buchanan. Sally Buchanan. Comes from one of those Scotch-Irish families. Kind of like you McNauls, only Texan. I've known her since high school."

"Thanks, toots. It's important, and I'll make it up to you."

"It better be. And you better. Isn't there a better job in Santa Fe than working for you and Willie?"

"Not a chance."

Tom was fading and called for his tab. He settled into his room's only soft chair and stared at a print of a shapely cowgirl smirking back at him over her left shoulder. He liked the artist's style, not to mention the woman. She seemed to own this room, and her bandana matched the color of the bedspread. There was an info tag taped to the wall in case he wanted to take her home. She was art to live with. But in the morning he was going after art people would die for. Or maybe kill for. He checked his guns one more time and crawled into bed, but he wasn't quite ready to give up on the day. What the hell. He called the phone number written on his cast and conjured up an image of those inviting eyes. After four rings a recording thanked him for calling the governor's office in Santa Fe and suggested he call back during normal business hours. She got me. He turned out the light. Ski parties in the neighboring rooms seemed to be the order of the evening. The revelers finally crashed around midnight, but Tom continued to thrash until two.

* * *

The alarm went off well before sunlight could work its way to the valley floor. Tom dressed quickly in a government-blue suit and tie. The unbuttoned left shirtsleeve concealed most of his cast. He slipped the Glock into his shoulder holster and a smaller pistol into a clip-on in the small of his back. Dawn was thinking about it as Tom stepped outside to sample the weather. A few of the brighter stars were hanging on in the cloudless sky, and the air was colder than a sled dog's nose. The forecast said a storm was roaring in from the west. A sudden gust cut through his clothes like a saber. He longed for an insulated parka but wore only a loose shell as his outer layer. This mission wasn't supposed to get physical, but then, neither were the last two. Based on recent experience, it was best to maintain maximum agility. He retrieved his bags from the room, tipped the maid like it was Judgment Day, and loaded the back of his SUV. The only place open was a bakery two blocks from the hotel. A freckled girl at the register chewed her pencil and stared at him. Maybe she'd never seen a man drink three cups of coffee in five minutes. As he left, she refilled the empty milk pitcher on his table. He eased the SUV through the quiet downtown streets and turned onto the road back to Mountain Village.

The plan was far too risky. Bluff his way in the door and try to scare the oilman into giving up the Vermeer. Might work if the guy didn't think the FBI was onto him. Yeah, right. The bastard didn't make his billions by running for cover. Surprised or not, he would put up a fight, assuming the painting wasn't already buried in a Swiss vault.

Tom drove back to the previous evening's observation post and parked in the same secluded spot behind the panel truck. Couldn't stay there long, but he wanted to check out how Kinkaid's morning with the mistress was setting up. He didn't see anyone watching, so he pulled out the binoculars. The sun was still below the top of the ski mountain, but there was enough indirect light to provide a clear view of the north side of the house.

The hot tub on the upstairs deck was empty. There were lights on in some of the rooms, but he saw no movements beyond the windows. Tom settled into a routine of making quick scans of the house every five minutes. During the intervals he demonstrated great interest in yesterday's newspaper. He was finishing the eighth scan when one of the house's four garage doors opened and spit out a red Porsche Panamera. The stylish panache-mobile disappeared down the wooded driveway. Tom tossed the paper in the back and started his engine. He was only a quarter of the way to his target when the Porsche blew by him. The driver was male, gray haired, and alone. That might make it easier to get through the front door.

Tom pulled the SUV up to within two feet of Kinkaid's gate. Ignoring the keypad, he set the brake and left the engine idling as he jumped out. There were no cars in sight, so he vaulted the gate and ran to a spot just inward from the motion detector. The gate began to swing toward him. It kept swinging as he dashed back to the SUV and drove into the grounds. The driveway curled through trees and ended in a broad loop on the uphill side of the house. Wooden pillars like old growth redwoods flanked the entryway. The chime of the doorbell was disappointingly meek—the setting called for Wagner, Ride of the Valkyries perhaps. Tom forced himself to take a deep breath and exhale slowly. After a dozen repetitions of this drill, a faint shuffling sound managed to penetrate the fortress wall. He heard a tight click as the left half of the door swung inward.

A mass of blonde curls topped out six feet above floor level and tumbled around a long face with cowgirl skin, angular features, and a wary smile. Despite the early hour, she wore full makeup, and long turquoise earrings dangled almost to her shoulders. Her embroidered long-sleeve shirt was tucked into jeans that clearly had no coin in any pocket. Fuzzy pink slippers accounted for the shuffling sound. Pale brown eyes gave him the once over and stopped when they met his gaze. She tapped his chest with the hairbrush in her right hand. "Who are you?" She tilted her head to peer over Tom's shoulder. "And while you're at it, how the hell did you get in here?"

Tom showed her the counterfeit badge. "Special Agent Thomas Mc-Naul, FBI. Are you Sally Buchanan?"

"Yes."

"I need to talk to both you and Mr. Kinkaid. May I come in?"

Sally rallied. "Don't you need a warrant or something?"

Tom forced a laugh. "I'm not here to search the premises. I just need to talk to both of you, and I need to do it now. May I come in? It's damned cold out here."

"Don't you guys work in pairs? Where's your partner?"

"You've been watching too many 'Law and Order' reruns. I'm not with the police department, Ms. Buchanan. I'm a special agent of the Federal Bureau of Investigation. Just a few questions." Tom dialed the hardness up a notch and leaned in a couple of inches.

Sally stood her ground but was clearly wavering.

"Look, Ms. Buchanan. I'm not here to investigate your love life. My team is following up on some information provided by a private investigating firm in Santa Fe, New Mexico. I got your name and whereabouts from one of their employees, Ms. Myrna Malloy. If you'd like to call her for verification, be my guest, but let me stand inside while you waste our time."

Her eyes tightened, but she moved aside and let him pass. Tom unzipped his shell and paused to let her take the lead. After a substantial hike through the entry hall, they emerged into a great room with dark wooden walls and a soaring cathedral ceiling laced with open beams. They stopped facing a long wall consisting largely of tall windows and a door opening onto the deck. Tom could see the hot tub through the rightmost window. Flickering light and radiant heat drew his attention to the right wall. It featured a stone, walk-in fireplace large enough to serve as a billiard room in a pinch. The line of metal logs must have stretched for twelve feet, but only half the gas jets were lit. Two open windows on the back wall kept the temperature below sauna levels.

"You didn't answer my question—how did you get through the gate?"

"Trade secret, but don't worry, nothing's broken. Is Mr. Kinkaid at home?"

"I have a feeling you know he's not. He'll be back in a few minutes, though, so don't get any big ideas." Sally started toward a stairwell leading to the lower level. "I think I will call Myrna. You wait here. My phone's downstairs."

She had to be telling the truth about the phone—it clearly wasn't anywhere on her person. Tom nodded and stood staring at the flames until he heard her steps move away from the bottom of the stairs. He

saw two closed doors in the wall opposite the fireplace. The first opened
to a library lined with floor-to-ceiling shelves supporting expensively
bound books. The bookcases were separated by occasional gallery
nooks adorned with heads of large beasts shot down in their prime.
Carcasses with less stuffing covered much of the stone floor. There was
no time to fan through the pages of several hundred dusty books, so
he backed out. One minute gone.

Tom opened the second door and walked into what had to be James
Kinkaid's local office. It was large enough to house the legislature of a
small state but was sparsely furnished. A corner to the right of the door
contained three wing-back chairs surrounding a carved table with a
crystal decanter of amber fluid. The room's only window was centered
in the long north wall. It was a stained glass depiction of John Wayne
in a cavalry uniform. Probably not by Tiffany, but not bad. Tom
couldn't tell whether Duke was looking outward toward the ski area or
inward at him. He shook it off. Kinkaid's vast desk and accompanying
throne were a few feet past the window and backed against the opposite
wall. Tom walked to the empty desk. He tugged at each of the drawers,
but all were locked.

On the north wall, a few feet to the left of Duke and directly in
front of the desk, was a painting of a smiling woman, naked but for
her cowgirl hat and red boots. The painting was at least five feet tall
and three wide, and it protruded a few inches into the room. Tom
checked out the other paintings. Most were western landscapes, and
all were hanging flat against the walls. The nude dangled by wires from
two six-inch brass brackets. Tom peeked behind the saucy lady and saw
she was hanging an inch inward from another, smaller painting. The
hidden one was unframed. No decorator did this. Tom grabbed the
frame of the naked lady with his right hand and squeezed the left side
between his elbow and ribs. He lifted it enough to unhook the wire
and then set her on the floor against the desk. He turned back to the
shy companion piece. It was a much older painting, unframed and relatively small—just over two feet wide and a few inches taller than that.
It showed three musicians, two women and a man, gathered at a harp-
sichord. And, if real, it was painted by Johannes Vermeer in the year
1664, or thereabouts.

My God, The Concert! Tom moved his face close to the surface of
the paint. He could see the expected fine lines of craquelure and some
signs of stretcher marks. Not conclusive—a good forger could turn

fresh paint into an old master in relatively short order. Tom curled the fingers of his right hand around the top stretcher bar and lifted the painting from the wall. He rotated it until he could see the back. Marks and materials looked authentic, but again, this proved little. The best forgeries were done on period canvases after removing the paint of a less-revered artist. Authentication wasn't his forte. He would turn the piece over to Kate's team. They would compare the back to photos from the Gardner archives and have the style analyzed, the materials tested. He was feeling dizzy and forced himself to concentrate. Time to get the hell out.

Tom turned toward the door but stopped when he heard footsteps from the stairwell in the great room. He leaned The Concert against the back of a wing-back chair and closed the door behind him as he stepped out of the office. Sally watched him from the top of the stairs. The fuzzy slippers were gone, replaced by tight leather boots with two-inch heels. The hairbrush was gone too, replaced by a beaded handbag. "What were you doing?"

"Interesting place. I just wanted to see more of it. Nice window in there." Tom tilted his head toward the office doorway.

"You think? That surprises me. Kindly refrain from further exploring. Jim can show you around when he gets back. So, what do you want to ask me?"

Tom downloaded a prepared spiel concerning an alleged theft of artifacts from a museum in Dallas. He counted on Sally's being more familiar with details of Kinkaid's mating habits than his art activities. She didn't seem suspicious when Tom said Kinkaid would know the history of the stolen pieces and might be able to suggest persons with motive. What crap!

Sally's eyes were glazing. "I wouldn't know much about that, but your FBI story checked out. Myrna said you're a real G-man, or something like that. Let's sit over by the fire and wait for Jim."

Sally chose a sofa far enough from the inferno to prevent roasting, but it was still uncomfortably hot. "I called Jim, too. He'll be back any minute. A bit early for a drink. Would you like coffee?"

"Always."

Sally mounted her heels and headed for the kitchen while Tom stretched and made a show of adjusting cushions. She disappeared through a door ten feet to the left of the fire. He waited until the clicks of Sally's boot heels had faded in the distance and then rushed to the office. Grasping the Vermeer by the top stretcher, he scurried back into the great room and headed toward the front door. As he passed the fireplace, a cold voice from his right stopped him.

"That's far enough. Turn this way, please."

James Kinkaid was standing in the doorway of his library. Has to be another door. He was a slight man whose sharp nose and chin jutted out together, giving the impression of a bird of prey. The pistol would not have looked large in his slender hand if Tom weren't looking down its bore. "Who are you really, sir? Sally called and said an FBI man wanted to talk to me, and I had to return without finishing my bagel. To find this." He pointed the gun toward the painting. "Times are tough in Washington, but I don't think the Bureau is reduced to stealing art."

"I'm not stealing it, Mr. Kinkaid. Just taking it in for appraisal, shall we say."

"You're not FBI, Mr. McNabb. They don't operate this way."

"McNaul. The name's Tom McNaul."

"I don't really give a shit. Now be a good fellow and set that painting down on the sofa. Gently."

Tom adjusted his position until the painting shielded his torso. Will Kinkaid put a bullet through a hundred million bucks? Maybe, but he'll think first. Then again, if the guy is a good shot, he won't have to. Tom's head and legs were exposed along with at least part of his crotch. Just like a Dutchman, too cheap to paint on a large canvas. Kinkaid moved to his left and began to circle his target. Tom turned, keeping the painting between the pistol and his chest. They came to a stop after a quarter revolution. Kinkaid was backlit by morning light from the north windows. Tom could feel the heat from the fire on his right side.

"Come on, now. Put it down. I'm not going to shoot you and get the police all stirred up."

Tom didn't figure any neighbors would hear a shot from inside this fortress. He clung to his canvas shield and tried to think of a plan.

"You must know what you're holding, Mr. McNaul. That's one of the world's great cultural treasures. Neither of us wants to see it damaged. I purchased it recently from some worthless goons with the goal of returning it to the Gardner Museum. Restoring a stolen masterpiece to the world. I just wanted to reward myself with the pleasure of having it on my wall for a couple of weeks."

Tom wavered. He didn't believe Kinkaid, but despair began to pulse through his veins. How many days had it been since the shootout in

Lexington? How much blood spilled? And what was left of his life? Or his love of art? Wasn't it all about the art? This wasn't some Picasso sketch lifted from a rich man's summer house. It was the jewel of the biggest art heist since the Mona Lisa. Shouldn't he take the risk?

Kinkaid was gaining confidence. He lowered the gun until it pointed at the floor halfway between them. "Put it down, and let's talk. I'd like to hear your story. Maybe we can return the painting together. Couple of heroes. I'm not in this for a reward."

Tom began to lower the painting, but he saw a sudden tensing of the muscles around Kinkaid's eyes, and the world lapsed into slow motion. As Kinkaid's gun began to rise, Tom whipped his right arm in a backhanded throw. The Vermeer floated toward the fire, wobbling like a poorly thrown Frisbee. Tom recoiled to his left and dropped, twisting his right side backward as he spun away from the gun. The old man never hesitated. He cracked off a shot that clipped Tom's sleeve. Glass shattered somewhere in the room, and there was a soft thud as the Vermeer landed in the fireplace. Tom hit the floor and continued his roll until he lay facing Kinkaid, the Glock now in his right hand. They froze, each man trying to stare down the enemy without looking into the maw of his gun.

Tom caught a whiff of burning paint and canvas. Neither of them looked toward the fireplace. "Why don't you put the gun down? You might have time to salvage something."

Kinkaid didn't waver, but he didn't shoot either. He appeared to be contemplating his chances.

"Do the right thing, Kinkaid. Set the gun down and live another day." Tom tensed the muscles of his gun hand. The man facing him relaxed and lowered his pistol. He set it on an end table and stepped back.

"Sure, why not? It was a forgery anyway. You figured that out, didn't you?"

"Yeah, eventually." Tom retrieved Kinkaid's pistol, slipped it into a coat pocket, and holstered his Glock.

Sally gained the top of the stairs. "I heard a shot. Are you guys OK?"

Kinkaid ignored her. "Turns out the micks in Boston hired a forger not long after they stole the real one. I'm not sure why, but I can guess. Nice job, wasn't it. Takes a pro to tell."

Tom frowned. "How did you get it?"

"They tried to sell me the real one. No way I'd pay what those bastards wanted, but they showed me the copy. I figured it was politic to buy something from them. I could hang it in my office and play with it now and then. Seemed best to keep it out of public view, though. It's too good a copy—people would ask questions."

"Don't bullshit me, Kinkaid. You bought the original. My source is solid."

"Your source is mistaken, but that story does seem to be getting around. I got a call from a woman in Boston saying the FBI was barking up my particular wrong tree. I don't know where the painting is, but if I had to guess, I'd figure someone stashed it long term in one of those unlisted Swiss bank vaults. The ones where the Nazi art loot is hiding out, or so people tell me."

Kinkaid coughed. "So if you're not a fed, who are you?"

"Private investigator. Working on my own. On spec."

"That so? Just a goddamn shamus? Well then, your little game is over. You've got nothing to take home, and my shot missed. How about we call it a draw, and you get the hell out of my life?"

"No deals, but I am going home now. You'd best keep looking over your shoulder, Kinkaid. I may give up, but the feds won't."

Kinkaid snorted and stretched an upturned hand toward the front door. Tom tarried. "What is it with you rich bastards. Why is owning a splash of old paint so damned important?"

"I don't really know about the others, Mr. McNaul. But I like the feeling that everyone wants something, and only I have it."

Tom glanced at Sally and then turned to leave.

"Hold on, McNaul." Tom stopped, still facing the door. "I don't follow one thing. You were holding up that painting, daring me to put a hole in it. Why'd you do that if you knew it was a forgery?"

Tom stood motionless, waiting in silence.

"You bastard. You didn't know, did you? Not then. What tipped you off? When did you catch on?"

"When your shot almost got me. You shot fast. You're a rich man, but even you would hesitate if you saw The Concert sailing into flames."

"But, when you threw it . . . my god! You thought it was real?"

"Yeah. But I didn't know for sure."

"So why did you do it?"

Tom thought for a moment. "I just didn't give a damn." He took a couple of steps toward the door, then turned to face Kinkaid and Sally. "A lot of people, like you, think that Vermeer is priceless. But it isn't worth me." He spun on his heel and never looked back.

~ 26 ~

Snow swirled as Tom reached the main highway. Visibility dropped to a few hundred feet, and the radio reported the usual closing of the Telluride airport. Most of the ice crystals danced off his windshield without sticking while the wipers mopped up stragglers. The road was turning white, so he slowed to thirty to avoid surprises from concealed ice patches. As he plodded toward Durango, he kept picturing The Concert spinning into Kinkaid's crematorium. He bit the inside of his lower lip until he tasted copper. The pain ended his vision like a breaking filmstrip. He tried to focus on the road, but the death of the painting gnawed at him. Good thing it was a forgery. If it was a forgery. Kinkaid wasn't exactly a man to be trusted.

The drive took almost four hours, but the snow in Durango was lighter. His flight took off half an hour late, and he pulled into the parking lot at Juanita's just after five. As usual, the skies were clear in Santa Fe, though the wind was beginning to whistle. The restaurant was quiet ahead of the dinner crowd, and he found a table in the aged bar to gulp his margaritas in peace. The waiter arched an eyebrow, suggesting a third as he set down a plate of blue-corn enchiladas smothered with red chile. Tom approved the refill and looked down into the bloodshot egg staring at him from atop the stack. He punctured it with his fork.

There was still an inch of margarita lapping at the rocks as Tom swirled the glass above his empty plate. His mind wandered to the Vermeer, stripping the alcohol of its allure. He slapped the glass on the table, paid, and left for home. The empty condo didn't beckon, but he needed to call Kate from a spot with no witnesses.

Tom spent forty-five minutes squirming in the purple chair trying to decide how much to tell his former partner. Colleen had given him Kinkaid's purchase of the painting in return for a stay-out-of-jail-free card, and a deal was a deal. Her tip was real. Kinkaid must have the piece stashed somewhere. He hadn't put much effort into his lies, as if he didn't care what Tom knew. Was he also lying about being tipped off by a woman in Boston? Tom needed to keep Colleen's name off the

FBI suspects list, at least until he was sure she'd slipped another dagger into his back. He grabbed his phone from the coffee table.

"Tommy. Nice surprise. You got something for me, or is this a social call?" Kate sounded hopeful it might be the latter.

"A little of each. I just got back from Telluride. When I left, there was a painting burning in the mammoth gas fireplace of a private ski lodge. It was a damned convincing forgery of The Concert. To my eye it was too good to have been done from a photo. The painting and fireplace both belong to a Texas oil tycoon named James Kinkaid."

The phone was silent for a few seconds. When Kate's voice returned, the levity was gone. "Let's hear the rest of the story." Tom told her the rest, the anonymous source version. "Tommy, I've got to hang up and make some calls. Don't go anywhere —I'll call you back."

"Got nowhere to go, toots." But Kate was already gone.

She called fifteen minutes later. "Some local police are on the way to the scene, and FBI field agents from Denver will be there in a few hours. I'm scheduled for a dawn launch in the morning—taking an authentication expert with me. That's assuming the Denver agents find any remnants. Otherwise, I'll go it alone." Her tone switched to accusatory. "Don't think that I buy the crap about you getting a call from some shy snitch. But we'll put that topic on hold just now, for old times' sake."

"Good luck with the remnants. It was burning pretty fast when I left, but Kinkaid might have salvaged something. I take it you're well enough to travel?"

"Yeah, for this. Long way from a hundred percent, but I can take it." Her voice softened. "I guess I'm kind of a hardass like you—must be why we get along. Last of our breed. Say, I haven't booked a return flight. How about I route myself home through Albuquerque? I'd like to look you in the eye when we discuss your so-called anonymous source. And I'd like to kick back and down a few with you. You game?"

"Anytime, partner." Tom was surprised at how eager he felt to see Kate again. Maybe Colleen was right to snarl at her.

* * *

The Lionel train whistle wailed twice, and Myrna yodeled accompaniment through the open office door: "Grab your gun, Tommy. Trouble's a-comin'."

Tom looked out the window. The top was up on Tracy Lee's red BMW convertible as it swerved to the curb and ground a layer of rubber off the sidewalls. Seconds later she clomped into his office wearing a beaded leather coat with fringes on the sleeves, matching boots and shoulder bag as red as her car, and a scowl like a bulldog with a toothache. "I suppose you heard I got my soup can back. I had to drive in to the damned police station to pick it up."

"How awful."

"Don't be a smart ass." Tracy Lee looked toward Willie's empty desk. "Where's your bozo brother? Don't tell me he managed to make it out the window this time?"

"No, he's on the road somewhere—and out of contact, for that matter." Tom sat up straighter in his chair. "Are you here to pay me? I estimate the value of Tomato Soup at thirty thousand bucks, so my twenty percent would be six grand—that's the finder's fee. Myrna can work up my expenses."

"Six grand my ass." Tracy Lee stamped one boot on the wooden floor and braced both fists on her hips. "You didn't return my soup can, the police did. And besides, it wasn't even stolen. Eddie Romero said Bryce just had it in his vault for some reason. Now the damned fool has run off somewhere—laying low till I cool off." Tracy folded her arms and reduced the steam by a few PSI. "I'll pay your expenses, but that's it. No, wait." She dug into her shoulder bag and produced a short stack of hundred-dollar bills. They were pinched in a hair clip studded with enough diamonds to make the bills seem cheap. It looked like there might be a thousand bucks in the clip, but she extracted only five Franklins and tossed them toward his desk. Two fluttered to the floor. "You deserve something for your trouble. It was a mistake, but after all, I did hire you."

"Stow it, toots. Willie and I found the prints; the cops just made the delivery. I'll knock off twenty-five bucks for that." Tom's right hand struck like a viper as he clamped his hand around her slender wrist and squeezed until she dropped the clip. He let go of her, picked up the clip, and released the remaining five hundred from it. "You still owe me five grand, but I'll keep this as the rest of the down payment."

"You asshole, I'll see that you never work again in this town."

"No you won't. Doesn't sound like Honest Eddie told you all of the circumstances. But don't worry, he will. Your husband was running a print forgery scam, and he was skimming from you while he was scamming the customers. Oh yes, there was a murder involved. Maybe you weren't part of it, or maybe you were, but either way, I don't think you ought to run around telling folks about why you're stiffing me. So go cool off, and then send over the rest of my money."

Tracy Lee was clearly stunned, but she recovered in a flash and stormed out of his office without a word. Tom watched through the window as she abused her car door and roared down Staab Street. He didn't think he'd ever see the rest of his money, but he had some compensation in mind.

Tom closed the door to his office and stretched out on the sofa. It was a Tuesday afternoon, three weeks to the day since he'd stepped onto the train platform in Lamy, running back to his homelands. Seeking sanctuary, or at least a place to catch his breath. Ready to start a new life with Colleen and Cassidy, and a new career, of sorts.

Tom took stock of his progress. His wife had tried to have him killed and seemed to be getting away with it; daughter Cassidy had left home and was hiding from her parents in New York; his violently inclined brother and business partner had split for parts unknown. The family still needed improvement.

A Boston gangster had tried to kill him, and the resulting truce was of dubious stability. Six people were dead, though perhaps the two back in Boston shouldn't count. Two cases were solved, but the gross receipts amounted to a lousy one grand, and he'd had to wrestle a woman for that. The Southwest Cultures case might have brought in forty grand if they hadn't blown it to save a dog. Laurie was pissed and had repossessed said dog. He'd made a break in the Gardner theft case, but there was a chance he'd tossed the Vermeer into a fire. And add one broken arm. He looked at the cast—the nurse's taunting phone number was still visible. A snigger worked its way down to his torso, and he convulsed in laughter.

Still no report from Willie, so Tom tried a call. He left a message on voicemail with little hope it would be heard. He was worried about his brother. Willie had been an honest man once, but now he seemed out of control—his violence was escalating, the justifications fading into mere convenience. Tom suppressed a shiver. He loved his brother, but he couldn't let himself slide that far. Well, the road trip might do Willie some good. A few thousand miles of cold winds in the face might push away some demons. He wouldn't give up on his brother just yet.

*   *   *

Willie saw the call was from Tom. He pulled into a rest stop, walked off the cramps in his legs, and sat on the picnic table farthest from the restrooms. Need to set something right. He called Laurie.

"Willie! Where the hell are you? We've been worried about you."

"I'll bet. I'm at the side of a road. Doesn't matter where, but I'm OK. I just need to tell you something."

"Like what?"

"It was Tom who found Stella. He's the one who tied her to your front door handle."

"What? He said you guys ran off chasing a lead. I chewed Tommy's butt for abandoning her like that."

"We were working a case, but after we split up, he went back and found Stella and took her to your place."

"Where was she?"

"He didn't say. Look, Laurie. Tom's a good guy at heart. And he's not like me. He'll get his act together someday. Don't sell him short, OK? You know he likes you."

"Yeah, well maybe I like him too. But I don't get it. Why didn't he knock?"

"Don't know. Hey, I gotta go. Good talking to you." Willie cut off the call before she could reply.

* * *

Georgia moonlight was no match for the dense overcast. The narrow road disappeared into darkness as a rider in black cut the lights on his motorcycle and eased off the throttle. His bike slowed and murmured as he coasted through the forest. As he rounded a curve, the woods were suddenly lit by the neon lights of a lone roadhouse. At least a dozen bikes and several pickups crowded the lot, and the front door was propped open, spewing music and voices into the night. He drifted a hundred yards past the lot, braked, and cut the engine. There was room to hide the bike behind a stand of trees tangled with kudzu vines. He removed a revolver from the left saddlebag and slipped it inside his leather jacket.

The night was cool, but the inside of Jimmy's was crowded and hot. Annie set down her empty tray and wiped sweat from her forehead. Business was good when the local bikers blew in, but they kept her jumping. Outlaw country wailed from the jukebox near the door, competing with the roar of voices from a long table in the back. The boys were tanked and ordering more. Langston was holding court again, roaring about how he was heading back to New Mexico soon to set things right. His ninety-pound tattooed tag-along giggled while fellow riders whooped approval.

Annie turned her head as a large man in black leathers and a balaclava stopped just inside the door. Only his dark eyes and gray eyebrows were visible. The stranger stared for a few seconds at the table of bikers, then turned his back to the room and perused the jukebox menu. He gave a faint nod and inserted a five. She watched him punch the same button five times before he walked out into the dark. Takes all kinds. Time for a smoke.

Annie stepped out the side door of Jimmy's and sat on the top step. As she leaned forward, elbows on her knees, she noticed the man in black standing in a grove of pines across the road from the lot. She didn't think he could see her—he was staring toward the front door, and anyway, the bulb in the porch light had burned out a month ago. The jukebox paused, then fired up a new song. She smiled and exhaled a slow stream of smoke. The Charlie Daniels Band, one of her favorites. The music stopped, and she ground her cigarette out on the porch. As she stood to go, the song began again. Had to be the stranger's choice. She listened to the familiar opening words: "The Devil Came Down to Georgia. . . ." as she slipped back inside.

*   *   *

It was almost five, and Tom shivered as he zipped the collar of his parka until it hugged his neck. From his narrow upstairs balcony, he watched the sinking sun paint the clouds. For a few minutes even the stubby piñons and junipers cast long shadows. God, he had missed the sunsets living back east. Too many tall trees. You could never see the sky. Not a problem here. He must have watched a thousand New Mexico sunsets as a kid. Time for a whiskey. As he stepped back indoors, he heard the sound of a key struggling in the front-door lock.

Tom emerged from his bedroom to find Laurie looking up the stairs. She smiled and let go of Stella's leash. "Hope you don't mind me letting myself in."

"Hardly, toots. It's good to see you … both. I'm about to crack open my best whiskey. Care to join me?"

"Sure, any occasion?"

"You'll do." Tom thought he saw a quick flush in her cheeks but wasn't counting on it. He sauntered down the stairs and produced two small glasses and a sealed bottle with no label attached.

"What the hell is that?" Laurie arched an eyebrow.

"The right stuff, but I soak off the label for modesty."

"I'll bet." She opened a different cabinet and selected a beer stein. He considered filling it but instead poured a portion two fingers short of the certain-sex line.

They clinked glasses and slouched into opposite corners of the sofa. Tom was startled to see Laurie wearing real girl shoes instead of her usual runners or hiking boots. She made a show of kicking one off but was out of practice. It shot like a line drive into the kitchen, almost taking out the bottle. Undeterred, she rested the bare foot on Tom's thigh and managed to slip the other shoe off without damage. She placed the second foot beside the first. "I got a call from Willie."

Tom sat as upright as he could without shedding her feet. "Where is he?"

"Wouldn't say, but he claims to be OK. That's not why he called, though." She sipped her mug of single-malt Irish and waited.

"I give up."

"Why didn't you tell me? About Stella? Willie said you were the one who tied her to my door." Laurie's jaw muscles tightened as she turned up the pitch and volume. "You creep, you let me make a fool of myself ragging you for running off while she was missing. What the hell's wrong with you?" She looked genuinely pissed, but Tom noticed her feet were still on his leg.

"Guess I'm shy." Damn it, Willie. What's your game? Now what do I tell her?

"Bullshit. But thanks, I guess." Her feet slipped to the floor, and she sortied barefoot into the kitchen, returning with a larger share of his eighty-dollar whiskey. She set the stein on the table and resumed her previous position on the sofa, her feet a couple of inches farther up his thigh.

"I don't get you, Tommy McNaul. You were pretty much a straight arrow back when you were my guy. Honest. Caring. Nobody was surprised when you ended up in the FBI, though I admit I was hoping you'd come home instead." She stretched toward the table to retrieve her drink, allowing one foot to slide along his leg on her way back. "But the feds gave you the boot after twenty-five years. Your wife seems to have done the same." She arched an eyebrow for confirmation. Tom just stared at her. "You got off the train and made love to me the next night, but now you're so gun-shy you won't even ring the bell when you've found my lost dog. You've changed—you're a loner now. You can't figure out whether you're running for home or off into the dark."

"When do I get the advice?" He cringed—shouldn't have said that.

Laurie swung her legs free and bounced to her feet. She stomped into the kitchen and poured a heartbreak of fine whiskey down his disposal. "No advice. But damn it, I think you're a decent, honest man at heart. Am I ever going to see that Tom again?"

Laurie grabbed her coat, remembered the shoes, and headed for the door. She opened it a few inches, admitting an eddy of frigid air. "You still need time, Tommy. You've got to figure out who the hell you are now, and where you're going. Hell, so do I." She pointed at the purple chair. "Stella's staying here. You need each other. But I get full visiting privileges, and I intend to use them."

It was a clever move, if a bit obvious. Tom slumped deeper into the cushions and gave Laurie a relaxed smile. "Thanks."

She let him see a smile back, then vanished into the night. Tom stood up to freshen his glass but left it on the counter as he began pacing. Laurie missed on one count—he wasn't a loner. He was aching to be close to a woman. His spirits had sunk when Laurie walked out the door, but she'd made the right call. She needed a man she could depend on, not one who's still married to the Wicked Witch of the East and seems better at shooting people than harvesting finder's fees.

Maybe Kate was right—the only match for one hardass is another. He'd loved working with Kate, and they did seem to be two of a kind.

Thirty years earlier, when Tom was still in high school, his father had advised him how to make tough decisions. "Flip a coin, Tom, and promise yourself to abide by its result. When the coin is in the air, you'll know what you want." Tom dug a quarter out of his pocket. His thumb sent it spinning almost to the ceiling. As the coin fell, he snatched it from the air, grinned, and put it in his pocket without looking.

His mind switched to a more somber issue. Laurie thought he was still an honest man and a seeker of justice. But was he? Honesty and justice didn't seem all that connected anymore. The law had been sacred to him once, but now he seemed to bend it to satisfy his personal sense of justice. He was inching along a slippery ledge. Was he following Willie?

Well, enough with the angst. Time to get back to work. Tomorrow he would resume tilting at the windmills of justice for the good citizens of Santa Fe, and this time he needed to get paid. The rich folks seemed to be good at dodging remuneration, but perhaps not as good as they thought. He pictured Tracy Lee Jackson storming out of his office, dripping with wealth and refusing to pay his modest fee. Pure spite. She knew he couldn't afford to challenge her in court.

Tom walked upstairs and slid the cardboard print box from under his bed. He brought it down to the kitchen table. The tape peeled off easily, and he folded back the cardboard flaps. Bright light from the overhead fixture brought out the red and silver inks particularly well. A can of Campbell's Tomato Soup had never looked better. He inspected it for a while and then leaned forward until his right eye was barely an inch above the tabletop. With thumb and forefinger, he carefully lifted the bottom right corner just far enough to admire the signature scrawled in blue ballpoint: "Andy Warhol." The stamped number was #9/250. He laid the corner down and took a step back from the table with his eyes fixed on the iconic image. Tracy Lee would have to make do with the forgery. This was much too beautiful to hang on a greasy kitchen wall, fading in the New Mexico sunlight.

About the Author

Although William Frank is a fourth-generation New Mexican, he spent his childhood at U.S. Naval Air Stations ranging from French Morocco to Guam. He studied aeronautical engineering at MIT and served as a flight test engineer in the Air Force before earning a Ph.D. in Atmospheric Science. He spent thirty years as a professor of meteorology at the University of Virginia and Penn State, studying hurricanes and their somewhat calmer relatives. Along the way, he developed a deep love of storytelling, and in particular, the American detective novel.

He retired from academia a bit early to return to New Mexico and write detective fiction. He lives just north of Santa Fe with his wife, Kathleen Frank, a noted painter of expressionist landscapes, and two corgis.